© Eleanor Swift-Hook 2022.

Eleanor Swift-Hook has asserted her rights under the Copyright, Design and Patents Act, 1988, to be identified as the author of this work.

First published in 2022 by Sharpe Books.

Table of Contents

Warwickshire, 22 October 1642

Chapter One

Chapter Two

Chapter Three

Chapter Four

Chapter Five

Chapter Six

Chapter Seven

Chapter Eight

Chapter Nine

Chapter Ten

Chapter Eleven

Chapter Twelve

Chapter Thirteen

Chapter Fourteen

Chapter Fifteen

Chapter Sixteen

Chapter Seventeen

Chapter Eighteen

Chapter Nineteen

Chapter Twenty

Author's Note

THE DEVIL'S COMMAND

Warwickshire, 22 October 1642

It was creeping close to twilight and the air had a sharp edge of cold.

Gideon Lennox, weary from two weeks of continual travel and just recovered from several recent wounds, was glad that they were nearing journey's end.

The main body of the king's army was spread out in quarters over some nine miles of countryside, in farms, villages and hamlets. Gideon would have been grateful for any shelter, but his commander, the infamous mercenary leader known to the world as the Schiavono and to his close associates as Philip Lord, had insisted that they should press on. He wanted to join the advance guard, which was under the command of Prince Rupert, the king's nephew and his general of horse. The prince, they had been informed, had taken up temporary residence together with his brother Prince Maurice, at a house called Wormleighton Manor. So ten mounted men, Philip Lord and Gideon, together with one woman riding pillion, pushed on ahead of their single baggage wagon and its escort.

The woman with them was Zahara. It was she who held Gideon's heart and soul in her keeping. She rode behind Shiraz, a man who seemed to be as careful of her as a brother and just as loyal to Philip Lord. He was, Gideon had learned recently, Persian. Although he seemed able to understand more languages than Gideon himself had ever learned, he was unable to speak any of them, having had his tongue sliced away. Instead, he communicated fluently with his hands to those who understood that silent language. His dark eyes were ever watchful, and despite the fine traces of silver visible sometimes in his thick black hair, he was one of the most dangerous men Gideon had ever encountered.

Three months ago, Gideon had given little or no thought to the existence of such people as Shiraz and Philip Lord. For an up-and-coming attorney in the inns of London that was not too difficult. Then he had been offered good money to travel north to Newcastle-upon-Tyne to undertake some work for the powerful Hostmen coal cartel. It had seemed a good opportunity to further his career and get away from the increasing political tensions in the city. However, having disappointed the cartel members with his honesty and integrity, he had been cozened into becoming a pawn in another powerful man's plans. That led to Gideon meeting Philip Lord and eventually joining his mercenary company.

A thousand miles removed from his safe and familiar world and having learned what it was to have to fight and kill to survive, Gideon was more philosophical than he might have been about the fact that he was riding to war. But then most of England had been pulled from its comfortable complaisance by recent events and was being forced to come to terms with the war.

Now, riding in the wake of Philip Lord, Gideon was

THE DEVIL'S COMMAND

uncertain of where they were heading or how far it still was to their destination for the night.

The challenge, when it came, was from a Royalist foraging party, seeking more places to quarter troops and secure supplies. As before, when they encountered soldiers of the king's army, in place of the word of the day, Lord offered them a document. It bore a seal that seemed to have a magical effect on whomsoever saw it. This time the effect was perhaps not so impacting as Gideon would have hoped.

Instead of being apprised of the direction they should take and perhaps offered a guide, the man commanding the foragers made fulsome apologies that he could not immediately escort the troop to the house. It seemed that either he didn't trust the document, or perhaps the hard-bitten and hard-biting look of the men with Lord gave him pause. Enveloped in the midst of the foraging party and with Lord himself riding alongside its commanding officer, white hair a clear marker to his men, they went first to visit the village outside Wormleighton Manor.

From the rather uniform look of the houses, Gideon assumed the settlement had at some point been transplanted. That could have been done to make way for an expansion of the house or perhaps the owners disliked having their view marred by cottages. The countryside around here in the Vale of the Red Horse provided wide fields and the gentlest of rolling hills, so any shabby row of buildings would create an immediate eyesore if not well screened by distance.

Those speculative thoughts were shattered when a shout went up. Every man around Gideon instantly had a weapon in his hand and he pulled his own sword free. His first instinct was to see where Zahara was and be certain she was safe. But the broad-backed black gelding she rode with Shiraz was right beside his mare and with an agility that surprised him, she slipped from her pillion to sit behind his saddle.

The mare protested a little and danced a few paces, but Gideon soothed the little chestnut as Shiraz shot off, bow in hand, in the direction being taken by Lord and the others. The warm pressure of Zahara's presence almost made Gideon forget the reason for her being there. Of all those in the troop, they were the two who were the least combat competent. The clear expectation was that instead of charging in with the rest to whatever had raised the alarm he should hold back and be prepared to run or fight to protect Zahara as needed.

He reined a little, glad of the docility of his mount that made her possible to manage with one hand and watched the confusing melee in which, somehow, all the participants seemed to know what to do. He heard Lord's voice the loudest, shouting orders to his men and those of the foraging party. The orders were obeyed even by the commander of the foragers himself.

"It is another troop seeking quarters," Zahara said from behind him. "One for the Parliament soldiers. It means their army must be nearby."

If there was an army close by it wasn't near enough to intervene in the skirmish. Lord's men, assisted by those who had been escorting them, secured some twelve prisoners, killed four men and ran off the rest of a force that had been twice the size of their own.

THE DEVIL'S COMMAND

They had sustained a few cuts but taken no losses.

As they reformed and Gideon returned Zahara to her pillion behind Shiraz, Lord took the time to address both his men and those of the foraging party they had joined with.

"You did that very well, gentlemen, and thanks to the courage and skill of your quartermaster here, we can ride to the prince bearing the gift of a fine bouquet." That brought laughter and even the quartermaster seemed mollified from having his authority usurped by a man he had treated with suspicion.

When they rode up to the gates of Wormleighton Manor, Gideon noticed that the men pushed into their midst were the sullen and frightened prisoners, where Lord's men were now welcomed as comrades.

Chapter One

I

Riding east across the northern hills of England at the head of forty of his men, half of whom were on foot, it occurred to Sir Nicholas Tempest that this was not how he had ever imagined he might begin married life. Not that he had put too much thought into the matter over the course of his twenty-one years, but when it had crossed his mind, it was always with a vague image of a graceful and beautiful woman who worshipped him, and whom he would hold in gentle affection.

He hadn't intended to marry but had been given no choice in the matter. The death of his uncle, Sir Bartholomew Coupland a month ago meant Nick inherited the baronetcy, becoming Sir Nicholas Tempest of Howe. But Howe Hall was a fortress rock in the harsh lands of Weardale. It lacked the means to maintain itself on the entailed lands of its estate. To be granted the mines, the copyhold lands and all other property and interests Sir Bartholomew had gathered in County Durham and elsewhere, Nick was compelled to marry the woman chosen for him by his father and uncle. Had he refused he would have been left with an empty title and a house crumbling into poverty.

Nick understood very well that it was not just his

THE DEVIL'S COMMAND

father and uncle who had placed the demand upon him. They had done so under the malign influence of the powerful men to whom they were bound. The mysterious Covenant. An organisation which shrouded itself from public awareness and sought to further its political ends.

The issue was not so much the idea of marriage, but of the woman to whom he was now bound. Christobel Lavinstock, the daughter of a gentleman farmer of Durham. She loathed him to the extent that he had needed to use force to take her to Howe and find witnesses well paid to swear that she had spoken her spousal vows. The priest owed his living to the Couplands and had said the needed words with tight lips.

It was not as if Nick had wanted things to be that way.

When they first met, he had tried hard to be as kind and generous as his father was with his present wife. But Christobel had rejected him in the most humiliating manner and left him with no choice but to act as he had done. His future, the future of Howe Hall, had depended upon it.

So now he was wed and his wife, declared by an obliging physician to be suffering from a severe imbalance of the humours which had afflicted her mind, was held against her will at Howe. If for the present, she was little better than as a prisoner, Nick was confident that given time she would accept her situation, become content, and go on to be the required adornment of the house as his wife and the eventual mother of his children.

But as a result, he had been more relieved than anything when the few days he had been granted in absence by the Earl of Newcastle, to see his new wife was safe and settled, had expired. Nick had seen as little as possible of her in that time, using the week instead to gather as many new men of fighting age and strength as he could. Now he was returning with them to Newcastle to take up his command in the king's northern army. He did so secure in the knowledge that through the marriage he had control of the means to maintain the men he had raised, along with the rest of his uncle's original muster, and Howe Hall itself could be furnished as might be required for both his comfort and its defence.

The weather had turned cold. The ground was hard under boot and hoof, which carried its own issues but allowed for faster travel than when soft and wet. As a result, they made better time than Nick had expected.

There were few other travellers. The rumours of war encouraged people to keep to their homes and trade had begun to falter again. Recent occupation by Scotland had left the people here wary of soldiers and tired of the travails of conflict, but conscious of what they needed to do to ensure they and their families were as safe as they could be.

When Nick saw the small group of horsemen approaching from the south, he was alert. These didn't seem to be local travellers. Apart from anything else they were too well mounted. When he saw a glint of armour, he ordered his men to halt and moved them into a defensive order. He counted eight men approaching and at their head a ninth, but whether this was a gentleman attended by armed servants or some small military patrol Nick couldn't at first tell.

When they came close enough, he could see that the leader was a man with unruly hair the colour of fresh leather, a scrappy beard with a moustache to match, and a face full of freckles split by a cheerful grin. It was a face he recognised as belonging to a man called Daniel Bristow. Bristow served Nick's illegitimate cousin, a mercenary commander known as Mags, who had been granted, and then lost, lands and titles in the German wars and returned to England at the outbreak of war, to redeem his fortunes.

Bristow reined in, as did the men behind him, and swept off his hat with a flourish.

"Sir Nicholas," he said, with an admirable degree of deference in his tone. "I'm glad to have encountered you so soon. I've been sent by the Graf von Elsterkrallen to support you as your most loyal and faithful servant and attendant. For you to use, sir, as you think best to promote your interests and further your ends." He completed the flattering speech, holding his hat to his chest, the plume in it catching in his hair, and sat his horse head bowed and bared.

It seemed an appropriate gift from the man who had spoken to Nick of the means by which he might ascend to take high place in the nation. These would be skilled mercenaries, sent by Mags as a token of good faith to leaven Nick's troops. Although Nick's impression of Bristow himself was that he had little more use than as a messenger. He no doubt stood merely as the mouthpiece, being the one man amongst these Nick would recognise.

Addressing himself to all the men rather than to Bristow alone, Nick issued a brusque order for them to join his troop. They didn't move to obey. Instead, Bristow, still holding his hat clutched against his heart as if it were some kind of talisman, spoke again.

"My lord. Sir Nicholas. Sir. Would you have me attach myself and my men to your cavalry, or perhaps I might do you some better service by acting as a rearguard?" This time there was a note of obsequious apology in his tone as if it grieved him to have to ask for clarification. And, curse the man, he even seemed to be implying that he had been sent in some position of command and not as a regular soldier.

Nick was sure Bristow was no gentleman for any pretensions he might have. His clothing might not be that of a common soldier, but then none of the men with him was so dressed either. They all wore the extravagant, but practical clothing typical of the soldiers of fortune who had returned from the German and Dutch wars. Regardless, the middle of a road some miles east of Medomsley did not seem to be the best place to discuss such matters.

"To the rear, then," he said and managed a gesture with his hand that he hoped was a good imitation of his late uncle when showing dismissive disregard for an issue brought unnecessarily to his attention.

Bristow straightened in the saddle, restored his hat and said a brief word to the men behind him. They wheeled with precision and made for the tail end of the small force. Feeling his authority had been somehow slighted, but uncertain quite how, Nick ordered the troop to move on.

Matters didn't improve when he arrived at his billet,

THE DEVIL'S COMMAND

an inn on the edge of Newcastle where he, his lieutenant, cornet and quartermaster had rooms together with officers from other regiments. He was greeted by Lieutenant Cummings in the common room and Nick instructed him to set Quartermaster Bayliss, the task of finding adequate accommodation for his recruits. Then he became aware that Daniel Bristow was standing at his elbow.

"Good God, man," Nick snapped, "what are you doing in here?"

His hat off, Bristow bowed, speaking as he straightened up.

"I was wondering, Sir Nicholas, if you wished me to make arrangements for myself and my men, or if you have space for them with yours?"

"*Your* men?" Cummings' voice was close to a growl, "How dare you speak that way about Sir Nicholas's troops?"

Bristow's eyes widened. "I would never be so presumptuous, lieutenant. I'm not referring to Sir Nicholas's men. I speak only of my own."

"This man is impertinent, sir," Cummings said. "Who is he?"

The lieutenant wasn't asking for a name but whether it would be appropriate for Cummings and Bayliss to remove the offending individual and beat some proper humility into him. Nick was wondering as much himself and the man in question must have sensed something of it too because he took a step back.

"Daniel Bristow," he said and gave a neat bow as he did so, before restoring his hat. "*Captain* Daniel

Bristow presently." He smiled and Nick wondered if he was dealing with a lack-wit suffering delusions. "However, since I have been charged by my employer to enter your service, Sir Nicholas, I will accept whatever rank you are willing and able to provide. Lieutenant, perhaps?"

"Why you little—"

Cummings made a grab for Bristow, but the smaller man was not there. He was two paces away towards the door, his expression cold and his right hand resting in the intricate metalwork guard on the hilt of his sword. Cummings was reaching for his own sword when Bristow spoke again.

"I would suggest you reconsider." Bristow's voice had lost its amiable air and carried a new authority which made Cummings hesitate. Using the sudden silence, Bristow went on. "You, lieutenant, are an excellent gentleman I am sure, and no doubt oft praised by your neighbours for your civic duty with the trained bands. But I kill people for a living, those with your kind of training and those with, much, much more and I am *very* good at my work."

There was a tense silence. For some reason, Nick didn't doubt for a moment that Bristow spoke the truth. Neither did Cummings who released his sword and stepped back, as a retriever might from a mastiff. Seeing that, Nick's anger at Bristow's impertinence evaporated. Mags had sent this man to serve him and that meant the leash was in his hands.

"Then you deserve a place with rank in my company," he said, ignoring the pained frown he got from Cummings. "Quartermaster Bayliss will find your men somewhere to stay."

THE DEVIL'S COMMAND

The smile was back, and the easy-going appearance restored. Bristow let go of his sword, pulled himself up to his full height, which was somewhat below Nick's own, and executed a smart bow.

"Thank you, sir, I will inform them forthwith. May I ask where I shall be quartered?"

Which was of course an impossible question. Nick already knew from previous tussles with Cavendish's commissar-general that there were no other decent quarters available in the inn, or indeed in all of Newcastle. Every available house was occupied. The one room large enough to accommodate another occupant was his own. Gritting his teeth, Nick hoped he managed to make the words sound as if he wasn't displeased.

"You will have to have a truckle in my room. There is nowhere else."

Bristow's eyes gleamed. "A truckle you say? Do you play cards, Sir Nicholas?"

II

As the cavalrymen milled into the stable yard of Wormleighton Manor, Gideon would have been happy to stay with Zahara. But she vanished as soon as they dismounted, the gathering dark making it impossible to see where she had gone.

When it came to being included in the activities of Lord's company, Gideon often found himself as neither fish nor flesh. His social status and his increasingly close relationship with Philip Lord tended to mean he was included with the officers. But sometimes that left him an awkward outsider, uncertain where to go or what to do.

He was rescued by Lord who appeared briefly with the steward of the house, before vanishing again. The steward took him inside, explaining that the family were not in residence and the guests of the house of any note were at supper, but if the gentleman would be willing to wait in the winter parlour.

It was cosy for such a big room, with groups of chairs and in one corner a harpsichord. There was a large hearth, tapestry hangings, even a carpet on the floor and what looked at first glance like a large white sheepskin which had been scrunched up in front of the fireplace. When the sheepskin uncurled itself and stood up, before padding over to investigate him, Gideon realised it was some variety of dog with a woolly coat. It stood as tall as his hip and as it sniffed the hand Gideon held out, there was a marked intelligence in the dark eyes that made him feel he was being appraised. However, the judgement seemed to fall on the side of approval as the dog wagged its tail a few times and even encouraged Gideon to pet it.

He was still making friends with the dog when the door opened with an abruptness that suggested whoever arrived through it had no need to ask anyone's permission to enter the room.

Gideon was an inch or two short of six foot in his bare feet. Both these men were taller than him, one perhaps by as much as half a foot. From their dress they were officers of some status. They looked to be in their early twenties and were similar enough in appearance for it to be obvious they were brothers.

THE DEVIL'S COMMAND

Both had the same red-brown hair, long, wavy and dark. Both had the same penetrating gaze, fixed in tandem on Gideon, the same long nose and the same sense of intelligence, but he could tell in a moment that the taller brother was the older and the one who led between them. The white dog trotted up to him, tail wagging happily.

"There you are, boy, who let you in here?" The older brother glanced at Gideon whilst making a fuss of the dog. His speech carried an accent Gideon couldn't place. "You have been making friends, I see. Who are you, sir?"

Gideon made a swift bow. From their behaviour and the fact their dog was in the house, he assumed they must be close friends or relatives of the owner of Wormleighton Manor.

"Gideon Fox," he said, using the nom de guerre he had earned in Lord's company. "Philip Lord's man of law and your servant, sirs."

"Boy likes you," the older brother said, "which speaks well. He has an impeccable ability to discriminate. The first time he met George Digby he all but pissed on his shoes."

Gideon tried to look as if that was as amusing as this man thought it was, but he was struggling now as Lord Digby was one of the king's known close councillors.

"I had better take your dog out, Robert," the younger brother said, pronouncing the name in the French manner. "You should thank God he doesn't shed. The housekeeper is a termagant and could shrivel a man's balls with a glance." The two shared a grin, then the younger brother clicked his fingers in command. "Come on, boy."

As he was leaving Lord arrived, stepping aside for the dog then making a respectful bow to the departing man. The older brother crossed to him in two brief strides and gripped his shoulders before he could repeat the bow. Instead, Lord smiled and stood passive in the other man's hold.

"Highness, I am glad to see you so well."

"Philippe, I am glad to see you at all." The tall man had shifted to French.

Highness? Gideon blinked and looked again at the man. He had an odd epiphany as all the clues he had been given came together at once. This would have to be the king's nephew, Prince Rupert, Lord-General of the King's Horse. The other would be Rupert's brother Prince Maurice.

Gideon stomach lurched at his own lack of recognition and the inadequate respect he had shown as a result. Then realised that he had already been forgotten.

The prince released his grip on Lord's shoulders. "I was wondering if you would ever come. You brought me men?"

"Far fewer than I planned, sir," Lord said. "I hope more will come. Those I did bring are worth many times their strength in what they will provide to your troops."

The prince nodded. "That I would not doubt, but it is you yourself who is the greatest strength and I hear you captured some enemy foragers on your way in. Would you believe I had Digby out with four hundred men earlier, because I knew the main enemy force

THE DEVIL'S COMMAND

had to be close by, and he reported nothing? *Nothing.*" The prince's voice rose with a tight anger. "He is beyond incompetent."

"If Essex has foragers out seeking quarters here, he must be close," Lord said.

"As soon as we can get some sense from the men you took, I will send scouts so we can discover what strength he has with him. The last reliable word I had was from Lady Catherine's sources. From what they said, he has his army so scattered we might yet manage to avoid fighting his full force. But first..." He lifted one hand and reached into his coat. "I have been carrying this for the last month against your coming." He produced a well-folded document and held it out.

Lord took it. As he did so Gideon could see that whatever it might be it was written on vellum, not paper. As Lord unfolded it, the prince watched, his expression that of someone who had presented a gift to a friend, one he was confident would be received with joy.

Instead, Lord glanced at it then folded it again and held it out to Gideon who crossed the room to take it.

"I thank you, highness," Lord said and completed the bow he had been unable to make before. "It is most generous, but I cannot accept."

Gideon had opened the document and the first thing he saw was the privy signet of King Charles and his fingers seemed to grow numb where they touched the vellum. It was constructed in an all too familiar mix of English and Latin and he sought the key phrases that told him what he held and the implications of it.

Having ascertained that, he looked up to see the darkening expression on the prince's face. Gideon decided this was not a man who was happy to have his will thwarted. Someone inclined by nature more to anger than compromise.

"It is not something in which you have any choice. If you are to serve me, it is essential, and that is why I persuaded my uncle to this." Then the prince's expression shifted and in a voice that held more of confusion and disappointment than anger, he added, "I thought you would be pleased."

Lord bowed his head.

"You do me much honour, highness, more than I deserve, and that you thought to intercede on my behalf has left me humbled by your condescension. But there is more at stake here than perhaps is clear. If I may explain?" The prince frowned but nodded and Lord turned to Gideon. "Mr Fox, would you tell me what that document is and what it signifies?"

It took Gideon a moment to understand the second part of the request. It was his growing knowledge of the kind of man Philip Lord was, that enabled him to make sense of it.

"This is a pardon," he said, speaking in French as they had been and holding up the document. "It states that you are not held accountable for any crimes you have committed to date, that you will not be pursued for your treasonous deeds and lifts the act of attainder passed against you." He drew a steadying breath. "As your attorney, I would advise you to consider the consequences of this. By its existence, it leaves you guilty of treason, even whilst lifting the penalties for committing treachery against the king's late father."

THE DEVIL'S COMMAND

Lord nodded and the prince shared his frown between them.

"And the problem is?"

"It leaves me guilty of treason," Lord said, echoing Gideon's words. "Whilst I am most grateful to be pardoned for the many crimes I am sure I have committed in my lifetime, treason against King James, your grandfather was never one of them. If you make me accept this, you make me admit to a guilt I do not bear, and worse, a guilt it would pain me to have held to be true."

The prince had the grace to look disturbed.

"I had not considered that aspect of it," he admitted. "I was seeking a remedy which would meet the needs of the time." His face cleared. "And whatever else it might do, this does that. It means you would be free to accept the colonelcy I wish to give you. Besides, it exists. It is done. It cannot now be undone. Were you to disclaim it in public you would offend both myself and my uncle."

"And," said a new voice in English, as a woman stepped into the room, closing the door behind her, "if you renounced it you would have to be detained as a traitor."

Lord spun around and for a moment his raw emotion was visible, though only the woman herself and Gideon would have caught it. It was the look of a parched man hearing running water, or one exhausted and hunted, sighting his sanctuary.

The woman wore a dark green gown with a deeper neckline than modesty should allow. Her hair, dark red almost to black, fell in fashionable ringlets about her face. She was not beautiful but was striking in the way that made beauty seem something commonplace beside it. Gideon had last seen her clad in male garb outside an old fulling mill where Lord had made his temporary headquarters some two months since. He knew, although from this angle he could not see it, that there was a scar marring her face on the other side, running from eye to ear. Then, Gideon had not known her name. Now he thought he might.

"Kate," Lord spoke the syllable lightly and crossed to her, taking her hand in both his and bending over it, kissing it as any friend might, before drawing aside so she could make her curtsey to the prince.

"I apologise for Philip, highness," she said as she rose. "He has a poor way of showing you his gratitude and of course he will accept the pardon." She held out her hand to Gideon and dropped an eyelid in a conspiratorial wink at him as he handed her the document.

Lord let out a breath in a heavy sigh as she passed it on to him, holding the vellum in his hands. He looked as if he wasn't quite so unhappy that it existed as his previous reaction had suggested.

"It seems I am outflanked, outnumbered and outranked." He made a deeper bow than before to the prince. "Highness, forgive me, I am most grateful that you have secured this pardon for me. I may yet hope there will come a time I can prove my innocence in the matter for which it stands."

The prince smiled and put his hand back on Lord's shoulder.

"I am confident that you will, and then I shall speak for you with my uncle, and all will be made right in the way you most wish. But now, if Lady Catherine will excuse us, we should find what has been said by the men you captured. If it is as I suspect, we may need to move quickly." He made a brief bow, more of the head than the body, towards the woman as he spoke. She curtsied again and Gideon saw her fingers link with Lord's as they passed, then the two men were gone. Gideon found himself alone in the room with Lady Catherine.

"Thank goodness we have that sorted. There is a reason the prince earned the sobriquet 'le diable' with his family. He is not happy to be crossed. You must be Gideon Lennox," she said, unabashed at any lack of formal introduction. "I have heard much about you, but not," she gestured to the harpsichord standing in the corner, "if you play?"

Uncertain quite how to take that, Gideon shook his head.

"I regret, my lady, it is not a skill I have ever had the opportunity to acquire. My father was of the belief that music was a gateway to Popery, so it was not something I was ever allowed in my youth."

"I am sure he was mistaken," she said and crossing to the instrument ran her fingers along the keys in a stream of clipped notes. "Oh good, it is in tune." She sat on the stool beside it and arranged her skirts, then tried a brief melody with one hand. "You see, if your father had been correct there would be parlous few who were not of Rome in the entire world." She began playing then something stately and slow. "Who was it that wrote: *every soul's alike a musical instrument, the faculties in all men equal strings, well or ill handled; and those sweet or harsh?* You don't know? Me neither. Philip, of course would. He has a memory for such things, Zahara tells me that were he of her religion he would have become a *hafiz*."

Gideon felt the colour flood his face. It was an unsettling experience talking to a stranger, who knew better than he did, those he was coming to know and care for—in one case cared for more than he felt able to admit.

"*Hafiz?*" he asked, uncertain how he was expected to respond.

"Is someone who is much respected for having learned the Quran by heart." She looked at him. "You do know what the Quran is?"

Gideon realised too late how he must seem.

"Yes, my lady, I know that."

She smiled at him as if he had done something she found pleasing.

"I am glad to have this chance to speak with you privily," she said. "You must forgive me for being blunt because it is too important to leave unsaid, and we may not have such a chance to talk like this again in the foreseeable future. So, there is no opportunity for us to do as usually happens and learn to know and trust each other over time, whilst in company with our mutual friends. Instead, we must both pretend that has already happened and we are now ourselves good friends." She lifted her hands from the harpsichord and turned her body towards him, the candlelight catching a spark in her eyes. "Do you think you can do that, Mr. Lennox? Gideon?"

Struck speechless, Gideon stared at her. He had never met a woman like this before, or a man, except perhaps Philip Lord himself. He had the odd image then of twin souls, or even more profound, one soul in two bodies and as if she had read his thoughts she smiled.

"I feel as if you already have," she said, answering her own question. "And before you ask, I am Kate. Lady Catherine de Bouquelemont is a woman who is gilded for court, well-mannered and demure in all things. Kate…" She set her hands back to the harpsichord and played the opening notes of a marching song. "Kate is a warrior."

"I am honoured, Kate, to be counted as your friend," Gideon said. "I promise I will always hold that friendship in the highest esteem."

She continued playing and sent him a delighted smile.

"I think, from what I hear, that you must be good for Philip. He is too inclined to be *le plus beau des plus beaux*—or as Danny put it once and perhaps better, *la plus belle des plus belles*. But I do not see you being caught up in that. And since he has lost Matthew, he needs someone with him who has their feet on the earth as you do. And so does Zahara."

The music stopped and Kate got to her feet in a soft rustle of silk. She moved to the group of chairs set by the hearth, gesturing to Gideon to join her.

"And it is Zahara who I would speak to you about because I know what you are to each other." She held his gaze and somehow, he mustered the courage to sustain it, unable to deny the truth and not wanting to do so. For a terrible moment he thought this woman might be seeking to warn him away from any involvement with Zahara. But then something in her expression changed and she nodded as if satisfied by what she saw in his face. "I wish I could promise you an understanding of her that would unlock the gate of the garden you crave. All I can do is what I always do. Tell you the style and size of the earthworks and fortifications you need to overcome, describe for you the walls of the citadel and the strength and weaknesses of its making and count the number and nature of the enemy within."

Gideon took the seat she offered then and shook his head. None of that made sense, but if it was to do with Zahara…

"I don't understand your allegory," he admitted.

Kate drew a deeper breath and sighed.

"What man could? Let me try to explain." She sat back and the flames from the hearth reflected in the red of her hair as embers. "Zahara was born to a woman stolen from her home one night in a coastal raid on a village in Devon by pirates from Barbary. The woman was sold to be a slave."

Gideon heard the words and felt his heart constrict.

"But Zahara was never a slave," Kate went on. "She was raised in her father's religion as his daughter. He was a merchant, and he was travelling in Shiraz twelve years ago with Zahara and her mother when terrible floods came. Her parents perished and she was rescued by the man we all call Shiraz. And Shiraz…" Kate went silent then, her eyes looking into the fire as if seeing visions there. "He had lost everything shortly before: his status, his voice, his wife, his children. Zahara gave him purpose and his life a new meaning. So, there they were, two lost souls, travelling together. Shiraz teaching, Zahara learning and studying. Then, when taking ship on a pilgrimage to the burial place of some of those revered in their faith…" Kate seemed uncertain how to go on.

Gideon held up his hand. "Zahara told me. She was captured as a slave by pirates from Algiers."

Kate nodded, her face sad. "She was thirteen years old."

Gideon's heart seemed to freeze in his chest.

"*Thirteen*? She did not tell me that."

Kate reached out a hand and gripped his briefly, as a friend might, before releasing it again. "And did she tell you how she spent a year being subjected to the worst a man might do to a woman? That she was used and abused, beaten, raped. And that it was all done with no mind to the consequences because the man who had taken her knew he had scant right under the law of his own people to have done so. He was powerful enough to get away with it."

Gideon heard the words and felt as if someone had flayed every inch of skin from his body, leaving each nerve exposed and raw, agonised by a pain he could not encompass. From somewhere else, another universe, he heard Kate's voice.

"Philip learned of her plight from Shiraz. It was a hard fight for him politically, financially and ultimately physically, but he freed her and brought her to me, small and broken."

She stopped speaking and the room was quiet, so quiet that the soft sounds of the fire seemed loud.

"But Zahara is resilient. Under my care she regained

much of what had been beaten from her: her confidence, her courage, her ability to trust in others. Shiraz stayed with her, guarding her as you will have seen, and when I could no longer keep her with me, they went with Philip." Then Kate reached for and squeezed his hand again, this time keeping hold of it. "And that is what you need to understand, Gideon. She loves you as you love her, but she is not now as other women and may never be. Her body has healed, and her spirit is strong. There may yet come a time… be a way… But it might be asking too much of any man to wait for something that may never happen. I am telling you now that if you can't wait, perhaps in vain and can't endure the pain and disappointment, then you must let her know and let her go. That she could bear, I think, and accept your friendship in its stead, but if you promise her more—" Kate stopped speaking and Gideon realised then how hard she was finding this too.

His throat closed on the words he wanted to say. Instead, he shook his head. The image he had seen before floated in his mind of twin souls or one soul shared between two bodies. He had thought the barrier between himself and Zahara was that of religion, but now he saw the ugly truth and he felt beyond anger, beyond grief. Simply lost.

"She knows she has my pledge," he said when words could come, but even then as little more than a hoarse whisper. "For as long as I live, and beyond if God is merciful."

Kate smiled at him then and released his hand.

"I think I knew that already," she said. "After all those of us who love are never given much choice in such things, are we? But I am glad to be sure."

Chapter Two

I

The silence in the room had no time to settle before the door opened and Lord came in. He had changed from travel-weary clothing to a stylish doublet and breeches in deep blue, decorated with silver braid and lace.

Gideon stood up and made a bow.

"I will leave you—"

"No." Lord's voice was sharp, and Gideon froze, aware that Kate was just as shocked by the brusqueness. Lord moderated his tone as he went on. "I wish you to stay. I will need you for something."

"Then, of course. What…?"

But Lord's full attention was fixed on Kate, with a yearning, close to hunger. As if he wanted to imprint every detail of her in memory or expected her to vanish from his grip. He crossed to where she sat and held out his hand, which she took so he could draw her to her feet.

"Zahara told me about Matt," she said. "That Mags killed him and has taken most of your men. I'm so sorry."

Lord bowed his head. Matthew Rider had been captain of Lord's company, and his good friend. Mags had arranged Matt's death in a way that meant no blame could be set at his door. He had then secured

THE DEVIL'S COMMAND

Matt's place as Lord's second-in-command, only to betray that trust in a most terrible way and take most of the company with him, leaving Lord only a few of his most loyal men. The memory of it was still bitter for Gideon.

"I have sent Danny to deal with Mags," Lord said, "and to bring back the men he stole. If it can be done Danny will do so."

"But he can't bring back what you have lost."

Lord looked back up to meet Kate's level gaze and something passed between them that needed no words. Then Lord lifted her fingers to his lips and kissed them briefly.

"I do not have too much time, but the prince has given me leave until we hear back from the scouts."

"The prince found what he expected?" Kate asked.

"The prince wanted us all out to beat up the enemy quarters. An entire army of them, which would not have ended well. I prevailed upon him instead to inform the king."

"Then there will be a battle tomorrow?" Kate asked, studying Lord's face, her own caught in a troubled frown. "Essex might prevaricate if he can. The last I knew his army was more spread out than our own."

"Yes, but we control the road to London now, so he has no choice but to engage."

Kate smiled. "Then Sir Faithful will be pleased."

"Sir *Faithful*?" Lord echoed the name with obvious doubt.

"It is indeed a true name," Kate said. "Sir Faithful Fortescue. He was to have left for Ireland with his troop but was instead coerced into joining Essex. He had me bring word to the prince that in a fight he and his men will throw down their field signs and join him. He wished to wait for a battle so as to have the most effect."

Lord laughed. "Then your Sir Faithful will be happy for a battle and the princes are, of course, delighted at the prospect."

"But you, I see, are not," Kate said and moved her free hand to brush a strand of hair from his face.

"I find it more a matter of necessity than a cause for delight."

"But it is still only a battle," she said. Gideon could hear the slight strain in her voice. "You have fought in many, what is different this time?"

Lord kissed her fingers again. "This time it is different because I have something to lose. Because between you and the prince, you have given me a future I did not have before. I find life more precious and harder to hazard."

That surprised Gideon. Despite Lord's initial reaction to it, the pardon must have impacted more than he had shown.

Lord was still holding Kate's hand and now unfolded it in both his own, studying her palm.

"*I have a heart, Lady. A loving heart, a truly loving heart. I would you had it in your hand, sweet Lady, to see the truth it bears you.*"

Kate smiled up into his face.

"*And you shall see I dare accept it, Sir, tak't in my hand and view it: if I find it a loving and a sweet heart, as you call it, I am bound, I am.*"

Lord moved one hand and in it was a ring. A ring Gideon had seen before, always worn on Lord's smallest finger, a gold band set with a ruby. He placed it in her palm.

"The pardon frees me to do what I would have done a dozen years ago if I had been able. I cannot offer you a church or a feast or at least not yet, and I know that no man on earth could ever make of you an honest woman. I would be the last to seek to do so. But I can offer you my name now it is no longer attainted." He inclined his head towards Gideon, but his gaze had not left Kate's face. "We have here a lawyer who can write words for a contract that will stand in law, should anything befall me on the field tomorrow. So, if you will accept me, *per verba de praesenti*, I do take you, Catherine, to be my wife."

Her hand cupped the ring, but she did not close her fingers about it. Instead, she studied his eyes as if seeking something there. Then, satisfied, she folded the ring into her hand, her gaze still locked with his.

"I do take you, Philip, to be my husband."

Gideon realised then he had been holding his breath, as Lord must have been, awaiting Kate's response. Part of his mind was shaping already the form of words he would need to put in such an *ad hoc* marriage contract for it to have some legal standing, but he also understood that the words, the vow, added nothing to what already lay between these two. He was still wondering why Lord wanted this. What difference would it make if anything were to happen to him upon the morrow whether he left Kate as his grieving lover or grieving widow? Unless, of course, there was wealth, land or title involved, but the pardon had not made mention of any such restoration.

"I assure you I have no presentiment of doom," Lord said, as he finished slipping the ring onto his wife's finger, "but I want your promise that if anything were to befall me you will endure and persevere for us both, keep to all we have avowed our lives to, and strive for happiness with all your heart."

That sounded to Gideon as much a vow as the one they had both taken a few moments before, but from the way it was spoken and received, one which held a much more powerful impact than stating their union as a fact.

Kate shook her head, eyes widening. "Philip, that is not fair. You can't ask me to—"

He still held her hand with the ring glistening like a drop of blood and he lifted his other hand to place the fingers over her lips, silencing her words.

"I know you too well," he said. "I know if I were lost, without good cause to do so you would not linger, and I cannot keep taking the field knowing your life rides with me."

The sparkle of sudden tears, unshed but there, was captured in the candlelight as it caught Kate's face. In his heart, Gideon understood then. Would he wish to live if Zahara were gone?

"Then I will swear so," Kate whispered, "before God and by my honour... But only *if*—"

"Oh Kate, my sweet Kate." Lord shook his head and was smiling as he did so, the white of his hair shimmering on the blue of his doublet as much as the silver points that laced it. "How did I know there would need to be some condition you will set upon me in return?" His face grew serious again. "Anything. I will promise you anything, in exchange

THE DEVIL'S COMMAND

for your word on this."

Kate drew a breath. "Before me, before God and before a witness, I ask you to swear the same." Then, "Oh no, don't you dare shake your head at me Philip Lord. You can't deny me what you ask for yourself."

Gideon, seeing the hard determination in Lord's expression, was pretty sure that he would. But then something changed in the turquoise eyes and for a moment Lord buried his head in Kate's hair as it lay on her shoulder. When he lifted his face again it looked white.

"I would say you do not know what you ask, but of course, you do."

He placed both his hands about hers as if he was taking an oath on them as on a Bible.

"I solemnly promise what you ask of me," he said, "that were anything to befall you, I will endure and persevere, keep to all we have avowed and strive for happiness with all my heart." Then his tone lifted. "There, are you content now or do I have to tell Gideon to include the lines in our marriage contract?"

And the moment was resolved in their smiles.

Kate left first, drawing a reluctant Gideon into a brief embrace.

"Don't forget our conversation. Zahara knows of it. Sometimes it can be easier to have a friend speak for you of things you cannot yourself find a way to express."

Then she went in a sweep and rustle of silk skirts.

Lord waited for the door to close, his gaze lingering there until Kate was gone.

"Thank you," he said, turning to Gideon. "I am

sorry for imposing on you like that, but it was all very sudden, and we have little time. Will you be able to create a contract of the kind I need? Something that will prove the marriage even if challenged?"

Which was a difficult question to answer.

"Is it likely to be challenged?"

"I would hope it will not be needed at all," Lord said. "I have no plan to be pistolled or take a mortal cut from an enemy blade. It is my intention that we will be able to take our vows in a more usual way soon, before a priest. But were anything to happen to me before that, then yes, it could be challenged, and Kate's life might even be at risk."

"I don't see—"

"No, of course you do not. That is because you have no real notion of the lengths to which the men who would mould my life will go. That is why this was even necessary. I ask again, can you do it?"

Gideon nodded.

"I will word it so it will be difficult to challenge, and I can be your witness. But it would have been stronger were there two witnesses and best with a priest."

"That cannot be helped now." Lord put a hand on Gideon's shoulder. "I trust you to do what is needed. If you ask direction to a man called Blake, who is one of the king's personal secretaries presently here to serve the prince, he should be able to furnish you with pen, ink and paper. Kate and I will sign it before I ride. After it is written you should try to catch an hour or two of sleep. If the king agrees, which he will as he has no choice, the prince will march before dawn. He seeks to occupy the high ground on Edgehill and is insistent that any man who can wield a blade should ride with him." He lifted his hand and sighed. "I regret when he took an interest in you, I made mention of the fact that you have done so to some effect in the past. For that I must apologise. Had I realised it would be taken in such a way I would have refrained."

"I've never been in battle," Gideon said, thinking of the brief confusion of the skirmish he had witnessed as they arrived and little relishing a repetition on a larger scale.

"Tomorrow, you may have your chance," Lord assured him. "But now excuse me as my wife is waiting for me." He strode to the door then turned as he reached it. "My wife. I like the sound of that, but by God it seems a strange thing to be calling Kate." Then he was gone, no doubt to enjoy legally, as man and wife, that for which neither had found a need for sanction through marriage before.

Gideon sought a servant of the house and was sent up a back staircase and along a couple of passageways to the room where, he was assured, he would find Mr Blake.

Blake was a younger man that Gideon had expected, perhaps in his late twenties. He had turned what had been a guest room into a workspace and despite it being well into the evening, he was still working at the table. A pile of documents was beside him and Gideon was surprised to see some familiar-looking news sheets from London, dated to the last few days and one even dating from the day before. He had to push away an odd wash of homesickness at the sight of a copy of the *Perfect Diurnall*. He recalled reading the first edition in his chambers back in January. Blake seemed to have been perusing it when Gideon disturbed him, and he rose with a friendly smile.

"Ned Blake, and you must be Gideon Fox, here with the intriguing Philip Lord. I was privileged to be involved in the drafting and writing up of his pardon a month ago now. Was he pleased by it?"

Taken aback, Gideon nodded.

"I think he was. You have legal training then?"

Blake gave a modest shrug. "I was apprenticed for four years, but not enough to qualify."

Gideon tactfully refrained from asking why his apprenticeship had not been completed. Besides which, he knew any sympathy would be misplaced. In royal employment Blake would earn more money than many his age who were fully qualified might hope for in the provinces. More than Gideon himself had been earning fully qualified in London.

"That must be useful in your present work," he said, and Blake rewarded that with a smile and a few rapid nods which appeared almost as if his head were wobbling on his neck.

"So, Mr Fox, I was told to render you due assistance. What do you need?"

Gideon gestured to a space at the end of the table where Blake was working.

"A stool to sit there, another light, pen, paper and ink."

Within a short time, Blake had all provided and sat down to continue his own work.

Gideon had given some thought to the requirements of the document he was writing and decided in the end that it would work best if it was simply a statement confirming that both parties had *per verba de praesenti* declared their spousal vows each to the other. He added they were witnessed in that by himself and, having done so they, had then fulfilled the consummation of the marriage.

He was not at all sure it would stand up to legal challenge. But the argument would not be around whether the events had occurred so much as whether they, in the absence of a priest, constituted a proper form of marriage. In theory it did, but in practice? The form of words was straightforward enough to write, and he was blotting it when Blake looked up again.

"That was fast. What is it? Do you need a copy?"

"Good idea," Gideon agreed and was reaching for a fresh sheet when Blake placed a hand with ink-stained fingers on his arm.

"It is getting late. I am sure you would like to get some sleep. Please allow me to do that. I was instructed by the prince to make myself useful to you and no one is going to ask me to fight tomorrow." He finished with a self-deprecating smile as if he truly wished he was to take part in the battle.

Gideon thought for a moment then nodded. There was no reason he had to write both copies himself, and he did need to sleep. But there was something essential he needed to do before that.

"Thank you," he said. He pushed the paper over the table to Blake who picked it up and read it over, his face changing as he did so from simple focus to surprise.

"Lady Catherine is married to Philip Lord? He is a lucky man. I was just making a copy of her latest exploits to be sent to the king." He gestured to the pamphlets. "Amongst other things she has done for us, she secures these from London as fast as they are printed. They contain much of value about how those there see the war and what they know of our army's doings."

"I can imagine that must be useful," Gideon observed.

"I think that is perhaps to understate the matter," Blake said. "She has served the king so well in her role as an intelligencer. Were I not in possession of these proofs I am not sure I would believe it. I am amazed any one person, let alone a mere woman, could achieve even half of what she has done."

Gideon found himself thinking that as an adjective 'mere' was the last he would apply to Kate. But he was curious now about what Blake had said.

"She has been active in such work?"

"Indeed so. One of the very few who are bringing good intelligence to the king, though he will sometimes not countenance receiving it. Lord Falkland, the king's Secretary of State, has declared that all such methods are deceitful and dishonourable and those who engage in them therefore not to be trusted. He refuses to condone the work of any spies or intelligencers. But, despite him, Lady Catherine has done much to remedy that lack. It is well she works for Prince Rupert or much of what she has done and uncovered would have been wasted." He put the document down on the table and looked at Gideon with speculation. "Do you think now she is married she will give up these escapades? It is hardly seemly for an unmarried woman to act thus, riding around the country unaccompanied at times, but for one who is married it would be unacceptable."

Gideon answered honestly.

"I have no idea. I don't know the lady well enough to say."

Blake looked thoughtful and then shook his head.

"I hope she does. It is more appropriate that she keep to her hearth and her embroidery. She is a magnificent woman. It would be a tragedy were she to succumb to the dangers of such work."

"I am sure she is well acquainted with them and able to know her own mind," Gideon said, irritated by the way Blake was talking.

"But surely her husband would never allow—"

"I think her husband has more faith in her than you seem to." Gideon retorted. Then before Blake could launch into another veiled criticism of Kate's behaviour, he rose, repeated his thanks and a reminder of the urgency of the copy, made a brief farewell and escaped through the door.

It took him little time to get directions to where Philip Lord's men were quartered. They had taken over a small hayloft and were already asleep. Gideon had noticed it seemed to be the happy facility of every veteran soldier he had met, with one notable exception, to sleep anywhere, instantly, the moment the opportunity presented itself.

He found Zahara below the hayloft preparing food on a table she had covered with a cloth. As he approached Shiraz chose to reveal himself, stepping from shadow to light to greet Gideon with a nod, before withdrawing to the concealing darkness again.

It was his way of letting Gideon know they were not alone.

Zahara herself welcomed him with a warm smile.

"Have you eaten?"

"No, but I—"

Of course, she then insisted he sit and eat some bread and cheese. When he had done so she gestured to the table.

"Here, you can help me cut this. When they wake, the men will need food they can carry with them."

'This' was the best part of a chicken which she had procured from somewhere and she was cutting and placing bread, a little chicken, an apple and some cheese on squares of linen, to be wrapped. Without thinking about it, Gideon took the knife she offered and began cutting. His mind caught up in what he should say, what he could say, as his hands went through the motions required. In the end he started with the news he thought she might most want to know.

"I was asked to witness a form of marriage between Philip Lord and Lady Catherine."

Zahara stopped her work then and looked at him, her face radiant.

"That is good news."

"Who is she? She is not at all like other women I have met."

"No, she is not as most other women," Zahara agreed. "She is Lady Catherine de Bouquelemont. Her father was an earl in Ireland and her mother the daughter of a duke here. But both her parents died when she was very young, and she was raised abroad. She was in the service of King Charles' sister and is

THE DEVIL'S COMMAND

close to the princes, his nephews." Zahara went back to her work. "Lady Catherine is kind and I think she is good for the Schiavono. I am glad for them to be wed. It is better so."

"Yes," Gideon agreed. "It made them both happier I think, but I wondered..." and that was where this was hard. Gideon had not had any sense that Lord was being pushed against his will into something he would have preferred not to do, more that there was some compulsion which meant it had to be done now, today, rather than in the due course of time.

Zahara seemed to read his mind.

"It is because he knows she might be with child."

That night at the mill in Weardale. Gideon realised his mouth had opened.

"But how did he...?"

"I told him," she said, glancing back up from her task.

It explained then, the sudden necessity for a marriage that could be proved at need, both for the protection of Kate's good name and to ensure any child that might be born did not have to grow up with the terrible stigma of illegitimacy. It explained, even more, the second oath he had placed upon them both. Lord feared that in the throes of grief she might forget that another life was bound to her own.

"Lady Catherine came to see me when we arrived. It was she who found us space here." Zahara gestured to the hayloft. "She told me she was not sure yet, but she had missed her monthly courses. That was something she had never done before. Indeed, she had thought herself barren after so many years and being the age she is. She would say nothing to the Schiavono until she was certain as even if it were so, much can still go wrong this early. But I knew he needed to know that it was possible. Sometimes it is the place of one friend to speak up for another."

The words were the exact echo of what Kate herself had said to him and hearing them reminded him of all that had gone with that. A hollow pit opened in his stomach and for a moment he had to step back from the table as the very smell of food was nauseating. Then he remembered why he had come, what he needed to tell her. He put down the knife and wiped his hands on a square of linen.

"There is to be a battle tomorrow and the Schiavono told me I will be riding with him. The prince has required it."

Zahara looked up at him. Her expression held the slightest of frowns as she searched his face with her kitten-green eyes.

"I trust the Schiavono to do all he can to keep you safe," she said.

"I am sure he will put me where I will be least exposed because I will be the least effective of his force," Gideon agreed. "But the course of a battle, from all I have heard, is not one any can predict with certainty, and it is possible..."

She reached over and touched the back of his hand, resting her fingers there for a few moments. He knew better now than to try and reciprocate, to follow his heart and take her hands and draw her close. More so since hearing from Kate what Zahara had endured. He just accepted what she was able to give.

"I will pray for you," she said.

THE DEVIL'S COMMAND

Gideon struggled then to find the words he needed to say. He couldn't even meet her gaze and stared at her fingers as they rested on his hand.

"Philip Lord gave Lady Catherine his name. If he dies, she has that at least. But I—"

Zahara's fingers lifted, and her hand moved to clasp his. He looked at her then and was lost in her eyes.

"No one shall die," she said, *"whose heart has lived with the life love breathed into it.* You leave the gift of yourself with me always, even if you were to leave me bereaved."

He was not sure he understood, but he felt the reassurance flowing from her and a little of her peace took roost in his soul.

"I will come back to you," he said.

Zahara smiled. "I know you will."

II

Nick found himself torn between exasperation and a grudging, never to be admitted, admiration for his new lieutenant.

After what had happened with Cummings, he wanted the tone of their relationship to be established. So having got back from a brief interview with the earl to report he was ready to take up his duties again, he retired to the room they perforce would have to share, with the intention of making his authority felt.

The last thing he expected to hear was laughter as he opened the door. He found Danny Bristow sat by a candle reading and chuckling as he did so. Perhaps if it had been some amusing pamphlet or ballad bought in the streets, Nick might have understood, but the book in Bristow's hands was Nick's own well-fingered copy of *The Souldiers Accidence,* one of Gervase Markham's books of instruction for those learning the arts of war.

As he closed the door Bristow gave a fresh snort of laughter. Nick made a point of ignoring him even when he put down the book and stood to bow. Instead, Nick sat on the bed and started fighting to remove his boots wishing he had kept his servant with him.

"Allow me to assist you, Sir Nicholas." Bristow knelt to unfix the spurs and then cup the heel of the boot so it could be pulled free. In a moment it was done, as well as any servant might and with less fuss than many. "Did you require assistance with your points and lacings too?"

In the shadowland at the edge of the candlelight, it was impossible to be sure, but there was a note in Bristow's voice which seemed to suggest he found the situation hilarious. Nick tightened his jaw and snapped a refusal.

"As you wish, sir." Bristow sounded almost disappointed. "I hope you don't mind but I found that book on the table and it has provided me with much entertainment."

"Entertainment?" Nick shook his head in disgust. "That is a book on military practice."

"Written by someone who also wrote a book for housewives and another for gentleman farmers," Bristow observed. He walked over, picked up the book and tapped it. "I think you must be a courageous man, Sir Nicholas, and I would pay good money to see you or any other use this as it stands on the field of battle."

"It is an accepted military manual," Nick snapped, but it was clear Bristow was not listening. He had the book open and was reading.

"So how about this? Markham writes '*The men to be handsome yeomen or serving men, light timberd, and of comely shape, where it skills not much for the tallness or greatness of the bodie, but for the height of spirit, and the goodness of the inclination. In which little David—many times—puts down the greatest Goliath.*'"

By the end Bristow was laughing so hard he was struggling to finish. Nick snatched the abused text away from him, curbing his fury.

"Did you never realise the importance of having good looking men in your light cavalry?" Bristow gasped through tears of laughter.

"It is a book well thought of by many," Nick said, nettled.

Bristow recovered himself and shook his head.

"If you must learn your soldiering from a book, Sir Nicholas, please make it a decent one. I might commend to you Robert Ward, for example. Or John Cruso. At least he has a general grasp of what is significant and what is not and has been to war in this current century."

He said more, but Nick wasn't listening. He found himself studying the strange man Mags had sent to him. Bristow was little more than average height and had nothing about him beyond his dress to suggest any military background. Nick's eyes were drawn to the square, competent, short-fingered hands, no longer contained in leather gauntlets. The third finger on the right hand was bandaged from some recent injury and there were red patches of healing skin. He had a sudden and rare insight that he was not the first to underestimate this man. It dawned on him that there was a lot to be said for having such someone like this in his service, below the notice of most whilst highly capable in thought and deed.

From Bristow's damaged hands, Nick's gaze moved to the sword he still wore even here when he had discarded all else of his craft. The familiar shape of the cat's head pommel sent an unwarranted shiver across the skin of Nick's shoulders. It reminded him that there was something he needed to find out. He waved away whatever Bristow had been saying with a dismissive flick of his hand.

"Tell me," he demanded. "You know the one they call the Schiavono? You have served under him?"

The gaze that met his was assessing and appraising. It was also disturbingly astute.

"You mean Philip Lord? Yes. I do and I have. But you already know that sir. What is it you want to know about him?"

And that was more difficult to answer than he had anticipated. He was already regretting the question but to withdraw it now would make him look foolish. He threw out the first notion that came into his head.

"I have heard he is popular with his men. What makes him so?"

Bristow moved closer beside the hearth, the flickering light sending his shadow dancing up the wall.

"What makes any man popular with his fellows? He

THE DEVIL'S COMMAND

has wealth, he has wit, and he has women. And he gives all those to his men. Or perhaps Gervase Markham has it right when he says a captain should have virtue worthy of reverence, authority fit for command and experience able to direct and censure *'and he that hath these hath that sufficiencie that to disobey is to die'*. In other words, the Schiavono knows how to lead men and he is a ruthless bastard if you cross him." Bristow pondered his own words for a short time then added, "Rather like the graf, I suppose."

"So why do you serve the one and not the other?"

The other man shook his head and lifted his shoulders. "You ask some strange things, sir. I've not given it that much thought. I suppose it is a matter of who I consider offers me the better prospects and right now I think that is obvious. I am being paid exceedingly well to be here with you."

And that gave Nick an idea.

"You serve Ma—the graf because he pays you more than Lord and offers you good prospects?"

Bristow nodded. "Put like that it sounds a little simple, but yes, that is pretty much it."

"Then what if I paid you more and offered you better?"

The firelight caught Bristow's eyes and turned their chestnut closer to red.

"Then," he said, considering, "I suppose I would be your man. But it is hard to see what prospects you might offer. Sitting at the right hand of the graf gives me wine, wealth, women and the promise of comfort and command. Sitting at your left hand as the second and spare of two lieutenants? Not so much." He gave a disarming grin. "You can see my problem, sir, I am sure. And that is not to mention that the graf is not a man who would take well any change of allegiance."

"Cummings can be found another posting in time," Nick said, feeling as if he were being led by an inspiration. "I am not without wealth and can offer you what you ask, including comfort and command, as I gain promotion. And as for the graf, well he need not know."

"I don't see…"

"He would think you still served him. Besides, you were there when he made it clear he was pledging himself to support me."

"Is that what you heard him say?" Bristow sounded doubtful, but went on, "I think you are asking me to play a dangerous part. The graf is not a man to cross. Were he to discover that I—"

"How could he discover it? He sent you here to serve me and no doubt to report to him. You will say to him what you need to say, unless I have charged you not to do so, or you perceive it to be unwise for my—for *our* interests for him to be so appraised, but as things stand, I don't see it being so much of an issue."

Bristow was looking at him now as if suspecting a trap or at least as if doubting his words.

"You do know where the graf has taken his men?"

Nick thought about it. "I assumed south to the king since he has not come here."

The other man shook his head.

"He has taken them to Fairfax who is petitioning Parliament for the means to pay them. If whatever committee in London approves the exorbitant fee he is asking, the graf will be taking the field against you."

THE DEVIL'S COMMAND

Chapter Three

It was freezing cold, pitch black and Gideon felt as if he was clinging to his saddle like a shipwrecked mariner might cling to a spar thrown about in the waves. He could hear the sounds of other horsemen close by. The snorts of their mounts, the scrape and creak of leather, the slight jingle of metal and the soft sound of hooves on earth. But he could see nothing except the faintest of shadows.

Had there been a clear sky it would have been different. The moon was a few days from full, but under the weight of wintery clouds, it was hard to discern much at all. Despite that, those he rode with seemed to know the path to take and, like cats, had eyes that could see in the dark. Gideon trusted that his own little mare knew those she was with well enough that she would match their pace and pick her own way without his guidance.

Somewhere ahead was Lord, who he had last seen clad in borrowed armour, riding beside Prince Rupert and getting ill-looks from Daniel O'Neil, the prince's Lieutenant-Colonel of horse. But Gideon himself was in the charge of Roger Jupp, who had been promoted to be Lord's captain in the diminished remnants of the company. Jupp's orders to Gideon had been brief.

"Keep the nose of your horse up the arse of mine, Mr Fox, then I know where you are."

Gideon was in borrowed armour too. Zahara had

THE DEVIL'S COMMAND

presented him with an old and battered buff coat and someone had strapped a breastplate over his chest, the cuirass held in place with straps across his back. The long-barrelled pistol he carried in a holster slung from his saddle had been a gift from Shiraz. It was a beautifully made doglock cavalry pistol and Shiraz had shown him how to load it and secure it from firing by pinning at full or half-cock with the dog. With it came a pouch of cartouches for rapid reloading and a small powder flask.

Jupp had been strong on that too.

"You don't even touch that bloody thing until I tell you to, sir, and as I'm going to be right in front of you, be good and careful where you point it when I do."

It seemed they were riding in darkness forever and then, here and there, Gideon saw sparks of light spread out below them. It was as if some stars had come down from heaven and settled on the ground. He realised it was where fires had been lit and they were on top of an escarpment looking out over the Vale of the Red Horse. The scattered fires had no doubt been made to warm those troops who had no shelter. On Edgehill, where the Royalist horse were assembling, a handful more had been lit, which would show both friend and foe that the king's army occupied the advantageous high ground.

Eventually, they came to a halt and the order was given to dismount. It was too cold to sleep but once they had sorted the horses, Gideon wrapped himself as well as he could in his blanket and tried anyway.

He had no idea how much later it was when a voice called him.

"Fox."

He must have been dozing because whoever it was had to call him again.

"Gideon."

Someone was shaking him by the shoulder, and he was shivering as he moved to sit up.

It was still dark, though the first slice of light dividing the horizon presaged a chill dawn. A cutting breeze, made worse by the being on the high ridge of ground, was tugging at his hair and he realised from the stiffness of his shoulders as he donned his frost-rimed hat, that he would have been wise to unstrap the breast piece before trying to rest.

Philip Lord stood over him.

"I have your horse here. We are summoned to a meeting with the king."

Gideon struggled to his feet and pulled the breastplate back into place and realised that he looked as though he had been sleeping on the frozen ground in his clothes. He opened his mouth to protest he was in no fit attire, but Lord was already striding away. The lightening shadows showed where their two horses stood ready.

If there was one lesson he had learned in Philip Lord's company it was to trust that Lord would have thought of everything. If they were to be in the presence of the king, Lord would ensure that when it happened Gideon would be appropriately dressed.

So he let the protest remain unspoken, avoided treading on the recumbent forms of the men around him and, taking the reins of his chestnut from Lord, made a good attempt to mount. His frozen limbs failed to respond as they should and he was grateful

THE DEVIL'S COMMAND

when Lord gave him a leg up, before pulling himself onto his own mount. That horse was one Gideon hadn't seen before and was a powerful blue roan. It occurred to Gideon as he rode that if he had to be in a battle, he would much prefer not to take his sweet-natured and loyal mare with him.

Lord's voice floated back to him softly lifted in song.

"Hey! now the day dawis;
The jolly cock crawis;
Now shroudis the shawis
   Thro' Nature anon.
The thissel-cock cryis
On lovers wha lyis:
Now skaillis the skyis;
   The nicht is neir gone."

They made their way through dozing groups of men, and soldiers rubbing their near-frozen hands as they talked in low voices and lines of patient horses. Once onto the road, Lord picked up the pace to a trot.

"Can I ask where we are going?"

"There is to be a council of war on the battle to come," Lord told him. "The king and both princes will be there with the senior army commanders. The prince wishes me to be ranked as a colonel. So far with no more of a regiment than Jupp and the company men, but the prince believes that will be changed at this meeting, which is why he wants me there."

Which left one rather obvious question unanswered.

"And me?" Gideon asked.

"That is why I came for you. I am hoping to be able

to attach you to the king's civilian staff or those placed about him, so Jupp doesn't need to spend the entire battle cursing me for having you ride with him."

Gideon felt a flush of humiliation and shame, although he knew what Lord said was true.

"I am that much of a liability?"

There was light enough for Gideon to see that Lord was looking at the way ahead when he answered.

"No. Were you with any of the newly raised troops here you would shine as bright as the morning star for skill amongst them, from what I have seen. But my company work as a team, a single force, and you are not yet integrated into that. For them you would be someone to carry and protect and in a big battle that is dangerous."

Gideon absorbed the words and glanced at Lord to be sure he spoke the truth. Lord turned his head and smiled.

"Now the Gideon Lennox of a month ago I could not have said that about and given another couple of months with regular training I might expect you to take your part as any other member of the company. But for today, if it can be arranged, I would prefer to have you witness your first battle rather than be fighting in it."

In his heart of hearts, Gideon was glad at that and then he wondered if that made him a coward. Perhaps something of his thoughts were on his face, revealed in the new sunlight because Lord broke into song again.

"All courageous knichtis
Aganis the day dichtis

THE DEVIL'S COMMAND

The breist-plate that bright is
  To fight with their fone.
The stoned steed stampis
Through courage, and crampis,
Syne on the land lampis:
  The nicht is neir gone."

They reached the outskirts of a small village which had clear signs of military occupation as the sun was kissing the clouds with shades of pink and orange. Away to one side they were granted a view down the steep slope of the ridge of Edgehill over the lands below.

"The army will have to come off here," Lord said. "Having denied it to the enemy, we can't engage them on these heights. If we are to force them to fight it needs to be down there." He made a sweeping gesture over the farmland broken by ditches, hedges, patches of heathland and the odd stand of trees. Gideon stared and wondered how such a sleepy-looking bucolic scene could ever be a battlefield.

"Come on," Lord said. "Someone will be meeting us with something more suitable for you to wear."

Lord was greeted by those who challenged them as if he were a man of the greatest importance and no one made any attempt to delay them. They stopped by one of the houses and Lord spoke to a man who stood by the door. Dismounting, Gideon was taken inside and found a selection of second-hand clothes of varying qualities had been set out within. Where they had been gathered from Gideon had no idea, but the man who helped him dress was not a military man. Gideon assumed he was part of the civilian baggage train. A man who no doubt made his living selling second-hand clothes to those in the army who needed them.

A half-hour later, Gideon emerged dressed in good quality maroon worsted and with sword on hip. Shaved and fed, he looked much like the professional man that Lord wished to project him to be.

There were a few men gathering outside the largest of the houses in the village, from where there was a view over the potential battlefield. Someone had provided a large trestle upon which were several sketched maps. The men Gideon could see were all dressed for war and his own appearance seemed suddenly inappropriate.

"Wait here," Lord told him and then was lost to sight.

With little choice but to obey and wishing he might vanish into the background, Gideon remained where he had been left. He adopted his most lawyerly stance and expression and tried to look as if he knew he was entitled to be there as he studied the activity about him.

Troops were still arriving on the hill from their quarters and, listening in to the conversations around him, Gideon gathered it was not expected for much to happen until the king arrived. Beside which the artillery, without which the battle couldn't commence, was not expected until the afternoon at the earliest.

After what must have been over an hour, Lord still hadn't returned. Gideon went to look over the vale and was startled to see how much the peace of the dawn was gone. There were now signs of military activity, bodies of troops moving. As they were at a good distance from the ridge, he assumed they must belong to the Earl of Essex's force, but he had no way to be sure.

It dawned on him then that if this battle was lost there would be little to stop those troops from charging right through the places where the king's men had been quartered. Wormleighton would be in the main path of any such rout. Although diverted by the barrier of the ridge of Edgehill, it was perhaps five miles in a straight run from where the battle would be fought.

Would he be able to get there first?

He stood there for a long time watching the troops forming patterns on the farmland and trying to calculate if there were more or less than those standing for the king on Edgehill. It was an impossible task, and eventually he gave up and walked back to the spot where Lord had told him to wait. By then the height of the autumn sun told him it had to be past midmorning.

An argument had broken out between two men and a third, their friend moved to try and calm them down. There were a lot of complaints to be heard from some of the more recent arrivals, commanders of foot regiments, that their soldiers had little to eat for the last two days and saying that asking them to fight without food was sheer folly.

One man was looking over the land below with a perspective glass and making comments to another who seemed to be making notes on the maps on the table. Someone was complaining in an overloud voice about the accommodation they had been provided with overnight and the unreasonableness of being awoken before dawn and then having to stand around until dinner with no prospect of any being served. Another had a pocket watch and declared that it was close to noon and if they were going to have a battle that day then it was past time to be doing so.

A hand touched Gideon's elbow. To his surprise and mild dismay, as he had seen little to like in the man, he turned to see Ned Blake. But at least here was someone else not dressed for war.

"I thought you were to be in the battle," Blake said.

"I was supposed to be," Gideon admitted. "However, it seems I am considered more suited to other things."

Blake frowned and shook his head. "Come with me." Linking his arm with Gideon's would have dragged him in a most undignified way had Gideon not acquiesced. Unwilling to make a scene and considering that the sooner he satisfied whatever whim of Blake's this was, the sooner he could be free of the man, Gideon went along with him.

Blake took him into the house, receiving nods of recognition from the soldiers guarding the door. Inside, the place was thick with men in armour, but Blake pushed through making excuses as he went and drawing Gideon after him.

After an argument about Blake's right of admittance on an urgent matter and Gideon being required to leave his sword belt, they were allowed upstairs. There, after a voice within consented, the door to a final room was opened for them.

The room was bright with an east-facing oriel that

had captured the morning sun. Standing facing it, haloed by sunlight and elegantly clad for battle, wanting but his armour, was a short, slight figure, head bared and bowed as if in prayer. There were others in the room, but this man captured Gideon's attention completely.

He had turned at their entry and Gideon's first impression as the doe-brown eyes took in his own appearance, was of a man who felt the weight of an unbearable burden forever on his shoulders, one he had no means or hope of ever lifting.

With a shock of awe, Gideon knew this was King Charles.

He found the breath he had been drawing stopped short and for a moment he lost any ability to move, his mouth open. Then limbs unlocked, he made a bow deeper than any he had offered to anyone before.

"Ned, was there something more you needed?" The king addressed Blake and glanced again at Gideon as if puzzled by his presence.

Blake had risen from his bow and kept his hat in his hands.

"Majesty, this is Gideon Fox, a gentleman of my acquaintance and of your nephew the prince. He is one of your most loyal subjects who had hopes of taking his place with your army this day, but thus far been unable to procure a place in one of your majesty's regiments. I thought to bring him to you as such courage and devotion is something of which you would know."

The king turned and Gideon found himself the subject of royal scrutiny.

"I commend you, Mr Fox, on your diligence in seeking to fight for your king."

One of the other men in the room cleared his throat. "If you are ready now, your majesty?"

The king inclined his head at the speaker, then looked between Gideon and Blake.

"If you will accompany me, Mr. Fox," he said. "I shall see you are accommodated."

Gideon swallowed down the shoal of fish which seemed to have taken instant and uncomfortable residence in his stomach and were trying to swim up into his gullet. He bowed again. Was there a law he could recall which made it a crime to mislead the king on a person's name?

Blake clapped Gideon on the back with a smile of achievement before walking out behind him as they followed in the wake of those who were with the king. It was as if the man thought he had done Gideon some kind of grand favour and expected in due course to be rewarded for it.

By the time they were back at the gathering of senior officers and advisors, Gideon found himself relegated to a place behind and to one side of the king. He was scrutinised by a gentleman he heard addressed as 'Lucius' by the king, when explaining Gideon was to be kept to hand, and 'Falkland' by one of the bristling nobility, who were jostling for a place. Gideon realised it was this man, with the look more of a poet or academic than a soldier, who Blake had spoken about the night before saying he was so principled, he was against the idea of using spies. Falkland gave Gideon a hard stare then spoke with Blake, both of them glancing at Gideon now and then.

THE DEVIL'S COMMAND

When Gideon caught sight of the king again, he was small amongst the forest of his tall commanders, his nephews towering over him, geared for battle. An argument had broken out and he could see the king frowning, trying to follow what for him must seem, as it did for Gideon, a matter of military pickiness. The prince was demanding the infantry use one formation. Whereas the lord-general commanding the foot, much Rupert's senior in age, was insisting they adopt another, saying it was more usual, and what little training the infantry had been given was rooted in it.

The prince, becoming more animated, stepped forward and Gideon caught sight of Lord. Lord saw him at the same moment and his brows gathered into a questioning frown. Gideon shook his head to try and indicate it was not by his own will he was standing there.

The argument went on for several minutes, becoming heated, until at the king's insistence there was a brief explanation given by the two generals. As far as Gideon could tell, it seemed to be something to do with a difference in the depth of the ranks. Having listened and given it his consideration, the king turned to the infantry commander.

"Lord Lindsey, I hear your contention and I can see you feel most strongly about it, but in this I must stand with the prince, my nephew. He is well versed in the most modern methods of warfare and if he feels that is the most appropriate approach, then it is the one we must take."

The Earl of Lindsey stood unmoving for a moment.

The gaze he bent upon the prince was so venomous that it would have seared the conscience of most men. But the prince seemed oblivious, acknowledging the king as if it were what he had expected should happen and wearing a slight smile as he responded to Lindsey with what he no doubt imagined was a gracious inclination of his head.

That was too much for the Earl. White-faced with fury, he hurled his baton at Rupert's feet.

"If my command and decisions are not adequate to the task of the day, then I will have no choice but to relinquish it. If I am not deemed fit to be a general, I will die a colonel at the head of my own regiment." He made a proper obeisance to the king then withdrew to a murmur of comment.

The king looked as if he had been carved from marble and it was Rupert who picked up the baton and held it in one hand, his expression speculative.

"If I might make a suggestion, we have a man with us whose qualification for command excels. He has the experience and a record of victory which can be tracked across Europe." The prince turned and held out the baton as he did so. "Colonel Philip Lord."

The response amongst the high command was as voluble as it was predictable. The voices being raised in favour were the handful who were the strongest partisans of the prince. It was Lord himself who dealt with the moment as it needed. He made a bow to the prince and raised his voice above the rest.

"You do me great honour, highness, but the position is one that should go to someone all here know and trust. It should be the Earl of Forth. He has more experience than me, a full and complete knowledge of the methods you wish to employ, and the trust of all here."

The prince's brows drew together, and his expression darkened. For a moment Gideon believed he was going to insist. But Lord had already stood aside to make way for the man he had named.

That resolved, the arguments moved on, the next being around a petition from the King's Lifeguard to be allowed to ride at the front of the army to prove their courage and devotion. It seemed other officers had been casting aspersions upon them and implying they were chosen to be an ornament rather than a functional fighting force and they were keen to dispel the myth.

Gideon heard Lord's voice raised in protest. He was saying that to remove the lifeguard from their due place was to put the security of the king at risk. But he and others who made the same point were overruled by the king himself and the Lifeguard were granted permission to ride in Prince Rupert's ranks.

And so it went on for nearly half an hour. Some of the issues were serious and needed quick attention, such as the lack of food for the men and the need to make sure all regiments could confirm they had the supplies of powder and shot they needed. But some were trivial and bizarre, like the fact that although many leaflets had been printed offering amnesty to any of the Parliamentarian soldiers who surrendered or changed allegiance, nothing had been done to deliver them around the area.

At which point someone, Gideon was not sure, but he thought it was a familiar voice, observed that the artillery was now close to hand, and they needed to take the army from the hill if they were to indeed engage Essex that day. A general murmur of agreement carried the point, and all looked to the king, who had been joined by his eldest son, the twelve-year-old Prince Charles, already as tall as his father.

"My lords," the king said and there was silence. "Gentlemen. I thank you for your loyalty and that you all hazard your lives and fortunes with me, and in my cause. I deem not the effusion of blood, but since heaven has so decreed that so much preparation hath been made, we must needs accept this present occasion and opportunity of gaining an honourable victory."

The commanders gathered made clear their approval and agreement, and it was a few moments before the king could go on.

"I put not my confidence in the strength and number of our army, but confide, that though your king speaks unto you and that with as much love and affection as ever King of England did to his army; yet God and the justness of Our Cause together with the love I bear to the whole kingdom must give you the best encouragement. In a word, your king bids you all be courageous, and heaven make you victorious."

There was a cheer of assent and as it faded the king looked around and said something to one of the men beside him who pointed to where the unhappy-looking Falkland was standing beside Gideon.

"Lord Falkland," the king said. "The man with you, his name?"

Falkland straightened and bowed to the king.

THE DEVIL'S COMMAND

"Fox, your majesty, Gideon Fox."

Gideon felt the ground beneath him shift.

"Yes. This man has come seeking to fight for me but has no one yet willing to accept him in their ranks. Who will take a gentleman of such high courage?"

Wishing the ground might complete its threat and swallow him whole, Gideon was barely aware of what followed. He tried to maintain the look of the courageous man he was being presented as being but could see no way to tell in the erupting hubbub who, if anyone, had stepped up to claim him. He realised that the council of war was over, and the commanders were moving away.

His arm was taken in a vice-like grip.

"God, Gideon, I leave you alone for a couple of hours and you somehow become an exemplar for the loyalty and courage of all Englishmen and you not even fully English."

"I didn't intend—"

"I am sure not," Lord reassured him before he could explain. "To say it is out of character would be an understatement of epic proportions. But, because of it, I regret you will have to ride with me. Jupp is spared the task of your care as he is set with the princes on the right, whilst thou and I are to ride on the left and offer my experience and your enthusiasm to whomsoever Lord Wilmott feels is most in need amongst his commanders. I have a feeling I know who that will be."

THE DEVIL'S COMMAND

Chapter Four

*"The freikis on feildis
That wight wapins weildis
With shyning bright shieldis
   At Titan in trone;
Stiff speiris in reistis
Ouer corseris crestis
Are broke on their breistis:
   The nicht is neir gone."*

Lord sounded almost blithe, his expression abstracted as if as his thoughts were elsewhere.

Clad again in his battered buff coat and still with no back part to match the breastplate strapped over it, Gideon rode beside Lord down the slope of the hill, with two men behind them as an escort. The horse Gideon sat astride was not his little chestnut, but the sturdy bay Lord had ridden from Yorkshire. It was a horse that had once belonged to Danny Bristow who had given it to Lord as a parting gift, saying he was sure he could get better from Mags. It was a well trained and experienced cavalry mount, so as Lord put it, even if Gideon had no idea what to do in a battle, the horse would.

Wilmott had decreed they were to ride with Lord Digby, and as the troops had already begun moving it took some time to find him. When they did, Gideon discovered he was a man close to Lord's age, with red-brown hair and pleasant, well-rounded features that suggested he was given more to the table than the stable.

"Aren't you the man the king named?" Digby demanded, as they reached him on the hill. A steady river of horsemen was trotting by on the long looping path that would take the Royalist left flank of horse from the ridge and into position on the plain below.

"I was honoured to have the king mention me, my lord," Gideon said, wary again of lying about his name.

Lord had no such compunction.

"Gideon Fox, my lord, and a braver heart does not beat in the breast of any man in England."

Digby switched his attention to Lord with a frown which made his face look jowled.

"And you, sir, were the man who denied Prince Rupert the Devil his wishes. That takes a serious measure of courage too. He is a vindictive youth who dislikes having his will thwarted."

"Which may be why I am banished to serve you, my lord, whilst my men have the honour of riding with his own troop."

Digby stared at Lord.

"You say so? And you wish you were with them?"

Shaking his head, Lord shaped a bow as best he could on horseback.

"I believe I have the better place to serve his majesty at your side, if you are willing, sir."

Digby smiled then with a mischievous warmth and charm that embraced the two of them.

"Gladly, gentlemen. You are both with me. Let us see what the day will bring us."

They took a wide loop to descend from the ridge,

and after riding with them for a short time, declaiming freely his opinions of Prince Rupert and other influential figures about the king, Digby disappeared ahead to find Wilmott. Lord and Gideon were left as a peculiar, unaligned vanguard to his regiment with a rather disgruntled Captain-Lieutenant Harris behind them, his authority usurped.

As they moved around the hill and he caught his first sight of the enemy army spread wide in front of them, Gideon's stomach gripped at his spine.

He was going to fight in a battle.

He would need to kill.

He could die. Or worse, be left maimed and useless.

He might never see Zahara again.

It was as well his horse was so steady because Gideon's whole body reacted, and all the bay did was flip its ears back for a moment and shake its head in mild protest.

The day was overcast, and the empty fields were tracts of brown with green and golden hedges. There was heathland, thick with furze and gorse and on the other side beneath the same troubled sky, were lined up men like himself, knowing they must fight.

And he had not even chosen to be here.

Which was the bitterest irony of the moment. Had he stayed in London, had his entire life not been pulled apart and remoulded by events and circumstances beyond his control, it was even possible that he could have been standing now on the other side of the field. Because, truth was, if he had a loyalty to give in this war it would be with the cause of Parliament, whose principles he was much closer in alignment to than any belief in the divine right of kings. But he was here, about to fight and maybe die, for the king. And had been singled out as one whose loyalty and honour in the royal cause were exemplars.

"The strange thing about your first battle," Lord said, his words breaking into the bleak citadel of Gideon's thoughts, "is how little you will recall of it after the event. It becomes a thing apart, taken out of time, as if you have stepped through a gate into another world, a world of confusion and cataclysm so complete your mind has no capacity to order it into the known and so rejects it as unreal." He glanced at Gideon with eyes that could be diamond-hard but now reflected the sky, wide and embracing. "And the strangest thing is that the process begins from the moment the action starts. What happened with your last breath seems unreal in your next. Some men are overwhelmed by it, but obedience and training become their anchor."

They rode on in silence for a few more paces.

"And what of lust for battle?" Gideon asked. He had felt it himself and knew its potency.

Lord considered before he replied. "That is a place beyond anger and fear and thought. Where you rage like a god and do not so much know you are invincible, as forget that you are not."

"And in battle what do *you* feel?"

Lord gave a brief laugh. "It has become a part of me as much as my lungs or my liver. Like wine, the more you drink the more you become accustomed to it, and I enjoy wine."

Gideon wondered if he was being even slightly serious.

"What should I do?" he asked, tight-lipped.

"Keep close behind me unless I tell you otherwise," Lord said. "If I know where you are it is safer for both of us, and I can be your anchor." Then he smiled. "And don't look so worried, I have to bring you through safely, I couldn't face Zahara otherwise."

Gideon found that scant reassurance. But he knew it was foolish of him not to be grateful for what was being offered. When it came to it in a melee, Lord's consideration could be the difference between his own life and death.

"I will do as you ask," Gideon said, "and thank you."

Lord held Gideon's gaze and his lips tightened for a moment before he looked away.

"If it were not for me, you would not be here."

The cavalry brigade had to pick its way through hedges around clumps of gorse and over ditches to take its place on the left, southern flank of the army and Gideon could see they were the last units to arrive on the field. Even the artillery had already been placed before each regiment and more were sited on the high bank behind. By the time Digby rejoined them, Lord had his regiment deployed in two squadrons by company and three ranks deep, behind Wilmott's.

"We form the reserve," Lord explained in response to Gideon's enquiring look. "Which means if all goes well, we get to stand here for the remainder of the afternoon and admire the work of our fellows. If it goes badly, then we may be called on to turn the tide. But with the prince set to ride with his own horse, I will admit to feeling a little uneasy about who will

THE DEVIL'S COMMAND

have the overall direction of events."

"It can't be that hard," Digby said. "We'll watch for our moment and go in."

Lord settled his Baltic gaze on the man beside him.

"It is indeed not that hard, my lord, but in battle timing is everything. If we move before we are needed, we could leave the infantry exposed to an attack from the enemy cavalry."

Digby made a dismissive gesture.

"I still say you make too much of it, you professional soldiers. As if there is some kind of secret alchemy. You should have been at Powick. The princes led us through the scum there as if we were riding down wheat in a field and they fled."

"I have been at many Powicks," Lord said, his tone careful, "and I know well what such a charge can achieve. A skirmish such as that, is not to be compared to a battle like this."

Digby said nothing. His lips pushed out in what might have been an expression of deep thought but had the appearance of a sulk.

The short autumnal afternoon was well through, and Gideon realised sunset could not be more than a couple of hours away. He understood little of such things, but he began to wonder if there would be time for a battle to take place that day. He shivered and not from the cold wind, which was blowing towards them. Behind him, he could hear snatches of conversation from the waiting men and the occasional burst of nervous laughter. He wondered how many had ever fought for their lives before, how many had been forced, as he had been forced, to kill a man. Or did they not even see men on the other side of the field, just an amorphous 'enemy' to be destroyed?

Then the wind carried with it the sound of cheers from the main body of the army, in a slow-rolling wave. It was hard to be sure, but Gideon thought he could see a group of mounted officers at the front pausing a while and then fresh cheers following.

"The king is giving his speech," Digby declared. "It is a little more substantial than the one he sent us out with. Stirring stuff. I helped him write it. That must mean we—"

A sudden clap of thunder obliterated his words, and a black cloud arose before the enemy lines. Around Gideon, men with skittish mounts were working hard to calm them or force them back under control. Even Lord's fine roan side-stepped as if wishing to escape. But Gideon's borrowed bay stood as it might in a stall and responded with no more than a lift of the head and a curious forward flick of its ears.

Somewhere in the centre of their own army a scream was heard which stopped as if cut off. There was a half-breath of silence, then the king's ordnance answered with its own staggering roar and the battle began.

II

The exchange of fire from the big guns seemed to go on and on, the smoke from them forming and thickening, making it harder to see along the lines. Lord sat untroubled, occasionally needing to quiet his roan. He projected serenity and confidence, like a beacon shedding light. The men and horses around

THE DEVIL'S COMMAND

absorbed it, drew from it and spread it further through their ranks.

By comparison, Digby sat as if transfixed, standing in his stirrups to see further, his head moving around like an owl's, striving to view everything happening all at once.

In front, there was sporadic musket fire as their own dragoons worked to clear the way for the cavalry against the skirmish force of the enemy dragoons well hidden in furze and hedge, ready to bring them down. The clearing process seemed to be taking some time and frowning, Lord rode forward and spoke to Wilmott who nodded and ordered a company to move up in support of the dragoons. That was too much for the enemy skirmishers who wisely abandoned the hedge and fled on their horses.

There was a shift in Lord's mood as he returned to his place, reminding Gideon of the sensation before a storm when the atmosphere almost seems to crackle. Whether from his own imagination or from something he could not see, the hairs on Gideon's arms all stood up. A moment later he almost jumped from his skin at a sudden massive crash as many guns fired together. It was too much for some of the horses who began whinnying and dancing sideways in protest and one even bolted.

"Wilmott will go now," Lord said, as the boom echoed against the ridge behind them.

"Why? What was that?" Digby demanded, his head doubling the speed of its movement as he tried to find some clue.

Sure enough, the horses in front had begun to move

off at something beyond the gathered pace they should have, spurred in fear by the guns, the dust from the horses lifting with the gun smoke.

"The guns were the signal to advance," Lord said, lifting his voice so the men around could hear and there was a cheer from the reserve behind them. Gideon saw how, with his own quiet confidence and those few words, he lifted the morale of the men in Digby's battalion and helped them settle again. Digby himself was fiddling with his reins in his gauntleted hands and as if in confirmation of Lord's words, with a sharp tuck of drums the infantry moved forwards.

"Of course," Digby said, to cover the fact that he hadn't known but should have.

The ground before the cavalry on this side of the battle was problematic for horses. Soft and boggy, with tangles of undergrowth from which the enemy dragoons had just been rousted, so at least there was no risk of empty saddles from musket fire as they advanced. But it meant that it took Wilmott's men a while to be able to form into the tight grouping needed for a charge and then begin to pick up their speed.

"What the hell?" Digby froze, his hand lifted to his helm as if doubting what he was seeing.

Gideon realised what had taken his attention. The brigade of cavalry had reached its full canter but there was nothing now to oppose them. They had bowled into the single small regiment of cavalry that had been in their path and swept it aside with little delay. Now they were hacking at some fleeing dragoons, but the cavalry that had been in front of them when they formed up was already gone, broken and fled.

THE DEVIL'S COMMAND

Through the impenetrable smoke, swept apart now and then by snatches of wind, Gideon could see that what had been an attack was now transformed without any hesitation into a full-blown pursuit on and past the enemy lines.

"If he does this right," Lord said, as if he were commenting on a craftsman at work, "Wilmot will rein his men in and hook around to attack from the rear. With the prince there too, doing the same on the other flank, this will be over soon. No infantry is going to withstand that kind of punishment, attacked from the front and the rear, and not these who are mostly raw recruits."

Digby stared at him, appalled.

"You mean the battle could be over and we have not even moved from this spot?"

Lord nodded.

"If the prince and Lord Wilmott do their work then—"

Which was when everything went wrong at once.

"Then why are we waiting here? The battle will be done without us." Digby let out a full-throated hunting call followed by some loud whoops as he turned to his regiment, waving them on. Then, evading Lord who tried in vain to grab his bridle, Digby took the entire reserve of cavalry on the left flank into a canter.

It was madness.

It would have been madness if the ground ahead had been easy, but this was over land with streams and soft patches, the kind of ground even a hunt might hesitate to race over.

Pressed in on all sides, Gideon found himself helpless to escape the rush. The problem, he realised, with having a horse trained to battle, was that it knew to join such a charge. There was no way to stop or turn, and he was swept along in the midst of whooping horsemen who seemed more intent on catching their fellows ahead than troubling to attack the enemy.

It was not a military manoeuvre, just a crazy race over uneven ground, with the destination uncertain. The biggest danger would be for his horse to stumble and throw him, so he wound up under the merciless pounding hooves. Like a twig thrown about in a raging torrent, Gideon clung on, hoping that the bay would carry him through.

There was some shooting and a man beside him screamed and fell away which made Gideon press down low over his horse's neck. Then came a violent eruption to the right with shouts and swords, but it was gone as if swept by on a river and Gideon had an impression now that they were in pursuit of some fleeing horsemen. In the maelstrom, he could neither see Lord nor had any idea where he might be.

The ride from hell went on longer than he thought possible. His whole body was aching from the effort of keeping in the saddle as they rowelled through a small village and then splashed through a ford. There was fighting away to one side, but Digby either seemed oblivious or his mount was unwilling to turn, being lured on by the fleeing horsemen.

Finally, it ended. With screams and blood.

They had somehow come upon Essex's baggage train and from what Gideon could see of the mess

THE DEVIL'S COMMAND

around them it had already been plundered by the other wing of Royalist cavalry. Thwarted by having nothing of any value left to steal, the men around him became possessed with a viciousness they had not brought to the fight. They began hacking at the split boxes and chasing down anything that moved. The waggoners, their women, the servants left attending the baggage who had nothing to defend themselves with but their eating knives. All were attacked in a ruthless and empty vengeance.

Gideon found himself impotent, shouting in protest as one of men he had been riding with cut down a boy of about ten who was screaming for his mother and trying to reach her. Perhaps it was a mercy he died, because a moment later another soldier had murdered the woman who was screaming her dead son's name.

After the nightmare ride, he found himself caught in a vision from Dante as Digby's men began to rip apart what was left of the baggage train and hacked at any of the civilians they found there, young and old, men and women. Trapped still in the heart of the cavalry regiment, Gideon could do nothing but curse the men around him. Of Digby himself, there was now no sign, and no one was there with any authority to stop the slaughter.

Sickened to his soul, he saw a break in the press and managed to turn his horse away from the carnage and force a way out of the baggage train. With no idea in which direction he was heading, a sudden pistol shot that reminded him he was in mortal danger himself.

Fortunately, no one seemed to be taking much interest in him. Clusters of men on foot or horse were running or shooting or hacking with swords, and the noise was a cacophony beating at his ears. His horse carried him through it, choosing a path that avoided the worst of the fighting.

Then, in the milling chaos, he saw a banner he recognised. The royal banner held briefly aloft. Assuming that where the banner was, he would find more of his own side's soldiers and wondering what it meant that the banner was here at all, he set his horse towards it at a trot.

Someone shouted at him and tried to grab his reins, but his horse, wiser at such things than Gideon himself, evaded it. Then he heard another shout. This time, incredibly, a voice he knew.

"To me, Gideon. To me!"

Looking around he saw Lord with a tightly packed group of cavalry also heading towards the banner, but on a different course to himself. Changing direction, his desperation lifting into hope as he did so, the bay stretched its stride to cross the ground and nearly dislodged Gideon when it jumped a place where two dead horses and some men had fallen. Then he was behind Lord and the blue roan moved aside to allow him the greater security of a place within the small tightly wedged group.

It was then he learned what Lord had said about the way a battle might affect his mind was indeed true. They were in a melee, the press of men and blades, the sharp report of pistols, with scant room to move and Lord's voice, a harsh command—an anchor.

"Sword, Gideon."

He had forgotten to draw it but now he did and the man in front of him found his cut countered with the same movement. Before his attacker could recover, Gideon had sliced at his exposed neck. Then another man was there, pistol levelled, a man encased in armour against which his sword would do little. By a miracle, the pistol failed to fire and by the time the cuirassier had thrown it down, Lord had one of his pistols in the man's face and his didn't misfire.

Time was broken into single images, like vivid oil paintings. This man's screaming face. That one choking. A horse rearing right in front. A pistol firing, the flash and smoke frozen in memory. His sword moving almost with its own life as brain and arm worked apart from conscious thought. Gideon had no feeling of exaltation or the exhilaration of battle, just a montage of brief emotions which were cut off, stillborn, like each hack or thrust of his sword.

Lord was at the front carving a path forward, powerful and lethal, an unstoppable force, his face distorted, become demonic. The volume and ferocity of his battle cries unmanning those in his path even before his sword found their flesh. His whole body, his horse and his sword were a single weapon thrusting into the heart of the enemy. Those who flanked him were like gleaners in the field, taking what he left and slaughtering in his wake. Behind him now, Gideon was in the lee of the storm and sense returned with awareness and pain, the ache of his arm sharp as he brought his sword up one more time.

Suddenly they were by the banner, and it was then Gideon realised what had happened and what they were doing. This was the army's colours, the royal banner, captured and in the process of being taken back behind enemy lines. But the small group he was with were set on recapturing it and, with a ferocity of fighting he had no wish to be a part of again, they were succeeding.

The man holding the banner took Lord's blade under his arm as he tried to use the spear-tipped pole itself as a weapon in his own defence. The banner was blood-stained and cut, dropping to the mud with the dying man who held it. Lord leaned from his saddle with a careless ease and snatched the pole as it fell, then in the same smooth motion passed it to Gideon as he straightened up, while shouting an order to retreat to the other men.

Keeping the fabric furled against the pole, Gideon found himself now enclosed by the men around him, in a protective screen. He wondered how they were supposed to bear the banner back to safety. But they seemed to gather more men as they went, then found a temporary sanctuary on a piece of raised ground where one of the Earl of Carnarvon's commanders, a man he heard named by someone as Sir Charles Lucas, had managed to gather and rally around two hundred men. A disparate collection of survivors from the various regiments which had formed the Royalist left wing.

Charged now with protecting the banner with his life, Gideon didn't take part in the repeated forays they made against the Parliamentarian rear, half-broken units who took flight when confronted by unexpected enemy cavalry. He sat his horse, moving like a puppet whose strings were bound to the words of Philip Lord, too fatigued physically and emotionally to do more.

THE DEVIL'S COMMAND

As it began to get dark it became clear the battle was over, but there seemed to be no sense of victory or defeat. Both sides were exhausted and, in the gathering gloom, too uncertain where was friend and where was foe.

Perhaps three hours at most after he had formed up below the slope of Edgehill, Gideon rode with the makeshift regiment back towards it. Somewhere along the way, he was freed from the banner and at another point, he was able to dismount.

Later, he had a memory of sitting by a stable with a mug that contained wine, but it was not too clear to him where that fitted into the sequence of events, because he was with Jupp. when he was told the king wished to see him. Gideon mustered his scattered wits and hoped his majesty would not mind too much that he was covered with mud and blood, which by the fairest of good fortune was not his own.

He didn't think he had the energy left to mount a horse, but Roger Jupp had found his little chestnut mare and somehow that made it easier. He had an escort of two of the company's men to ride with him as well as the messenger sent to fetch him.

The king was still on the battlefield, determined to be with his soldiers. There was a fire that had been built for him although wood for such must have been hard to gather. He looked very different from when Gideon had met him before. Had it only been that morning? It seemed a week, a year, a lifetime ago. Now the king appeared to be as tired and worn as Gideon felt but maintained a patient calm as he spoke to those brought to him. And it seemed a veritable stream of men came and went as Gideon stood waiting.

The smell of woodsmoke covered all else that might have been on the night air, but not even the crackle of flame was enough to drown the sound. A continual ungodly dissonance of groans, punctuated by a sudden shriek or scream as the wounded and the dying lay freezing where they had fallen in the battle now waiting in the vain hope they might be tended.

But Gideon had the shriek of a mother seeing her child cut down echoing in the hollows of his mind and the cold of the night seemed not so bitter as the frozen cold that left in his soul.

A hand rested on his shoulder.

"*What sequel shall follow when pendugims meet together? Speak, Parrot, my sweet bird, and ye shall have a date...* You look more parrot than pendugim, I think." Philip Lord was there, somehow managing to look immaculate, his hair groomed and silvered by the firelight. He was dressed in dark blue velvet, bestrewn with sewn gems like stars in the night sky. Lord must have followed Gideon's gaze because he added. "Not mine, I assure you. It is on loan to be returned. And fear not, you don't need to take centre stage, all you are required to do is stand in the chorus."

With that Lord was drawn aside by a man Gideon recognised as one of those who had been leading when they were fighting for the banner. He seemed to be intent about making some point although Gideon could not hear what was said.

And then Gideon was being urged to step forward into the charmed circle of firelight and found himself placed with a small group of men. He recognised them as the ones he had fought beside in the desperate drive to reclaim the royal banner. Lord, flanked by the two other men who had led that attack with him, were being brought to the king. Both of the other men with Lord had been found some better clothing, but neither matched his exquisite elegance and Gideon felt certain that it must have been the prince who had arranged things that way.

The king nodded as the three bowed and were presented.

"Colonel Philip Lord, Captain John Smith and Captain-Lieutenant Robert Walsh, with a handful of men and against great opposition, they recaptured your majesty's Banner Royal and preserved it from the enemy."

Gideon swayed with fatigue and hoped whatever thanks they were going to be offered wouldn't take too long. A glance at the king left him convinced he wasn't alone in that wish.

"I have heard of your exploits, gentlemen," the king said. "I can see but one way to reward such courage."

And there before those of the high command assembled, Gideon bore witness to history. For not in more than a hundred years had such a thing happened as the king created the three men knights banneret, an honour that could only be awarded on the field of battle.

When it was done the king looked at those who stood with Gideon, the handful who had been with him in that desperate struggle and survived.

"Your courage is beyond question, gentlemen, and

for that I shall have struck a gold medal for each of you."

Then they were all bowing and being guided away from the fire. The cold even a few yards away from it was bone deep, for the sky was almost clear of clouds. Breath frosting, Gideon looked up at the stars, gemstone chips against the black velvet of night where the moon rode close to full.

"He hands them out like gewgaws," Sir Philip Lord said, suddenly beside Gideon with a man behind him leading the horses. "But Kate will like it. I am sure she will be the envy of her friends being able to add 'Banneress Lord' to her tally." He laughed and Gideon decided he couldn't see it as being a thing about which Kate would care at all. Lord sobered then. "I would have refused, but it seemed a bit churlish to point out I was just doing my job and might have offended someone, not least Captains Walsh and Smith who seemed to think it important." Then, "Good grief, Gideon, you look like a walking corpse. Come, we have a cold night ahead and there may be more fighting tomorrow. And yes, before you ask, I did send word to Wormleighton to say we were hale. Meanwhile, I'm hoping Jupp might have found the means for a fire, and we will have to see what food, if any, there might be."

Somehow Gideon managed to make it back onto his mare and set her to follow in Lord's wake, accompanied by the men who were their escort. From ahead, where Lord was lost in shadow, he heard lilting words.

"*So hard are their hittis,*
Some sweyis, some sittis,

THE DEVIL'S COMMAND

And some perforce flittis
　On ground quhile they grone.
Syne groomis that gay is
On blonkis that brayis
With swordis assayis:—
　The nicht is neir gone."

Chapter Five

I

Dawn came too late for some and too early for others. When Gideon woke, Lord was already roused and gone, and the view from Edgehill was over a haunted landscape of low mist. The mist lifted with the sun, revealing the battlefield below in all its misery. Despite his hunger, Gideon found it an effort to eat as the men around him made a scant and cold breakfast on the last of the food the company had left shared out between them.

Jupp said they had lost a man in the battle, a hard loss from the shrinking numbers of Lord's men. Not someone Gideon he had known well. Not someone to grieve. He was blessed in that. There would be few who remained whole on either side of the battle who had not lost a friend, a brother, a father, who had been fighting with them or against them. Or if not dead, one who was now missing, or maimed or injured. There were those saying, Jupp told him, that perhaps three thousand or more had perished on both sides and as many again injured of which some were like to die.

Gideon knew he was not the only man counting the cost of this war and thinking it already too high.

"Who won?" he asked, trying to raise the appetite to eat the stale lump of bread in his hands.

Jupp shrugged.

"They hold the field, not us. If that counts for

anything, but I'm not sure it does."

"Will we be fighting again today?"

That was the question no one could answer.

An hour later it seemed the answer was 'no'. The men of Lord's company went to assist those walking the field below, under flags of truce, to find out the living from amongst the dead and carry them back to the relative safety of the army. At least that was what Gideon assumed they were there for at first.

More than once Gideon saw Jupp or one of the men use a knife to end a life. The first time it happened Jupp caught Gideon's expression.

"It's a mercy," he said. "If it were me, I'd hope for the same."

But Gideon was not so sure that was always the case. Those wearing the orange field-sign of the enemy were the ones most often receiving Jupp's 'mercy' and looting the dead seemed to be as much on the minds of himself and his men as any thoughts of saving lives. It was depressing.

Gideon was close to heading back alone rather than be a party to such but stayed to help free a half-frozen man with a broken leg from under what had once been a magnificent horse. As he straightened, he saw something glitter, pressed into the mud where the horse had been lifted. Curious, he chiselled more of the frozen mud away and revealed a sword hilt. One of its curved quillons had been what caught his attention, glinting in the thin sunlight.

The lattice of the basket hilt was close and high up over the grip. At its extent it reached over to embrace the pommel, which was shaped as a cat's head of silver, with a Tudor rose embossed upon it.

"Before God, you are one lucky bastard, Mr Fox, sir," Jupp said from behind him. "Here, let me. I want to hold it at least." He reached down and pulled the sword free of the frozen ground like some latter-day Arthur freeing Excalibur. He wiped it down with a gauntleted hand and gave a low whistle. "This is some blade." Then with an evident reluctance, he turned it and offered it to Gideon, hilt first. "Here. It's yours. You found it."

With an odd mix of guilt and exhilaration, Gideon took the sword, sliding his hand beneath the basket to grip the hilt and, lifting it, feeling the balance that made the blade lethal in action and fast to recover. It seemed wrong that he should steal a sword from an unknown dead man, for this had not belonged to the pikeman whom he had helped to rescue. But simple logic whispered that if he left it, then another would take it. Nodding to Jupp, he claimed the blade as his own and, feeling fortified in some strange way, stayed to continue with the work of trying to save lives.

They saw Lord once. He was on his blue roan directing the capture of some enemy guns left exposed. But that was too much for the other side who soon after began to take the field again. Seeing it, Jupp ordered the company back to the safety of the ridge, their pockets and purses heavier with coin and jewellery and more than one with a new coat, sword, knife or pair of boots.

By late morning Essex had drawn up his men again, with reinforcements freshly arrived. Uncertain whether this presaged another battle, Gideon stayed with Jupp. Lord had not reappeared, and Gideon had no intention of rejoining Digby and his men, after what he had witnessed them do in the baggage of the Parliamentarian army, the previous afternoon.

A little after midday, which passed with no meal as they were now out of food, Gideon was cleaning his new sword when he caught sight of Lord riding with those around the two princes, He was easy to mark, his long hair silver in the grey light and the distinctive colouring of the horse beneath him. Even from a distance, Gideon could hear the group laughing and joking together. As they drew closer, Lord left the princely group and rode over, talking with the men and sharing a jest about his new status and the deed that won it. Then he greeted Jupp and Gideon.

"I don't see anyone with the stomach for another battle," he told them. "Essex is not going to try and assault us up here, and I know that the prince has no intention of joining him in the vale today. Besides, the king is all but heartbroken by the loss of so many of his men and it seems that his sons came dangerously close to being captured or killed yesterday too. The enemy cavalry Wilmott should have engaged sidestepped him and then went around to our rear and wreaked ten kinds of havoc there. Of course, if Digby had stayed back, we would have been in place to prevent that."

"So who won?" Gideon asked his question again.

Lord looked out over the vale where the army of Essex was lined up, seeming to Gideon a sure sign that they must have taken the day. There were still men from both sides out on the field and there were more dead than the living now being taken up.

"We'll know soon," Lord said, "If they withdraw, and I think they will have to, it is our victory. And then, if the king takes wise council, he will have a chance to reach London and take it before Essex can reorganise. If we can do so, it will be all over bar the executions."

The words had a prophetic ring and Gideon shivered. The thought of London, his home, being subject to what he had seen Digby's men doing sent a cold serpent slithering through his intestines.

"There are always the trained bands," he said, remembering and hopeful.

Lord laughed. "Who do you want to win, Gideon?"

He had no answer to that but needed none as Lord caught sight of the sword he had been cleaning. Expression frozen, still shaped in mild exasperation, Lord stared, then without asking he picked the sword up.

"Where did you get this?"

"Lucky bastard found it under a dead horse," Jupp supplied. "It's a beauty, isn't it?"

Lord said nothing, staring at the rose on the pommel, before he put it down again.

"Yes," he said. "A fine sword." Then he turned back to Gideon with a nod and a brief smile. "You have earned the right to such a blade, one with which you may prize open the oyster of this world. I did not yet tell you that you excelled yourself yesterday. *A wreathed garland of deserved praise, of praise deserved, unto thee I give.*" He inclined his head in a gesture of respect. "I must go. If all unfolds as I foresee and we are fortunate, we may be permitted to return to Wormleighton this evening, although I suspect if we are, it will not be for long."

He clapped Jupp and then Gideon on the shoulder, nodded acknowledgement to the rest of the men then remounted and trotted off after the now distant group around the princes, breaking into a canter to catch them up.

Lord's prediction was fulfilled later in the afternoon when the Parliamentarian army could be observed withdrawing from the field in good order. Soon after that, tired, hungry and with their horses in a like state, Jupp led Gideon and the rest of the company back along the ridge. Much of the army was withdrawing to their assigned quarters. Apart from the cavalry still working as scouts and patrols, the majority of those who had survived the battle on both sides were allowed, at last, to rest.

They were joined on the way by Lord who was now riding a different horse, this one a well set cremello of Italian stock.

"A gift," Lord told Gideon, no doubt catching his look of surprise, "from the king. *A horse of a strong & comely fashion, of great goodnesse, louing disposition, and of an infinite couragiousnesse. His heade, which beeing long, leane, and verie slender, doth from the eyes to the nose bend like a hawkes beake...*" He broke off and laughed. "I am not yet convinced. This one seems showy and flighty with a nose that bends ever after apples, but as I seem to be well equipped now with horses you may keep the bay. I think he will serve you better than your chestnut."

It was a very expensive gift. Gideon realised that in a day he had gone from a man who had no clothes he could claim as his own to one with two horses and two swords. Such, he supposed, were the fortunes of war and the attraction of it to men who had little in life. On the tail of that thought came another. That he was becoming accustomed and acclimatised to this way of life himself. He had taken the sword he now wore from a dead man after all.

Despite being tired and hungry, the mood of the company was cheerful as they rode. They were all heading for a hot meal and a warm place to sleep after two days and nights with neither. And some were returning to their women and the welcome they would have from them.

"The season excellis
Through sweetness that smellis;
Now Cupid compellis
  Our hairtis echone
On Venus wha waikis,
To muse on our maikis,
Syne sing for their saikis—
  'The nicht is neir gone!'"

Lord's voice slipped into the rhythm of the hooves and by common consent, they all pushed forward faster, the sooner to be there.

II

After two days in the company of Lieutenant Daniel Bristow, Nick had learned a couple of important things. The first was that other people seemed to find him less irritating than Nick himself did. The second was that if he asked Bristow to do something it was achieved. His new lieutenant seemed to have a happy

THE DEVIL'S COMMAND

facility to know when to smile and when to let the smile falter, something Nick envied, as it was a skill he knew he lacked himself.

But then Nick was aware of his own limitations and how to remedy them. He also lacked the skill to chase down a hare, nor could he run three times as fast as a man. But he kept dogs and horses which meant he could have those skills at his beck and call. He saw Bristow in the same way. The issue was, he could leash a hound and bridle a horse, but he had yet to find a means to be sure of his control over the man. Until he did, in the same way as Nick might employ a rope to temporarily tether a horse or hold a hound, he used the expedient of gold to keep Bristow in check and loyal enough to come to heel when called.

Which was why that morning when he received the message he had been dreading, his first response was to send his new servant to find Bristow. He had asked Bristow to find another room for himself in the inn and he had done so. How, Nick cared not, as long as he didn't have the man sleeping in his room. Not after that first night. Bristow had kept them both up late playing cards and then his uneasy movements on the truckle all night had kept Nick awake too.

When the efficient sounding double-tap came on the door, Nick was pouring himself some wine. His hand hovered the jug over the second cup as he called permission to enter. Then he set it down and turned with just his own.

Bristow came in, sweeping off his hat in a deeper than necessary bow. "Was there something you needed, Sir Nicholas?"

"I have a meeting to attend in Durham this evening. I want you to provide my escort."

"Do we need to all be *light timberd, and of comely shape*?" he asked. "Or are we going to be required for more than display?"

Nick studied Bristow's freckled face and decided it was probably not impertinence but a serious question.

"If you mean do I expect we will be needing to fight, then no, unless by mischance or common hazard of the road. But I do wish to impress those I am going to meet with."

Bristow looked as if he was thinking hard, then sucked in his cheeks.

"If you want us to dress to impress, I'm thinking we need a uniform, but that might be a bit difficult to put together at speed. When is your meeting?"

"This evening. We leave after dinner." The notice had been short, but that seemed to be usual for these men bound to the Covenant. Perhaps made more so because the war was intervening in everyone's affairs

Bristow pulled a face and rubbed his ear.

"As it happens, I might be able to arrange it anyway, as long as you are not too troubled if the coats are white."

Nick found himself frowning. "But the earl's regiment wears white."

"That is why I ask, sir."

"And how do you come to have access…?" He trailed off, not sure he really wanted to know.

Bristow grinned.

"I happened to be playing cards with a gentleman who I know for a fact could arrange it for me and he lost heavily. He works in the Earl's commissary so

THE DEVIL'S COMMAND

rather than trouble the poor man for payment when he has a wife and child to support, we agreed he would be willing to allow me a favour should I have the need." He looked speculative. "Of course, it is possible there are other colours there too."

Nick drew a breath to express his admiration, then changed his mind. It would sit better were he to act as if he assumed such behaviour. If Bristow were to realise the degree to which Nick was impressed by his accomplishments, he might try to take advantage of it.

"Very well," he said, giving a brief nod of approval. "If another colour is possible that would be preferable, but I leave it in your hands.

Which meant that when he had eaten dinner and was preparing to leave, he was both curious and a little apprehensive. He had given instructions to Cummings regarding his absence and a promise to be back in the morning if not before and noticed the look of relief in the man's face which made him wonder what it was Cummings got up to in his absence. He decided to ask Bristow sometime to see if he could find out. Then, on the tail of that thought, he realised that Bristow would already know.

The escort of eight men, Bristow's own, were all clad in Dutch style coats in a strange shade of green that seemed part way towards grey. They had burnished back and breastplates and new buff coats. They even all wore pot helms with faceguards.

Except Daniel Bristow. He wore the same green coat as the rest but with a cape of the same green as the coat. His hat had a green band and a silver buckle and even boasted a green plume he had managed to find from somewhere.

The effect was impressive and when they moved off in close order through the streets of Newcastle, Nick couldn't help but notice heads turning as they passed, and that in a city that had seen its fill of soldiers over the last few years.

Of course, it also meant he had to endure Daniel Bristow's company on the three and a half-hour ride south to Durham which he had expected to be unbearable. But for some reason unknown to Nick, Bristow retreated into himself and seemed content to keep to his place.

Their destination was a fine house a few miles from the outskirts of the city. It was not comparable to the sprawling fortress-grandeur of Howe, being smaller and less ostentatious. Nor was it of a modern elegance. Built in the style that was favoured over half a century previously, with brick below and beams above, there were high twisted chimneys and oriel windows. Before was a formal garden, designed to delight the eye. Behind was a courtyard, flanked on both sides and beyond with outbuildings that bespoke the wealth and industry of the place.

Such was Newhall, the Tempest family seat and a house Nick avoided whenever possible. Part of that was because he didn't get on well with his father's second wife, the woman chosen to replace Nick and Henry's mother. And though fond of her litter, his half-siblings, Nick found that distance and occasional encounters made them more endearing and delightful than prolonged exposure.

But the main reason he avoided the place was that

THE DEVIL'S COMMAND

the house was bound up in his memory with a time of his life he did not wish to dwell upon. A time of closed doors, furtive whispers and the leaden sense of inevitable doom. When his mother, so beloved and the source of all the joy and laughter in his young life, had lingered on her sickbed for almost a year before painfully departing this life.

He had been sent to Howe the day after her funeral, returning there with Sir Bartholomew Coupland to a life where love, joy and laughter had no place. Newhall had never felt like his home since then. Henry, less than a year his junior and his father's favourite, had stayed here in Durham and Nick had been raised at Howe. They had been as close as brothers could be. Nick and Hal, not even a full year between them in age and more like twins than siblings. But that moment marked the point at which he and Henry had been pulled apart and they had never been close since. Nick had been nine years old and every time he caught his first sight of the house, he was again that child, with the same resentment and anger, grief and bewilderment.

He was grateful that they arrived when it was getting into twilight and the house with its memories engraved in every feature was softened, more profile than painting, the colours greyed by the fading sun. There was still light enough for him to be sure he made an impressive arrival with his escort, essential now that he was no longer 'Master Nicholas' but Sir Nicholas Tempest with a status that outshone his father's own.

But the show was not for his father, who Nick knew

placed little value on any display or pomp and whose opinion of Nick had not changed since he was that nine-year-old child. No. The show was for the other men who would be there, men who represented the real power of the Covenant to which Nick and his father were both bound. He wished to prove to them that he was no longer the youth they had met at his coming of age, when their cold appraising stares made it clear they had found him wanting. He would show them that he was now a man of substance, a man with his own place in the world. A man to be reckoned with.

"Will we be staying overnight here?" Bristow asked, taking the reins of Nick's horse once he had alighted. Bristow's men were in a neat line, each beside his mount.

It was an unpleasant inevitability Nick could see no way to avoid.

"I believe we will be," he said and if Bristow thought the lack of certainty in any way strange, he didn't show it.

"I'll get the men settled then, sir," he said and gave a smart bow before striding over to talk to the best presented of the servants that had come out when they arrived.

Nick didn't see what came of that because his father had stepped out through the door to greet him, together with the lady of the house. Within moments the deep waters of family had closed over his head and, as always, he was left struggling to break the surface. He went through the necessary rituals, even achieving some degree of graciousness towards his hostess.

THE DEVIL'S COMMAND

Then, having dismissed his wife, Nick's father pulled him close and spoke in a low and urgent voice.

"This is not the time to be playing games, Nicholas, these men have the wealth and power to break you like a twig. Break me as well. You listen to them, and you do as they require. As we have always done. Then they will be on their way, and we can get back to our own affairs."

"Hardly 'our own' affairs," Nick said. "There happens to be a war going on, or had you not noticed?"

His father looked at him with eyes that had once ruled Nick with their fierceness, but which now seemed puffy with fatigue. His face was lined with weariness and the once magnificent hair looked thin and greying. It struck Nick then that whilst his father was ageing, he was ailing too. That thought made his blood run cold. The last thing Nick wanted was to be saddled with the responsibility for his father's wife and family on top of all else he had to manage.

"Don't be impertinent," his father snapped, but it sounded more as if from habit than conviction.

Once Nick would have reposted, but he was shaken by his discovery and no longer sure he wished to bring the man he had feared and respected all his life to any kind of defeat. He lowered his gaze as if chastised.

"I will be careful," he promised, and that at least he meant.

The meeting took place in the parlour at the far end of the house with windows curtained and the small chandelier fully lit to provide good illumination.

Paintings hung on the panelled walls: a Dutch interior of a woman doing laundry, a pastoral landscape, an old man sitting by a window with a young girl holding a rose, a family portrait of his grandparents with his father still an infant. They were all familiar to Nick from his childhood. It was a room that the child in Nick still wanted to enter on best behaviour, standing with his hands clasped behind his back, careful not to dirty the brocade cushions and curtains. So, this time, he made an effort to stride in with confidence a step ahead of his father.

The men who waited were the same two he had met before at his coming of age. One was an older man of the same generation as his father and Sir Bartholomew, portly but not obese, with a brush of dark coppery hair, shot through with steel. The other was a man in his late twenties, clad in black as if in mourning, his golden blond hair a stark contrast as it lay in curls over his shoulders.

As before they offered no names and greeted him stiffly.

"I hear you are wed, Sir Nicholas," Portly observed. "I also hear it wasn't the most regular of spousals."

Nick felt the colour rising to his face.

"I did what was needed to secure Howe, sir," he said. "I suspect it was your plan that I should do so. Indeed, you forced me into it so you can't complain at my methods." He included his father in the accusation, who at least had the grace to look away.

"No one is complaining," Gold said. "If anything, quite the opposite Sir Bartholomew referred to you more than once as 'that milksop nephew of mine'."

Nick drew a shocked breath.

THE DEVIL'S COMMAND

"Oh, don't mistake me," Gold said, his gaze holding Nick's like a vice. "A man with more wisdom and discretion would have managed the matter in a better way. But you made a tough decision and acted upon it, which is more than some would have."

"He was raised not to flinch at necessity," Nick's father put in.

"As were we all, Sir Richard," Gold said thinly. "As were we all."

Portly cleared his throat. "The woman, is she with child?"

Nick blinked. How to admit he had not even touched his wife? He had come close. But when it came to it, he found he had no wish to have her unwilling, to live with an enemy in his bed, raising his children and managing his house. He knew it would take time, but he had time and could be patient. She would be his because she wished to or at the least because she accepted it must be so. He had taken her to Howe, ensured the marriage was indisputable on paper and let all assume what they would.

"I have no idea," he said. "There was no sign of such when I last saw her." Which was the truth. He thought of how she had been when he last saw her, eyes like storm clouds, spitting curses at him when he asked how she fared. And the bandages on her wrists still red.

"You need to see to it," Portly said, his tone much the same as the earl when ordering a military patrol.

Nick opened his mouth to reply but his father got in first.

"Good God man, he has scarce had the time to bed

her, what with Newcastle demanding that he dance attendance. We have no time for family matters. We are summoned to fight for the king."

Both the other men looked at his father and there was something in their expressions that lifted the hairs between Nick's shoulder blades.

"Well, that is another issue we need to discuss," Gold said. And the way he said 'discuss' made it clear he was not intending there to be a frank and forthright exchange of views. "These times are indeed challenging for all of us, but in that challenge, there is also a lot to be had of opportunity and keeping our eyes fixed on old horizons may blind us to new ones."

Nick's father was frowning.

"You mean the new world? New Albion, New Hampshire, New England and all that romantic pap?"

Gold smiled, but the effect was more that of a predator baring its teeth.

"Oh, we have not lost sight of those possibilities, believe you me. But why set out to shape a handful of people in a land of forests and savages when we can take the heart of this nation and mould it in the crucible of conflict to the form our forefathers foresaw?"

Nick found himself reminded of a conversation he had a while before with Mags.

"You mean we can take advantage of this war, somehow?" he hazarded.

Gold nodded. "We can. We are and we shall."

Nick wondered then how big that 'we' was. He knew the Covenant had once wielded a lot of power, even across Europe. But as time went on, he found himself wondering more and more if all that was

THE DEVIL'S COMMAND

happening with the Covenant now was just the rattling of dead men's bones over the heads of the living. It had existed for a century and perpetuated, in secret, a bloodline of descent from Queen Mary Tudor and Philip of Spain. Originally that had been in the hope that one day such a monarch might reunite the Protestant and Catholic schism in Europe under a single ruler. Now though, Nick thought, they aimed less high. And Nick knew his father and uncle had long since concluded the best course was to free them all from the tyranny the Covenant had become and destroy the last legitimate remnant of that bloodline—Philip Lord.

"So, what do *we* do?" he asked.

Portly was the one who answered. "We do what we are told, of course. This is not about mere earthly splendour. This is about uniting humanity under one star, rescinding all the old hatreds and divisions of nation and creed." His face took on the look of a man recalling past glory. "The last of our founders to leave us used to speak often of the idea of an empire. An empire with its throne in England, a throne supported by the might of men and the power of God. God revealed anew through the words of his angels."

"Except no one now seems able to speak with those angels," Gold said. "We are left to work with what we have, as God wills."

It was as if they spoke of two different visions.

"You are talking of possibilities and ideals," his father said, an edge of exasperation in his tone. "My concern is here and now and the fact that my name and that of my family is caught up with the name of a traitor."

Gold lifted an eyebrow.

"Oh, of course, you will not have heard. Philip Lord is pardoned by the king, though he may not know it yet himself."

Nick felt as if his entire life had been packed in a small box and dropped into a river. "Then—"

"By the king," Gold repeated. "For Parliament to acknowledge that, it would require passing an act to lift his attainder and at the moment I don't see them having the time to do so even were they inclined to for someone who the king wished to relieve." He must have seen the confusion on Nick's face, because he went on. "We have two governments in England at this time, one by royal fiat and one by the passing of acts. We are no longer ruled by one set of laws but by two."

Portly nodded. "The question is, of course, who will prevail?"

"The question is," Nick's father said hotly, "who *should* prevail? The king is—"

"The king, as even his most ardent supporters know, is a weak fool," Gold said, cutting across him. "He has legitimacy, but he lacks the ability to wield it, or we would not be where we are now. On the other hand, Parliament has the wealth of London behind it and all that can buy, but it lacks the veneer of legitimacy. But we can provide that. We can give them a monarch with more right to rule than Charles Stuart."

Chapter Six

I

Gideon knew something was wrong from the moment they trotted into the courtyard at Wormleighton. There were servants to hand, carrying lights and ready to take the horses, but even before he had dismounted, Zahara pushed through to Lord. Gideon couldn't hear what she said, but she was talking in an urgent way, her face pale in the light of the lantern she held.

None of them had slept more than a snatched handful of hours over the last two nights, with a hard day of fighting and the tense inactivity of today adding to the strain. Of them all, Lord had slept the least, if at all. Despite that, his demeanour had been amiable for the entire ride back, laughing and joking with little trace of any fatigue. But as Zahara was speaking, his skin blanched and every moment of those two days and the sleepless nights between, became visible on his face.

And then, like a door closing on a private room, the bland mask was restored, but now it was edged with a fine outline of strain. Lord said something back to Zahara and went with her, into the building his men had made their own.

His horses being led away, Gideon wondered whether to follow. He wished above all things to talk to Zahara, but there was something in this that made him feel it was wiser to stay away, to let her speak with Lord about...

Perhaps it was Shiraz? Or had someone brought ill news from the north of Danny?

Kate.

It had to be Kate.

No one and nothing else could have provoked such a reaction in Lord. And suddenly, Gideon felt too exhausted to take on that emotional burden. With conscious cowardice, he turned and walked into the house. Perhaps with a glass of wine and some food he would have the wherewithal to—

"Mr Fox, or can I presume to call you Gideon?" It was Ned Blake, walking across the large and open entrance hall. "I am so relieved to see you returned. I heard of your heroism and the knighting of Sir Philip."

Gideon struggled to think of what he had done that might be called heroic. He had been swept along with a stampede of cavalry, turned and fled from a barbaric slaughter without even attempting to stop it and then had been pushed into an ugly fight in which he had no thought save for his own survival.

"My heroism?"

Blake smiled and his head wobbled with enthusiasm as he put a hand inside Gideon's arm to draw him towards one of the downstairs rooms.

"I heard you protected the Banner Royal with your own life to bring it back to the king. But you must be hungry. I was about to eat. There is supper served for those of the walking wounded we have here. Is Sir Philip going to join us?"

THE DEVIL'S COMMAND

Gideon shook his head wondering how to explain that he had been given the banner to carry as of all there he was the one deemed the least effective in its defence, not the most. By having that burden, he had freed the men about him to fight for its, and his, protection.

Blake led him into a room where a number of wounded men had gathered at the table and the smell of food was enough to bring Gideon's stomach near to cramp.

Blake piled food onto his own plate before pushing the dish at Gideon. "If we wait to be served, we will starve amidst plenty. Here, this is very good, you may have heard of it, potato pudding. A bit over spiced for my taste but quite delicious none the less."

Then Blake watched with a tyrannical solicitude as Gideon put some onto his plate and took the required mouthful. It was hard to taste much apart from the spicing, but he nodded anyway, just happy to be eating. A minute later or so later, the plate half empty and his brain perhaps restored somewhat by nourishment, it occurred to him that Blake would know if Kate had been taken ill or had an accident.

"Lady Catherine," Blake told him, "left on Sunday, soon after I got back and has yet to return."

The potato pudding turned to ashes in Gideon's mouth. He had to swallow it down with a dry throat.

"Where did she go?"

Blake seemed oblivious to Gideon's concern and was putting a helping of ham on his plate, then after a moment's hesitation moved to put a slice on Gideon's plate too.

"This is excellent food, you know. Some of the best I have had in recent weeks."

Irritated Gideon pushed his hand away and the slice of ham fell on the table between them.

"Where did Lady Catherine go?"

Blake frowned and put the ham back on the serving dish.

"When I got back from the council of war, Lady Catherine asked me what had passed and, knowing the prince holds her in high regard, I told her all I could of what had transpired." He beckoned to a serving boy who had appeared with a fresh jug. "She was most perturbed to learn that the amnesty notices had been printed and not distributed and asked where they were. Thank you, the half cup is fine." He gestured to Gideon's cup and the boy obligingly filled it. "As it happened, they were in one of the bags I had here. She took them, thanked me and said that she had a faithful friend who she believed would help put them to good use amongst the men of the enemy army even at this late stage. That was the last time I spoke with her. I believe she left the house soon after. I assumed she had gone to join Sir Philip or the prince after making her delivery."

Suddenly grateful for the wine, Gideon drank two great gulps of it then got to his feet.

"You will have to excuse me," he said, answering Blake's look of surprise. "I have remembered that I need to speak to someone."

He left the room and headed outside, the cold air hitting him like icy water. Driven by urgency he increased his pace to a run. Lord was in the stable yard giving commands to an unhappy looking Jupp, his

THE DEVIL'S COMMAND

blue roan furnished and ready.

"...gave my word and I am not about to let you break it for me. I am going to find Lady Catherine and you are going to lead the men onto the ridge of Edgehill an hour before sunup whether I am back by then or not." As he was speaking, he swung himself into the saddle.

"You can't go alone, sir. At least let me—"

"I am taking Shiraz with me. Your task is taking the men to join the prince and I suggest you make sure you get some sleep first." Then he caught sight of Gideon. "And now we have Sir Percival too. I can manage well enough without the entire bloody round table."

It had been a long time since Gideon had been subjected to this side of Philip Lord and for a moment, in his extreme of fatigue, it drew him up short.

"I came to tell you I know where Kate went," he said. "But you should eat at least before you go after her."

"God above, is this a gathering of nursemaids?" Then Lord drew a sharp breath, and Gideon could see what it was costing him to control his emotions, like a man taking an aggressive mount in check. "Tell me what you know."

"She took the amnesty letters, the ones mentioned at the council of war She told Ned Blake that she had a *faithful* friend who she believed could ensure they were distributed to the Parliamentarian army before the battle."

"Of course." Lord closed his eyes and lowered his head. In another man Gideon might have thought he was praying, but then he looked up again. "Thank you. At least I know where to begin."

A clatter of hooves made them both glance around as Shiraz appeared on his strong-backed, black gelding. He was a dark silhouette in the lantern light, his clothing like a patch of the night sky, bow and quiver on his saddle and sword and dagger on his hips. But behind him on her usual pillion sat Zahara, wearing a leather buff over her clothes.

"No," Lord spoke the word with such forceful denial that even Jupp stepped back.

"If Shiraz rides with you, so do I," Zahara told him, simply.

"Then, I will go alone."

"If you do, we will follow."

Lord let the air in his lungs hiss out between his teeth and changed language to one that Gideon had not heard him use before. His face twisted and the cold venom in his tone was enough to raise the hair at the back of Gideon's neck, even without being able to understand the meaning.

Shiraz drew a breath, his expression one of fury, but Zahara reached a hand up to his shoulder, her gaze locked with Lord's.

"You use words as barbs and blades to drive us from you," she said, in English. "There is no point. We are both riding with you."

"I am too," Gideon said.

For a moment Lord stared at him as if he could not understand what Gideon had said. Then he laughed, a harsh ratcheting sound that had nothing in it of mirth.

"Just what I need. A castrated Moor, a clingy whore and a useless lawyer. I think not."

THE DEVIL'S COMMAND

Goaded beyond the limits of endurance, Gideon had his sword half-drawn, but on the last word Lord rowelled his spurs against the roan who threw up its head in protest then shot forwards and was gone.

Gideon was shaking with anger. The words Lord flung at Zahara, laced with deliberate malice were unforgivable. He must have known when he spoke them the harm they could do. Shiraz had his teeth bared, and tears stood stark in Zahara's eyes. But it was Zahara's arm that stopped Shiraz reaching for his bow.

"Can you not see?" she said, a taut desperation overlying the ocean of pain in her voice. "It is not what it seems. He uses cruelty to try and cut us off from him so we do not follow him into danger. It is not because he cares nothing for us, it is because he cares too much. He is simply too exhausted to manage it any other way." Shiraz turned his head over his shoulder to look at her, frowning and must have seen as Gideon did her resolute expression. Gideon had been a victim of such vicious contempt from Lord before, and that with nothing of care behind it. But Zahara believed it, which gave him pause.

"Get your horse, Gideon," she told him. "Follow us. When the Schiavono calms enough to think and realises we have come after him, he will see he has to let us be with him. It is too dangerous for any alone."

"I'll get the bay," Jupp said and headed off at a run.

"I know where he will go," Gideon said, feeling as if a lead weight had been bound to his heart. "The company that defected in the battle, he will want to speak to their commander Sir Faithful Fortescue."

Zahara nodded and said something to Shiraz whose expression had shifted, the hardness draining a little from his features. He lifted his head in a single upward nod. Then Zahara held out a hand to Gideon and he gripped it as he might a rope in a turbulent river.

"We will meet you there. Ride fast and take care," she said. Then she wrapped her arms about Shiraz, as he pushed the black to speed in the vanishing wake of the roan.

As Gideon waited for Jupp to bring his horse, Ned Blake emerged from the house.

"Oh, there you are. I was quite worried when you shot off like that. You seemed somewhat disturbed. Sir Philip has left? I thought I saw him through the window, but I couldn't be sure in the dark."

It was hard to know what to say to that. Whilst it was not Blake's fault that Kate had gone, a part of Gideon found it difficult not to think that had the man not mentioned the amnesty pamphlets Kate would have been here, safe, awaiting their return.

He stopped his thoughts before they could run on.

"Lady Catherine is missing," he said.

Blake drew a sharp breath.

"If there is concern for her safety, someone should tell the prince. He will want to help. There might be a search made."

"Someone can be sent," Gideon suggested, "I will see to it." Jupp could send one of the men.

Blake gripped his arm. "I will go. I have access others may not have. It will be faster."

Which was true. Grateful for a simple solution Gideon nodded.

THE DEVIL'S COMMAND

"The problem is," Blake went on, "my horse is lame. I will need to find a mount."

"Take my chestnut," Gideon offered. "Captain Jupp will show you where she is."

Jupp was back leading the bay and Gideon thanked him.

"Do you know where I might find Sir Faithful Fortescue?" he asked.

Jupp scratched his chin for a moment.

"That the one who came over to us in the battle? His men were half of them fools and forgot to remove their field signs. I cut one down myself before we realised."

"Where would he be?" Gideon asked again.

"Up on the ridge. I expect Sir Faithful will be with them."

Gideon took the reins of the bay and pulled himself into the saddle, then with a brief word to Jupp to let Blake take his mare, Gideon turned the gelding's head and set off back to Edgehill.

II

"You are talking of treason," Nick's father said, appalled.

"And what do you call seeking to replace the existing monarch in the first place?" Gold asked, an edge of scorn to his tone. "For that is what we have worked to do as long as the Covenant to which you are sworn has existed."

"But that was different, that was to replace a woman first, and then a drooling buffoon of a paederast. This king—"

"Has no more right to rule than his father, the drooling buffoon," Gold said. "You can't condemn one and support the other. Perhaps it is because you are getting old and losing the will to stand up for the truth."

That made Nick's father bridle.

"I am as strong in the Covenant as always. It is you who seem to be changing what we stand for."

"We had fewer options before," Gold said. "Fewer opportunities. This war has opened up much that was closed to us."

"What is to stop Philip Lord offering what you are suggesting on his own account?" Nick asked, feeling they were getting pulled away from the important point. "If he wished he could present himself as an ideal alternative and as he was a traitor against the last king's person, not the country, they might have no problem with that."

Gold and Portly both looked at him. Gold with a slight smile of discovery and Portly as if Nick were a talking dog.

"That is a possibility," Gold conceded, "but you forget, he has no proof. If he wanted to walk that path, he would first have to come back to us and place his head in our halter."

Nick wondered if the halter analogy meant that of a horse to be lead or a noose on some gallows. For a moment he was back in time a month or so, lying by a muddy road with the blue-diamond eyes cutting into his soul. *You will die.*

Nick shivered. "He would never do that."

There was a silence.

THE DEVIL'S COMMAND

Delicate and attentive.

Then Nick realised what he had said, and the colour flooded his cheeks.

"You sound most certain," Gold said.

"Yes. I've met him." Nick closed his mouth on the words. This was his real test. He had to move these men away from what he needed to hide and push them into seeing him as a useful individual.

He had met Philip Lord twice. Once Lord had held him prisoner for a few hours and Mags had freed him. The second time he had captured Lord and Lord somehow managed to escape on the way back to Newcastle. Nick had no intention of revealing that humiliation. Those who knew of it, Cummings and Bayliss, were just as tight-lipped since the escape had made all three of them look incompetent.

With that in mind, Nick focused on the first encounter and hoped news of the second had not leaked out through his men.

"He had a sword to my throat at the time and he vowed my death at his hands."

Gold and Portly exchanged glances. His father looked shocked.

"Yet you live," Gold observed.

"He wanted to know the strength of Howe." The lie came easily enough. "He had left me placed under guard with two of his men as he attended to some other business. Two of mine then freed me."

"That sounds a little—"

"One of my men was Francis Child, the mercenary known as Mags who is also Graf von Elsterkrallen." This was the dust he hoped to throw in their eyes to distract them. It seemed to work because this time the quality of the silence was very different.

"Francis Child?" Portly echoed, a note of keen interest unmistakable in his voice. "The Coupland bastard?"

"You said nothing of this before," Nick's father said, his tone accusing.

"I was embarrassed to admit what had happened," Nick told him and that at least was honesty.

"He is still with you?" Portly asked, expression intense.

"Who?" Then he realised, "No. Mags has a mercenary company now, but I have one of his officers with me."

"With you? Here?"

Nick cursed himself. If these men decided Bristow was a better connection to Mags, he might find that far from establishing himself, he had killed the goose that laid the golden egg before it had even produced one.

"Yes, but he is my man now," Nick told them, hoping that was true.

Gold nodded. "And where is Francis Child and his men?"

"With Fairfax. He is selling his sword to Parliament."

It felt as if the room had suffered a sudden frost.

"Send for this man of yours. I want to speak with him," Gold demanded.

Whilst they waited, Nick's father took the opportunity to refill the cups of his guests with wine and even found one for Nick himself.

Bristow arrived looking as if he were dressed for an

THE DEVIL'S COMMAND

honour guard. Considering he was wearing the same clothes he had travelled in, Nick realised he must have spent much of the time since their arrival with a brush. His bow and stance were immaculate, and under the mass of tawny hair, his eyes were wide and guile-free. Gold, Nick saw, glanced first at the sword then at the man who wore it. Portly was frowning in disapproval.

"Lieutenant Bristow," Nick told them.

Gold gave a brief nod. It struck Nick then that despite looking an immaculate soldier, Bristow still managed to give the impression he was an unprepossessing individual. He wondered at the trick of it.

"Whom do you serve, Lieutenant Bristow?" Gold asked.

"I am Sir Nicholas' man, sir," Bristow said. "Lieutenant in his company."

Nick's father looked confused. "I thought Cummings was your—?"

The question was mercifully lost as Gold spoke across it.

"And before that?"

Bristow considered. "How far back would you like me to go, sir?"

"Imagine," Gold told him, "I am someone seeking to employ you, lieutenant. I would like to hear of your career."

"Before being employed by Sir Nicholas, I was serving with Graf von Elsterkrallen as a captain of cavalry. Before that I was employed for some years in various capacities by the mercenary commander known as the Schiavono, mostly as his Master of Ordnance. In addition, I led both infantry and cavalry companies, conducted sieges and defended them, commanded the occasional garrisons and did whatever else might be required from carrying messages to digging ditches." He paused as if considering, then smiled. "I am something of a jack of all trades, I suppose."

There was a strong silence when he finished speaking and Nick had a moment where he wished the world could turn back to before he had opened his mouth about Bristow.

"And you will have known this man, this 'Schiavono', well?" There was an edge to Gold's voice that spoke of suspicion.

Bristow nodded.

"Very well, sir."

"But you have given up all you have so eloquently described to be a humble lieutenant," Portly observed.

Bristow rubbed at his ear as if it was sore. "Yes. I have," he agreed. "And put like that I can see how it might seem a little unorthodox."

"Most men seek to ascend in their military career," Gold said pointedly.

"I am no different," Bristow assured him, "but circumstances change. Men change. The Schiavono I found when I came to England was not the same man I left in Germany." There was a bitterness in his voice that was hard to miss. "We parted company on less than friendly terms and I transferred my allegiance to the graf, who is one that counts the Schiavono an enemy."

"And now to Sir Nicholas? As a *lieutenant*?" Gold

THE DEVIL'S COMMAND

made no attempt to conceal his incredulity.

"The graf expected me to prove myself and sent me to Sir Nicholas to do so. Sir Nicholas, on the other hand, has not suggested I am lacking in any way and has promised me good pay and fair prospects should I decide to remain in the country. Besides," the hint of a grin broke his lips apart, "at the moment I am doing the work the graf asked of me as well as that Sir Nicholas requires."

Portly was frowning. "You seem to have little problem with admitting your duplicity."

"If it were indeed duplicitous, then perhaps I would," Bristow replied. "But the graf charged me with ensuring the welfare and wellbeing of Sir Nicholas and Sir Nicholas pays me for the same thing. I see no problem being paid twice to do the same job."

"No man can serve two masters," Gold said, his voice now cold.

"I am Sir Nicholas's man, sir, as I told you before," Bristow said, unruffled, "His man against any."

There was another silence, this one more speculative and assessing.

"I almost believe you," Gold said, then shook his head. "Alright, you may go."

After the door had closed behind the departing Bristow, Portly and Gold exchanged looks.

"This could change things," Gold said. "This could change many things."

"If he is to be trusted," Portly added.

Gold looked thoughtful then.

"I know the type and I think perhaps he can be. We just need to be sure the carrot is golden and the stick lethal." He smiled at Nick for the first time and patted him on the shoulder. "You have done well. Very well. I think you may be the man we need, especially as you have the services of Lieutenant Bristow."

THE DEVIL'S COMMAND

Chapter Seven

I

Finding Sir Faithful proved impossible, but Gideon caught up with Zahara and Shiraz who had found his men and were asking about Kate.

None of them had seen her, they said, but one recalled having heard that word had been passed amongst the officers in the Parliamentarian ranks to look out for someone who might be trying to spread word of an amnesty or give out papers. Another said he was almost sure someone had been caught doing that, but bearing in mind their own fragile status, intending to turncoat, they had been careful not to show any interest at the time.

Gideon's heart plummeted at the implication.

"Where would any prisoner have been taken for secure keeping?" Gideon asked. It was a slender hope. If, as it seemed, Kate had been captured and was still alive, then she would be held in the heart of Essex's army and inaccessible. He wished he could be confident that her gender and her gentility would protect her, but after what he had seen happen in the battle, Gideon could no longer be sure of anything.

"Warwick," his informant said with certainty and the men around him nodded. "Warwick Castle most likely, and if you have ever seen the place, you will know why. I doubt the king has the men or the guns to ferret Essex out of that stronghold. They tried to take it back in August, but Lord Brooke's men saw them off. That is where the Earl is pulling back to, and I heard he had sent a couple of suspected spies there to be questioned."

It was news to Gideon that Warwick had a castle. He had never been to the city.

"I think," he told Zahara and Shiraz as they rode along the ridge, "it is safe to assume Lord will have heard the same from Sir Faithful by now. He will be riding for Warwick."

"We have to catch him up or he might be taken too," Zahara said.

Shiraz nodded and having sent Gideon an enquiring look to be sure he was ready, touched heels to his mount who was away like a shadow into the night.

The journey from the ridge of Edgehill to the bridge over the Avon before Warwick must have been a little over ten miles. It was so cold that the breath of man and horse froze before the face and crept under clothes to pinch the flesh beneath. They were not helped by the fact the moon was full, the night clear and much of the way was through open countryside. But as they rode, a sweep of lowering cloud offered some friendly shadows and the hint of a thick mist to come.

The traffic on the road was mostly Parliamentarian. Messengers or troops escorting specific officers, wounded men or prisoners. Had he been alone he would have been taken at the first encounter, but Shiraz seemed to have a preternatural ability to predict men on the road, to find places in shadow where they could conceal themselves or even keep moving whilst invisible. But there were too many

THE DEVIL'S COMMAND

heart stopping moments when discovery seemed a breath away and Gideon had to trust the skill of Shiraz and the surefootedness of his own horse. Despite the dark and the need to avoid detection they managed it in much better time than Gideon would have imagined possible.

The rugged outline of the castle was cast against the sky, lit by the high, bright, moon. Gideon was wondering how they might hope to cross the guarded bridge let alone find a way into the town or castle, when a young owl called from some trees not too far from the road. Shiraz stopped and turned back. From somewhere in memory, Gideon matched the sound he had heard to another occasion so was not surprised when a familiar voice spoke from the dark shelter.

"*Forgive me, what I am now returned to, sense and judgement, is not the same rage and distraction presented lately to you. That rude form is gone for ever. I am now myself, that speaks all peace and friendship, and these tears are the true springs of hearty penitent sorrow for those foul wrongs which my forgetful fury slandered your virtues with...*" Then in a very different mien, "God, that is pathetic. I have no words I trust. Like a parrot, I offer another's. I cannot unsay the unspeakable, but I am hopeful you did not all follow me here simply to strike me for my insults." Lord sounded as close to humility as Gideon had ever known him but by speaking, he reminded Gideon of what he had said before and of the tears of pain in Zahara's eyes.

"It is not for us to forgive," Zahara said, her face invisible in the cold darkness. "First you must forgive yourself, then perhaps we can forgive you."

The silence seemed to last a small eternity.

"I find I am not sure I can." Lord stood beside his horse in a patch of shadow. His voice held a chastened note. "It seems I will have to hope for your tolerance, if not your forbearance, in the meantime because there are matters most pressing at stake here. If Gideon were not sitting there on Danny's old bay, I would have sworn he had stopped at the Bridge Inn. I saw his chestnut there. I was hoping to intercept him when he left, but..."

For a moment that made no sense at all. Then suddenly and chillingly it did.

"I leant her to Ned Blake," Gideon said, feeling sick. "His horse was lame, and he said he wanted to tell the prince what had happened to—"

"Blake?" Lord was taken aback. "The obsequious privy chamberlain who pens all the prince's letters?"

"The same man," Gideon agreed. "He who took me to see the king. The same man who told Kate of the amnesty leaflets and just happened to have them with him for her to take."

"Perhaps he has fear for her safety too," Zahara said.

"He said he did," Gideon agreed, "and that was why he wanted to tell the prince in the hope that might lead to a general search. But if he is here before us, he didn't ride to the prince."

Lord let out a tight breath that rimed the air, caught in moonlight. "I think I need to talk with the man." Then he stopped again. "That is, if you are all willing to assist me."

"We wouldn't be here if we were not," Gideon said,

trying to keep the acid from his tone but knowing it was still there. "We are here for Lady Catherine's sake."

"As am I," Lord said curtly, "allies in this at least then. The problem is Blake knows us, which means we cannot walk in and see what he is up to."

"He does not know me," Zahara said, "or Shiraz. A woman travelling with her servant to Warwick."

"No."

Gideon's instant negative clashed with Lord's words.

"You are *sure* he does not know you?"

"I have seen him, but he has never seen me." Zahara sounded confident. "He only ever saw Lady Catherine."

Gideon, dumbfounded that Lord might consider Zahara going into the inn, missed the implication of her words.

"He was *enamoured* of her?" Lord said, voice cold.

"She told me he was like a puppy with big eyes whenever she was near, would invent excuses to need to be in her company and had done his best to be as useful to her as he might."

Lord bridled. "Why did she not mention that to me?"

"Because she knows you too well and had no wish for the man to be run through by your sword. She thought it harmless."

"Then why would he…?"

"He knew you had married her?" Zahara suggested.

"Yes, of course, I sent—" Lord broke off. "Gideon, did Blake seem angry at Kate, to you?"

Gideon thought back over the conversations and shook his head.

"It was more as if he hoped being married would dissuade her from taking any more risks. If anything, he seemed careful of her."

"Then why give her the amnesty letters in the first place?"

"Maybe, if I go into the inn I might find an answer," Zahara said gently.

"No," Gideon said again.

"A little bit louder next time, Lennox," Lord said, "I think there were a few over the river in the castle who didn't hear you. And before you say 'no' again, at whatever volume, I would ask you why you believe you are entitled to deny Zahara the right to do what she can that might save Kate? Were you in that place you would not hesitate and think yourself a coward were you to do so?"

A hundred answers offered themselves: that Zahara was a woman, that it was too dangerous, that... He found himself silent inside. He didn't doubt for a moment that she was capable of doing what she suggested. The issue wasn't Zahara, it was himself. He was making the same mistake Lord had made in trying to shun the three of them at Wormleighton and Lord was trying to stop him before he, too, said something unforgivable.

So instead, he reached out a hand towards her in the dark and found Zahara's held out to him as if she had known he would do so. Reassurance flowed from her, and it was as if a little piece of her determination and strength settled deep within his soul.

"I will come back to you," she said.

THE DEVIL'S COMMAND

Gideon gripped her hand. "Be sure you do."

Lord gave a purse of coins into Zahara's keeping then Shiraz turned the head of his horse back to the road.

After they had gone Gideon slid from the back of the bay to let the horse rest a little and silence stretched into the night around them.

"I didn't mean it," Lord said, after a while. "Any of it. You are far from being useless as a lawyer or in other spheres."

"And Zahara is not a whore?" Gideon said, keeping his voice to the same uncarrying level. That was hard when the emotional burden of the words was so great.

There was another silence.

"Oh God, did I say that?" Then, "No. I know. I did. I have no excuse for it, I hope she will forgive me."

"I think she already has, although I'm not sure I am able to," Gideon said, feeling the brittleness in his voice. "And you called Shiraz a eunuch."

"He is," Lord sounded bleak, "though I should not throw the fact in his face. He is more of a man than most who are fully endowed, and I do not mean his fighting prowess, that is not the mark of a man. I mean his wisdom and courage, his forbearance, humour and fortitude. A man could not ask for a better friend." Lord drew a breath and let it out as a sigh. "Shiraz never mentions his past, though Kate and I have pieced together something of it. He was once a man of some standing in Persia, a diplomat, a scholar and a philosopher. A man who held high rank before dark political tides turned against him on the death of the monarch he had served faithfully and tore everything from him. Even his voice."

It was an image of Shiraz Gideon struggled with. To him Shiraz was a menacing figure, unimaginable without his sword and bow. Lord must have heard that in the quality of the silence that followed his words.

"You think a man who wields the sword can have no power with the pen? That a warrior must never be a thinker? War is the common state of humanity. Those who fight have still to consider how to live, still reflect on what matters, still grapple as any might with the eternal verities. We are not like the little clockwork figures that run out to chime the hour then vanish into oblivion the times between." There was a cold tightness in his tone and the distance between them seemed to expand.

In the wait that followed Gideon tried not to think about it and focused instead on the wisps of low cloud that were beginning to assemble. There would be a dense mist before dawn.

It was getting late but there was still movement on the road, more soldiers in troops and companies heading to Warwick. Some heading, no doubt, for the fortress itself. He wondered how, if she were there, they could ever hope to redeem Kate from its walls.

As if reading his thoughts Lord spoke from the darkness, voice changed from before.

"I think we will need more of guile and gold than strength of arms to get in there and out again, sharp minds more than sharp swords." Then after a moment, "I am glad, therefore, that you are with me, and I was both foolish and churlish to think I would fare better alone."

THE DEVIL'S COMMAND

Gideon knew an olive branch when one was offered. The matter was simple. He could cleave to the anger and feed it, let himself be towards Philip Lord—Sir Philip Lord—as he had been before when first they met. Could choose to see him solely as the cold, brutal and ruthless soldier-of-fortune he most assuredly was. Or he could recognise that this was a man not at ease with his emotions any more than Gideon himself, and who had fallen in extremis. It took little imagination to know how he himself might respond if Zahara did not come back from the Bridge Inn. He made a conscious effort and unclenched the bindings of self-righteous indignation he had wrapped tight about his anger and let it go.

"I'm glad to be here," he said and, with a slight shock, realised he meant it. "But how long do we wait for Zahara and Shiraz?"

There was no need for an answer; the sharp report of a pistol shot split the night from the direction of the inn and a moment later, Gideon was on his horse and riding, for once ahead of Lord's roan.

II

Nick had lived with a knowledge of the Covenant all his conscious life. At first, it had been little more than the awareness that there was an expectation placed on him that was not placed on Henry. Then, when he had gone to live at Howe, it had crept out of the shadows and lurked in every corner of the house, passed in whispers behind closed doors, concealed itself in secretive looks and sudden changes of conversation.

At a young age, he had learned to play the game of secrecy himself. Learned to keep close anything he saw or heard, turn it over in his mind like the piece of a puzzle and then fit it into the whole. And that meant that by the time he was first told of it, he already knew enough to be neither surprised nor to ask too many questions. His uncle had tried to convince him that to be born to the heritage of the Covenant was to be chosen by destiny. Nick knew it to be otherwise. It was an intolerable burden, making of his life a playing piece in someone else's game of chess. And now he was beginning to wonder if to these men it was indeed nothing more than a game they played with the affairs of the nation.

They were, of course, insane. They and their schemes would fit best in the walls of Bedlam. For the first time in his life, Nick felt the smallest sliver of empathy with Philip Lord who sat at the heart of these grand designs. Like Nick himself he had been born to be the clay these men would mould to their ends.

But the empathy did not extend beyond that. Despite what was demanded of him, Nick had not become a murderous traitor. At least he could comfort himself that the ideals of the Covenant aimed at the weal of humanity. Unlike that piratical mercenary who was set on its destructive woe.

"This is the time God has sent us and man has wrought," Portly declared. "If we can't tame the wild stallion to the bridle, though I believe it can be done, then we will need to begin again. For that we must look to you." He nodded at Nick.

THE DEVIL'S COMMAND

"Me?" Nick struggled to make sense of the words. "What must I do?"

"You can't be that innocent," Gold said, his incredulity bordering on contempt.

"They mean that you need to have a son with your wife," his father said heavily, and not with the kind of enthusiasm most men might bring to the idea of their first grandchild. Nick felt the same sick sensation in his guts as he had felt when the women at Howe told him Christobel had tried to take her own life rather than face a future married to him. He had not told these men that detail, nor his father. A handful of loyal servants at Howe who had dealt with it knew, and he had no intention of telling anyone else.

"But why?" At the same moment, he knew the answer. The impossible answer. "Christobel is the daughter of a man of humble birth, she is not—"

Gold bared his teeth in a cold grin.

"From her looks alone, how could you think that?"

Nick had no answer he could give.

"It is what Christobel believes," he said, before realising how weak that must sound. The thought made him strike back with a challenge. "Is there any proof to the contrary?"

Portly and Gold exchanged glances. Nick's guts tightened. Those in the know against those not. The players against the playing pieces.

"The proofs themselves, the original documents, are beyond our reach," Portly said.

"And for good reason," Gold added, "but there are copies which are signed if not sealed. One set being the copies Sir Bartholomew guarded."

"Where are they now?" Nick's father demanded. "If they were my brother-in-law's property they should go to his heir, my son."

"To be the keeper of a thing is not to be its owner," Gold said, "and in these troubled times, we need to ensure they are secure." He turned to Nick. "But I am sure, given time, we can arrange for you to read the documents in full, so you can understand the true nature of what you will be risking your life for. That is fair." He finished speaking and looked over at Portly, who nodded assent.

"Risking my life?" Nick asked, confused now, "I thought you wished me to spend my days in bed with my wife?"

Portly lifted a hand as if to push the notion away. "All of us risk our lives in this endeavour, you should have no illusion about that. The Covenant has always had its enemies. But, yes, it would be useful if there was a child, though were you to find that aspect of your role beyond you it matters little who does the deed as long as the resulting child is male, hale and deemed legitimate, but—"

Nick had his sword half-drawn before his father could clamp a hand about his wrist.

"How dare you, sir," Nick snarled.

Gold laughed. "The cub has teeth, Michael, I would be careful." Then, to Nick, "Disregard what he said, he is used to dealing with those who are so committed to the cause that such niceties are irrelevant. In some ways, you should consider it a compliment. He speaks to you as one of us."

Nick released his sword and tried to make sense of what Gold had said, whilst still in a place of buffeting

THE DEVIL'S COMMAND

emotion.

"Do you mean that all this talk and insistence of bloodline is no more than a trail of paper and ink?"

There was a moment when all three of the older men stared at him, and he feared he had somehow spoken an awful truth none of them had heard uttered before. Then Gold smiled and clapped him on the shoulder.

"In the early days, all was done as the original signatories to the Covenant saw it should be done. Blood for blood. The last man of those died right after the culmination of his work was born. That culmination being Philip Lord. Since then, there have been those who feel that the appearance is more important than the reality. That what matters is what men believe. They hold that the belief in itself sanctifies the reality. When the cause is so important, sometimes it is more important to offer what is needed, than that what is needed is there to be offered."

"I am not sure I…"

"He is saying," Nick's father told him, "that your wife is not of the same unbesmirched and legitimate bloodline as Philip Lord. She is by way of a compromise."

"She would be a compromise anyway, were her antecedents precise to the paper." Gold sounded dismissive. "She is, after all, a woman. But needs must. Besides," he smiled between Nick and his father, "would you not wish a new royal dynasty to have the Tempest name?"

His father looked thoughtful, but Nick found he wasn't at all sure that he did wish it. If only because were this whole conspiracy to fail, which in his view was very possible, the name 'Tempest' would be painted throughout the rest of history as that of the worst kind of traitor, alongside such names as Fawkes and Warbeck.

"So Christo—my wife is not a *full* sister to Philip Lord?"

Gold stared at him without expression.

"Does it matter? The key thing is we can prove her to be so. Much as you can prove that as your wife, she chose to wed you."

And that made him close his mouth. He had done that to achieve Howe Hall, so how much further might these men go to achieve a nation?

"Do we even need a child to be born?" Nick's father said. "You have the means to find some brat which looks close enough to Nicholas and myself to fit the bill."

"I am sure we could," Portly agreed. "The problem is that you will have noticed both Philip Lord and Christobel Lavinstock have a rather distinctive appearance. That would be harder to match."

"I don't see the problem," Nick's father went on, "after all, who is to know how they look and who is to care when all that matters is what is given in ink on paper?"

Now the hostility from both Gold and Portly was tangible.

"You are being difficult, Sir Richard," Portly said, his tone stiff. "Though those stratagems and deceits are there to fall back on in need, our first and foremost duty is to ensure that such are not required. If the intentions we have set in motion come to fruition,

THE DEVIL'S COMMAND

then there will be blood not ink sustaining the endeavour." He covered his mouth and gave an apologetic cough. "I for one would find it difficult in the extreme to bend a knee to a street brat dressed in silks and with a crown upon its brow and for all her lack of legitimacy, the true bloodline flows in the veins of your son's wife." He looked at Gold. "Most who remain are much of my mind, but admittedly there are some of the younger generation who don't appreciate that there is an irrefutable sanctity in the blood of great kings which makes them divine vessels with the God-granted right to rule."

To Nick, it sounded very like the arguments of the day, between the divine right of the king and the pragmatic power of his parliament. He tried to bring the conversation back to the issues that most affected him.

"You said I was the man for the next step and that I would need Bristow, which sounds to me as if you have something specific in mind."

"We do," Gold agreed and then turned to Nick's father. "I apologise, Sir Richard, but I will have to ask you to retire for a time. Perhaps you would be kind enough to see that supper will be ready soon. I think my dear friend, Michael here will waste away if he has nothing to eat before we have to leave."

Nick's father bristled visibly.

"You are having secrets from me with my son?" He sounded outraged.

Portly lay a soothing hand on his arm.

"Richard, Sir Nicholas is a man grown now and a full member of the Covenant, your guardianship of him has therefore run its course. Thus far you have known much that has been kept from him, but now it is safer if he alone knows what is required. The fewer men who know the less chance that any will learn of it."

"You are accusing me of—?"

"No one is accusing you of anything," Gold snapped. "This is how we have always done things. Only those who have to act need to know what they do. Were it otherwise we would have been betrayed a dozen times by accident if not by design. In your life you will have performed deeds and held secrets on behalf of the Covenant which none of us in this room will ever know. But your time bearing this burden is done. Now it falls to Sir Nicholas, who is a true son of the Covenant, to pick up the Tempest and the Coupland share and see it through."

If the weight of the words pressed down on Nick, his father was crushed by them. There was something broken in his expression as he gave in to the inevitable and left the room. Nick watched him go, a new bleakness taking root in his soul. Then he realised the two men were both studying him. He straightened up and met their gaze.

"What is it you want me to do?"

Gold looked hesitant, which was strange after his being, of the two, the more confident and sure.

"As Michael here has told you, our ideal result is to still use one we know is of royal blood and can prove so. The depositions and other documents in the archive would convince the Pope himself, I am sure. Yes, there are those who still hold that there is some sacred alchemy in the bloodline itself and who am I to say they are wrong? The common people think so, even those who despise the king we have."

It was as if Nick had fallen into a lake and was treading water. He had his head in the air but was making no progress towards firm land.

"And that means?"

Portly, or Michael as Gold called him, cleared his throat.

"What Gabriel is trying to tell you is that we still want Philip Lord. Either the man or his legitimate seed."

Nick tried to make that fit into his previous understanding of the Covenant's aims.

"My father and Sir Bartholomew told me he should be killed," he said. "That these things had run their course, that—"

"I am sure that would suit many," Gold, or Gabriel, said. "You see there are many now bound to the Covenant who wish to be free of it. They regard it as outdated and obsolete and believe if Philip Lord were no more all their problems would die with him." Nick said nothing because that was indeed the view both his father and Sir Bartholomew had held—and had raised him to hold also. He understood then that his father had been sent away because these men knew that too.

"And if I were of that line of thought myself?"

"Then," Gabriel said, his voice gentle, "you would be of no more use to the Covenant, and we would have to see if your brother Henry could show more wisdom."

Every hair on Nick's body stood on end and the

flesh across his shoulders tightened as a thin line of sweat sprung out on his scalp. He thought for a moment he might vomit. As it was, he had to swallow hard twice before he could produce any words and even then they had a hoarse rasp to them from a throat that was dry.

"You want me to capture Philip Lord?"

There was a bark of laughter from Michael and Gabriel smiled thinly.

"I think you might find that task a little beyond your capabilities," he said. "No. We have other work for you to do. For you and your man Bristow."

Chapter Eight

Whatever the cause, the furore at the Bridge Inn had spilled out onto the road and was drawing attention from the troops guarding the bridge itself. Even in his haste Gideon noticed them. They were well-armed men who were uncertain whether they should run over to intervene or stand at their posts. Seeing that, he recognised in time that flying out of the night at a gallop was going to draw too much attention and reined to a trot, stopping at the side of the building. Moments later Lord was beside him. He dismounted and threw his reins to Gideon.

"Wait here. I should not be long."

Then he was gone.

But the urgency driving Gideon was too great. He pushed his horse into the stable area and blocked the path of a boy who was running to get a look at what was going on out front.

"Hold these horses here and you can have a shilling when I return."

The boy's eyes went large, and greed warred with curiosity, then he took the reins.

Gideon left him with the horses and ran towards the inn. A side door stood open with tempting rich smells of ale and savoury food, blending with the promise of a warm wood fire. But as he stepped inside he ran into Philip Lord and to his immense relief, an unharmed Zahara. Shiraz was right behind them supporting what seemed to be a very drunk Ned Blake.

Lord's eyes widened at his sudden appearance.

"Where are the horses?"

"I left them with a boy in the stable yard."

Lord's expression changed.

"Tell me you don't mean that?"

"I did. I—" Then he realised what he had done and the heat of horror and shame washed through him.

Lord shook his head. "I had better see to it. Wait here."

He closed the door of the inn and left them there sheltered in the shadows of its wall, invisible from the road. Feeling sick at what his folly might have brought upon the boy, Gideon was about to go after Lord, when Zahara put a gentle hand on his arm.

"The Schiavono will have some idea to make it right. He will not hurt a child." Her conviction was absolute, but Gideon was not sure he shared it. His own mind was still too raw with the brutality he had seen Digby's men wreak on the baggage train and he had a sour sensation in his stomach that told him such scenes were ones that soldiers-of-fortune knew well. It seemed an interminable time but can have been but a couple of minutes before Lord was back.

"We must be quick. The soldiers are intervening now." He took the semi-conscious Blake from Shiraz as he spoke. "You know where we will be."

Shiraz nodded then he and Zahara went back into the inn. Gideon found himself out in the cold helping to heave Blake onto the withers of Lord's horse, before mounting himself.

He wanted to ask why Shiraz and Zahara remained. He wanted to ask what the pistol shot had been and

THE DEVIL'S COMMAND

why there was a fight in the inn and what had happened to the boy. He wanted to ask why they had a semi-conscious Blake with them and where they were going. But there was no chance to do any of that before Lord was leading the way out across country in the dark, leaving the sounds of brawling behind.

Lord reined in by the stand of trees they had been hiding in before and Blake groaned.

"You will have to help me secure him better," Lord said. "Here, I have some match cord you can use to tie his hands. If he can't sit straight, we'll have to carry him broadside."

Gideon knew from personal experience how uncomfortable that was. To be laid over the horse like a sack, face rubbed raw on leather. But then Blake was perhaps too far gone in his cups to notice so much. He dismounted and did what he could to help Lord. Blake started throwing himself around and they had to gag him when he began shouting. In the end he was bound hand and foot and cast over Lord's roan, still wriggling enough to make the horse unhappy.

"You will have to take him," Lord said. "That bay is shot proof. It should not be for long. I am sure Shiraz will bring your chestnut with him. But I have no wish to linger here too long. We are nearer the road and the inn than I feel is safe and there will be patrols checking the surrounding areas at some point for sure."

"Where are we going?"

"Shiraz and Zahara overheard mention of an empty seasonal farm labourer's hut about half a mile from here. Someone who was too late for a room was given direction there by a local, but then was offered a place to share a room, so we can hope not to be disturbed."

"And the boy?" Gideon had to know, but the lack of trust was plain in every syllable.

"Good God, Gideon, what kind of monster—?" He broke off. When he spoke again there was a note of emotion Gideon was unsure how to place. "I gave the boy a shilling and a message to take to someone who does not exist who I said will be staying at the Two Virgins Inn in Kenilworth. He is promised another shilling if they are not there and he waits for them to arrive, so I think it will keep him well away from here for as long as we need."

"How did you know that was the name of the inn there?" Used as he was to Lord's strange and eclectic range of knowledge it came close to stretching Gideon's credulity.

Lord's hiss of breath held intense exasperation.

"I did not. This was a child. It was easy enough. He told me himself whilst thinking I knew it already." Lord drew a breath, and his voice resumed its more regular timbre with something of a cutting edge. "Next time, I expect you to obey the orders I give you."

There was nothing Gideon could say to that.

With some difficulty, they loaded Blake onto the bay, and with him still struggling, Gideon set the stoic horse to follow in the wake of Lord's roan.

Finding the hut was not easy, and had they not encountered the ghostlike Shiraz with Zahara pillion, leading Gideon's mare, they would have missed it.

As a shelter it offered no more than the walls about them. There was a hearth, swept out but empty, and

THE DEVIL'S COMMAND

two straw-filled pallets which were damp but not mouldy, a couple of candle stubs sat in holders, all suggesting this was not a place abandoned. Close by there was a stand of trees which offered both the chance of firewood and a place of concealment for the horses.

Lord took Blake from the bay and carried him like a sack into the hovel as Shiraz and Gideon led the horses under the cover of the trees and managed to gather a little firewood. By the time they got back to the hut, Zahara had lit a candle from her tinderbox and Lord was studying a document by its light. He handed it to Gideon and pointed to Blake now propped in the corner looking afraid as he seemed to be aware of his position.

"He was carrying this."

As Zahara built a fire in the hearth and Shiraz went for more wood, Gideon read the neat script. It was not Blake's own hand and the seal attached was not the prince's or the king's. It was that of Robert Devereux, Earl of Essex and it named Blake and instructed that he should be given free passage and assistance in the name of the earl.

His throat constricted, Gideon handed it back to Lord.

"What does it mean, though? If he betrayed Kate, then why would he have come here? Why get so drunk? Why was there a fight—?"

Lord's face was granite in the candlelight.

"The shot you heard was arranged by Shiraz for the creation of a massive distraction as was the fight. Blake appears very drunk because Zahara put something in his food to make him so."

At her name, Zahara looked up from beside the hearth.

"You will not kill him," she said. "It would be on my conscience as much as if I had."

Lord looked haggard. "No. I will not. My word on it."

Gideon had a strong feeling that on another day he might not have answered her the same way. But this night, he owed her an act of grace of such magnitude, no matter what it might cost him.

Lord crossed to Blake and drew his knife, cutting the gag, then pressing the blade against his neck.

"I am sure you noted that," he said in a voice Gideon had not heard from Lord before, something cold beyond hate. Gideon thought he had witnessed in full the ruthless and brutal hinterland which lay deep with Lord. Now he knew he had not. This was something inhuman. "Your life is protected by the will of the lady. But if you endanger her, I will have no choice. I want you to answer me and I promise you that there is a great deal I can do to you that falls short of killing, but which you would wish did not."

Zahara had looked away and her face in profile to Gideon looked haunted. He had no wish himself to witness the torture of a man, but this one held the key to Kate's whereabouts...

"You don't understand." Blake's voice was slurred but he sounded at least as if in command of his wits. "I came to save Lady Catherine. You can't, but I can."

At the mention of Kate's name Lord's head lifted, eyes widened, nostrils flared.

"You are a creature of Essex's betrayed by the pass

THE DEVIL'S COMMAND

you carry, why would you have any care for Lady Catherine?"

"She is…she…I…I mean I have the greatest respect for her. I would not see her harmed. I wanted to help her—"

"You wanted to help her by sending her into danger?" Lord's voice was a snarl. "You sent her to Essex with those letters of amnesty and then betrayed her to him. They knew she was coming."

The tip of the knife had dug too deep, and a bead of blood welled from Blake's neck and ran down the blade.

"I swear to God, I meant her no harm, I would never have hurt her."

"Alright. Let me accept as honest, for now, your protestations of care for Lady Catherine, but what were you doing in the inn? You were seen speaking to someone who left right away for the city. Who was it you spoke to and what did you tell them?"

"I don't know what you are talking about. I didn't—" The last word was swallowed in a scream, but Gideon had no idea what Lord had done because Zahara got up and left the hut and he went after her.

She stood with her hands behind her back, pressed against the outside wall, her breath ragged as if with sobs, but there was no sound of crying.

"I know it… that he… that we must…"

Without thinking Gideon was beside her, his arms about her but he felt her stiffen in his grip, her muscles tense, he stepped back.

"I'm sorry," he said. "I wanted to comfort you, to—"

There was another scream from within and Zahara was clinging to him like a frightened child, the silent sobs now shared with tears. He folded his arms about her as if she were fragile and tried to make of his body a fortress in the ocean of her misery and of his arms bastions against the horror of the world.

He didn't know how long it was they stood there. He knew only that Zahara needed him to be a rock and bear it for them both. So he did, even when the rain began, heavy and wet.

Then the door of the hut opened, and Lord came out, backlit by the fire he had finished from what Zahara had begun. He saw the two of them and stood aside.

"You had better come in," Lord said.

The promise of warmth and dryness was an invitation of its own, but even as Gideon thought to respond to that, a dark place within him was asking if that was tainted. Had Lord used flame as well as metal on Blake? In his arms he felt Zahara still shaking.

"Are you ready to go in?" he asked her, "We can stay here if you prefer."

For a moment he thought she would refuse, and he would not have blamed her if she had. He had no wish to see what Lord had done to Blake himself. But he felt her head nod against his chest. He opened his arms as she stepped away.

"Thank you," she said, then her head held high, she walked back into the hut. Before Gideon could follow, a hand from the darkness gripped his arm and he turned, about to shout, his hand clasping for his sword before he realised it was Shiraz.

In the light from the open door, he saw the dark glitter of the other man's eyes and wondered if in trying to comfort Zahara he had offended Shiraz. But Shiraz lifted his chin and then inclined it in a nod of approval and gratitude, and his eyes held something more which Gideon couldn't read. Feeling as if he had somehow passed a test, he followed Shiraz back inside.

Lord was sitting by the hearth eating some bread and cheese which Zahara had brought from the inn.

"Leave him," Lord snapped as Zahara moved towards Blake who was now a huddle in the corner, under his own coat. "He is not worth your care."

She hesitated for less than a heartbeat, then went over to the man and knelt beside him.

Lord was on his feet in a moment.

"I said—" To his eternal credit he stopped himself, though Gideon had taken half a step towards him, and Shiraz was watching him like a predator studying its prey.

Lord slumped down again and shook his head a hard breath escaping in a shuddering sigh. The fatigue of a man who had not slept in three nights, eaten too little, been pressed beyond the limits of emotional endurance and had fought a battle in the middle of that imprinted on his face.

"Blake has been being paid five pounds a week by Essex," he said, his voice rasping. "He told Essex that Kate was going to be handing out the letters *before* he even told her they existed. He wanted her taken. He was angry because she had married me. If I had not, then—" Lord broke off and drew a breath before going on. "He claims he regretted it and when he heard I was coming to look for her he hatched a new plan. To have me seized and Kate, somehow, freed. He believed he could persuade Essex to it at least. Then she would be grateful to him for her life and he could take my place in her affections."

Gideon's skin chilled and felt clammy. Any sympathy he might have held for Blake had gone. He glanced at Zahara who still seemed determined to tend him. Gideon was reminded of his friend, Anders Jensen, a highly skilled physician-surgeon who had left in part because he was sickened by the violence Lord inflicted on his own in a rough and wild justice. He too had tended those in need no matter their nature or allegiance. It bespoke a compassion in them both that Gideon could admire but never share.

"Essex knows I will be in the area and looking to free Kate," Lord went on. "That makes the task a dozen times harder than it would have been because Essex is no fool." He sighed and lifted a hand to brush hair from his face. There was blood dried on his fingers. "I don't know where Kate is being held because Blake does not know. They have taken some prisoners to the castle, but Blake says he heard there are others being held in Warwick itself."

He closed his eyes and leaned back against the wall and was quiet for so long Gideon even wondered if he had fallen asleep, until he spoke again.

"As to what we can do. Right now, I think there is little. The one way I could get into Warwick tonight would be to use the safe conduct Blake had on him. The entire city is in a high state of alert, and I am distinctive to say the least, with nothing to hand to make myself seem reliably otherwise."

Gideon swallowed hard.

"I could go. I am not known or that distinctive. The only person who has even seen me here, you sent to Kenilworth so there is no reason I should draw any dangerous attention."

Lord's eyes had shot open at his words.

"And what would you do?" he asked.

"I could try and find out where Kate is being held. That would at least take us forward and with the safe-conduct from Essex I should be able to get into the castle even, if needed."

Lord shook his head.

"I think you might not understand the degree of peril involved here, Gideon. If you were taken you would be hung as a spy and there would be nothing anyone could do to stop that. The castle will be—"

"In chaos," Gideon put in. "They will be trying to accommodate all the incoming men and if Essex has come here his army will follow. One man will not be noticed in all that."

Lord studied him with eyes that were still bright as diamonds, even if fatigue was leaving them set in hollows.

"You have had much too little sleep."

"I've had more than you."

Lord laughed at that, his head back against the wall behind him.

"That is true. But I am used to this. You are not trained to it."

Gideon's jaw tightened.

"The difference between going tonight and tomorrow is that tomorrow may be too late. I am not intending to act, merely to listen and ask questions. If

Kate is being held anywhere in the city there will be talk of it. It is too much of a grand story. The daring and beautiful cavalier spy. I am sure I will hear of it."

"If I let you go and something happens—"

"It will be on my own cognisance," Gideon said. "I know it will be dangerous. I know if I am caught then I will be killed. I also know I am the one hope Kate has."

Lord studied his face in the flicker of light from hearth and candle. It was easy to guess what was in his mind. What had Lord called him? *A useless lawyer*. And that must be how he saw Gideon in the dark recesses of his mind, no matter how much he might trust Gideon's good intentions.

"This is not work for a man of the sword," Gideon told him, trying to counter those unspoken objections. "You said as much yourself. That it would need guile more than strength of arms to get in there and out again. This is work for a man who knows how to ask the right questions to get information from people without them being aware they have given it. That has been my profession for some years."

It was Zahara who settled the matter. She spoke without ceasing her work.

"I do not understand why you will not let Gideon go. He believes he can do it and he is as a good a judge of his own skill as you are of yours. As he says, of us all here, only he can do this which might save Lady Catherine."

Lord had no answer for that.

A short time later, mounted on his chestnut, chosen because she did not have the look of a military mount, and carrying the bulk of such coin as Lord had with

THE DEVIL'S COMMAND

him and the safe-conduct from Essex, Gideon was riding alone towards Warwick.

Lord had promised to await his return. "We will stay here if we can," he said, lifting one of the large flat stones by the hearth. "If we have to go, I will leave a message for you here to say where we have gone. If there is no message, you must assume we are taken."

Zahara's farewell had been even more brief. She gripped his hand after he had mounted, her face invisible in the dark.

"You will find Lady Catherine," she said. "You will both come back."

Her confidence stayed with him as he rode up to the bridge and presented Blake's pass. He was nodded through with no more than a glance. It was late now, but there were still men arriving from Kineton. As he reached the city Gideon found himself delayed behind one group of soldiers and then hemmed in by another from behind.

Then it was his turn to be scrutinised and asked his business. This time his pass seemed to have a less magical effect. The man who took it and read it, frowned at the script then grabbed the bridle of his little mare and led him to the side of the road, amongst the men with muskets who were the guard on the city.

"Dismount and wait here," he was told and the man, together with the safe-conduct, vanished into the dark, leaving Gideon standing under the suspicious eyes of the soldiers. He had a sick lump in his stomach and a bitter taste in his mouth. Any attempt to leave, or even asking if he could, would add to whatever weight of suspicion he already carried. So he did the one thing he could do: wait and pray.

"You are to come with me."

The man who had taken his pass was back—with company. Before he could protest, Gideon was relieved of his sword and seated again on his chestnut, in the midst of a tight group of four men, riding at a brisk pace on the road that led to the castle.

Heart pounding and trying hard not to show how afraid he was, Gideon had a blurred impression of the monumental stone building. They passed under a gate and into a large courtyard then, hooves echoing on the stone, through the tunnel of another narrow gatehouse. He glimpsed huge wooden gates, a solid portcullis raised but ready to drop and from the floor of the building above, holes in the masonry where attackers who made it past the first defence could be slaughtered with weapons firing down on them.

Wondering if he would ever ride out of the gate again, Gideon was pushed by his escort into the expansive bailey. It was vast. The walls and towers fringing one side, disappeared beyond Gideon's vision at the far end. Opposite that was a long stone building.

Although it was late, there was light everywhere. Gideon realised that at some point in recent history this ancient fortress had been transformed to become a comfortable modern dwelling as well as a stronghold. The windows were glazed with expensive expanses of glass.

He had little time to give much attention to his surroundings, being ordered to dismount and then escorted into the main building. Gideon had an impression of gracious living, statuary, paintings, moulded ceilings and wooden panels. The building was thick with soldiers, and the men with him seemed to be well known to those there as they were not challenged until they reached a door part way along the main passageway of the building.

Then he was hustled inside the room and had the impression of comfort, grandeur, and the warmth from a large fireplace. But his attention was held by the three men there, none of whom he recognised. They were all clad in military dress that denoted wealth and status. Two were in their thirties, one with long light brown hair and the other with a curt style of the kind that a London apprentice boy might have worn. The third was an older man, his square-jawed face boasting a broad moustache and framed with grey hair that touched the wide white collar he wore. He was clearly the one in command.

Gideon made a bow towards them, and the older man squinted at him for a moment.

"Blake, isn't it? I know we've never met but your work I've seen. You have given us invaluable service."

"Invaluable, my lord?" one of the younger men echoed. "At five pounds a week I think 'expensive' might be a better term."

The older man frowned his companion into silence as Gideon's heart did a small galliard leap then settled back into the powerful pavane it had been pounding in his chest ever since he had been detained outside the city. Claiming to be Blake could be fatal if anyone who knew Blake were to recognise him. But on the other hand, denying that he was would at best earn him a closer view of whatever dungeons this castle might boast, and at worst a rapid execution.

"I am indeed Edward Blake, my lord," Gideon said, hoping his voice sounded as confident as he intended it should. He was certain now that whoever the two younger men might be, he was talking with the Earl of Essex, Lord-General of the army of Parliament.

"Good. But before we talk of other matters," Essex went on, "I have a couple of questions for you. Forgive me if they seem a little unrelated to the matter in hand and humour me with your best answer."

"Of course, sir," Gideon said, and repeated his bow.

"In a matter of inheritance, if I had a child of profligate nature, but wished to provide for his children, could I leave the house to him for his life and then to his heirs without needing to fear he might have the power to sell it to pay his gambling debts and leave my grand-children with nothing?"

Gideon stared at the earl, wondering what on earth such a question might have to do with his present circumstances. He was about to say he had no idea, as any scrivener might. But then he recalled what Blake had told him of his past.

"If I were to advise you in such a case, sir, it would be to suggest that you left the property in trust to the grandchild of your choice and found some other bequest for your son. The law would say that the grantor, yourself, can only bequest such an interest in an estate to the grantee, in this case your son, and not to his heirs." Gideon allowed himself a small smile. This was too easy. He had said the same thing to clients a score of times at least in his career and making such a well-rehearsed explanation had a

THE DEVIL'S COMMAND

calming effect on his emotions. He could feel his confidence growing with every familiar phrase. "In other words, sir, the profligate man inherits all the rights you would have bestowed upon his heirs. Or as Sir Edward Coke put it *that always in such cases, 'the heirs' are words of limitation of the estate, not words of purchase*."

Essex blinked.

"Words of purchase?"

"My apologies," Gideon said smoothly, "it is a legal term which is used to define one who acquires an interest in property directly through deed or will rather than through right of descent. In other words, those heirs do not have that legal and vital interest which you might wish they did."

The broad moustache twitched and then the earl nodded.

"You must forgive me, Mr Blake, not having met you before I needed to be sure you were indeed who you claimed to be. Haws told me some time ago of your legal background, so I thought to test you with that in his absence. I regret that after he came to me with your news, I needed to dispatch him to London with certain vital and secure messages and an account of events or he would have been here to greet you himself."

Managing a crooked smile with his bow, Gideon offered a brief and silent prayer of thanks that this man Haws had been sent away. Essex made a motion with one hand to the soldiers behind Gideon, who bowed and left the room. Essex waited until they had gone then nodded at the two men with him who inclined their heads and moved to the rear of the well-furnished room, affording some privacy to whatever the Earl wished to say.

Gideon had begun to hope he might somehow manage to walk out of the castle alive.

"I will not keep you long," Essex said, his voice moderated so as not to carry to the others in the room, "but I have read your most recent report concerning Sir Philip Lord and it matches with a request I was sent by the Committee in London. It seems he is seen by some as an important individual, traitor or no. I have been carrying instructions for his detention and urgent dispatch to London for the past several weeks, but until today I have not had any thought that I might have some means to execute that warrant."

"I am your lordship's most humble servant in all things," Gideon said. "What is it you would have me do?"

"I want you to set a trap to capture this Sir Philip and I think I may have the perfect bait with which you may do so to hand."

THE DEVIL'S COMMAND

Chapter Nine

"Those men," Bristow observed as they rode from Newhall the next morning, "if you don't mind my saying so, sir, they did not seem very gentlemanly at all. In fact," he paused as if in thought, "they reminded me much of myself on a bad day."

Nick looked at him and scowled.

"What did they say to you?" he demanded.

Bristow shook his head.

"They made it clear that if I wished to live long enough to collect on the generous payment they were offering, I should keep that to myself. But, in brief, they wished me to serve your every whim with alacrity and efficiency. It seemed to me they felt confident they had already directed the path of that whim."

After his own chilling experience with the two, who he doubted were called Michael and Gabriel any more than they were Portly and Gold, Nick was a little surprised to find Bristow so sanguine. It was clear he didn't dismiss or diminish the threat they posed, but he seemed almost not to care about it.

"I think you know well there is nothing whimsical in what they expect of us," Nick said, a bitter taste flavouring the words.

"What I think, sir," Bristow said, "is they are playing in a game of Tarocchi with many wild cards in amongst the trumps. The gamble they make is their lives and fortunes—and ours too, needless to say—

against winning a great political prize."

That made Nick look hard at the man beside him, his freckled face bland and unconcerned. Bristow must have felt the scrutiny because he turned to meet Nick's gaze.

"Perhaps, it is I who should be asking what they said to you, sir, because I have a feeling whatever it was it will be affecting the two of us."

And that was true. The issue for Nick was how much he should share. How far he could trust this man.

"I don't think you need to know all of it," he said.

"I'm sure not, sir," Bristow agreed. "Although the more I know the better I can assist you in achieving the goal. It might be some of my experience could be of service to you."

And that was the difficulty. The man was right. Nick knew that at some point he was going to have to make a decision on how much he trusted Daniel Bristow. The trick of it had to be to ensure Bristow's self-interest marched in step with his own.

Which was when he realised that he needed to try and find out more about the man.

After all, it was not as if Bristow had sprung fully formed from the ground the day they first met. He must have had a childhood, no matter how squalid, parents, siblings perhaps. He must have known some degree of education to be able to offer the kind of skills he spoke about. It was a strange sensation to think that. And to realise this capable and ruthless individual could have within him all the same kind of turbulence that Nick himself experienced.

He found he was looking at Bristow, seeing the

dishevelled exterior, the quick, intelligent eyes looking out from the misleading mass of freckles and wondering *who* he was. It was not an experience Nick had ever known before, and part of him drew away from it. To acknowledge those aspects of another was to, in some way, regard that other as an equal, which Bristow was not and never could be in any meaningful way. But Nick was aware he had undeniable admiration for this soldier-of-fortune and blatant envy for the way he carried himself and dealt with those around him.

As if sensing his scrutiny, Bristow turned to meet his gaze. Nick made a decision.

"Are you from a military family?" he asked.

"I did have an uncle who rode with Sir Horace Vere, if that counts? But no, I'm an eternal disappointment to my father who was, and last I heard still is, a merchant of some standing in Manchester."

"You were a younger son?" Nick hazarded. As with the landed classes he understood merchants were also caught in the same trap of inheritance.

"Sadly, for both me and my father, no. I was his one son and heir, though I think he is reconciled to having my sister's husband take things on after his demise. I am now a mere codicil in his will, or indeed perhaps not even that." If the thought in any way troubled Bristow at all he didn't show it.

Nick tried to take in what that meant. He tried to imagine telling his own father he had no wish to be his heir, that he would go and fight in the German wars instead. Somewhere deep in his heart he felt a resonance for that notion. It wasn't something he could ever have done. He might have wished away his destiny a thousand times, but he had never once tried to walk away from it.

"How did it happen?" he asked, the curiosity genuine to his own surprise. "Didn't you get on with your father?"

Bristow grinned.

"It didn't *happen*," he said. "I made a deliberate choice. Up until I made that choice my father and I had a very warm relationship. We agreed I would serve my apprenticeship as a mercer in London, where I would make valuable contacts for the future of the family business. After that he would allow me to attend university so I could indulge my passion for mathematics. He is a fair and reasonable man."

"You turned to a military career following your apprenticeship and time at university?" Nick was surprised. Bristow seemed too young to have such a high degree of education and the years of military experience he had described to the two Covenant men.

"Oh no," Bristow told him cheerfully, his gaze on the road ahead. "As soon as I got to London I broke my indenture, which was an informal one contracted between our two families. My new master was happy to let me go once I had persuaded him." Bristow grinned as if at an amusing memory

"But why leave the apprenticeship? You had your father's promise."

"I did. But who would ever want to be a *mercer*?" Bristow spoke the word as if it were a form of calumny. "It was all my childhood. Ribbons, lace, braid, comfits, candles and cloth. Oh, so much cloth.

THE DEVIL'S COMMAND

I can still name you the price of silk and linen of every kind. Know it by weight and weave and colour, price the rags on the back of a courtier or a whore and judge the exact worth of a man by the quality of his breeches. It is soul destroying."

"It makes some men wealthy." Which was surely the point of such trades. Nick knew of more than one of his contemporaries who had married into the merchant class for their money.

"It made my father so," Bristow agreed. "But I have no stomach for it."

"You left your education for soldiering?"

"Not exactly," Bristow told him. "I exchanged one apprenticeship for another. One I found more amenable. I was taken on by the Company of Maisters of the Science of Defence, they specialised in teaching excellence and proficiency in weaponry, and in teaching how to teach that. Turned out I had something of a talent for it. There was a proving held and I triumphed. Sadly, they were much in decline and had never been accredited as a proper guild. But that served me as it meant they had a looser understanding of apprenticeship. I was able, through a trial of arms in what they called 'playing the prize' as often as I was permitted, to be made a Provost by the time I was twenty. Of course, that would never have been allowed fifty years ago, but times change."

Nick stared at him convinced that this must be a lie. He had heard of the once great schools of swordsmanship, with their brutal contests for advancement in which a student might face up to fifty opponents in consecutive bouts. But he thought they had vanished at the start of the century, replaced by fencing studios where the fashionable and wealthy could learn swordplay much as they might learn dancing.

"And I would have been a Master by now I suspect," Danny went on, "had I stayed to see it through and not gone to study at Leiden." He turned his gaze back to Nick, "Mathematics has always been my first love."

"Then why take a career in arms and not academia?"

"Academia is by far the more dangerous, in my experience," Bristow said. "Besides, in my present profession, I can combine both my passions and the pay is good."

Nick wondered if he was being toyed with. There seemed to be something missing in all the explanation, but Nick couldn't quite put his finger on what that was.

"What do you seek from it all?" he asked, and as he did so, realised that was the question he most needed answered. The one that would hold the key to binding Bristow to him. "Renown? Advancement?"

Bristow tilted his head back as if to study the sky from beneath the brim of his hat. "The usual things," he said. "Wine, wealth, women, good friends, a game of cards and a good fight. And one day, if I live long enough, perhaps a place or my own where I can sit in the sunshine on a summer's afternoon and reminisce about it all." Then he looked at Nick, his gaze almost a challenge. "Isn't that what everyone wants?"

"Some people," Nick agreed. "Some seem more concerned about shaping the world to the image of it they wish it to have."

"And glad I am for that," Bristow agreed. "Those are the men who pay me. If every one of them was happy with the way the world is, there would be no wars and I would be forced into academia after all."

"But you have no care which of them you fight for?" It was something which cut into the root of all Nick himself had been taught. "There is no allegiance in your soul to cause or person, or even religion? Nothing you feel is worth dying for?"

The wind that they had been shielded from, caught him with its cold bite as they crested a rise and he shivered.

"I would die for my friends," Bristow said after a few moments more of thought and Nick started to wonder how one would come to make a friend of such a man as Daniel Bristow. "And for the man who pays me, of course. I think that is enough." Then, after a brief hesitation, "I know you feel it would be indiscreet to advise me fully, but can you tell me something of what we are required to do, sir? And who were those men?"

It was as if the answer to his own was being given to him in Bristow's question. Friendship was built on trust.

Nick glanced round and saw the nearest of the soldiers were out of earshot. But wanting to be sure, he picked up his pace a little. Bristow guessed his intent because he lifted a hand. So, as he too broke into a brief trot, the men behind them did not.

Their way lay through hills, open heath and rugged fields. It seemed an appropriate setting, beneath a sky snarling with rain clouds to talk about what was to come. But it still seemed so alien to Nick that it stuck in his throat like a fishbone.

"I can tell you nothing of who those men were," he admitted, deciding some lines needed to be drawn from the first. "Don't ask me about them further. It is enough for you to know they have the power to do all they promise or threaten."

"I believe you. They seem to have a long reach or deep pockets, perhaps. If we are to be working for them, then I hope the latter."

"I think they have both the reach and the gold," Nick said.

Bristow frowned.

"Very well. Who they are is placed to the side for now and I wait to hear what else is being served for this meal we must eat."

"I can at least tell you your part. You will need to take me to Mags. Our friends wish to engage his services and urgently. Before Fairfax can persuade Parliament to part with the coin he asks."

For some reason that seemed to silence Bristow. They rode on for a while in the wind and a sudden splatter of icy rain. Then he turned to Nick and there was something new in his face, some kind of gravity that Nick had never seen him show before as if for once he was taking the situation seriously.

"Sir Nicholas, were I not bound to your service by gold and blood threats, I would be seeking now to leave it."

The words seemed more chilling to Nick than the weather.

"Why is that?" he asked, not sure he even wanted

THE DEVIL'S COMMAND

the answer.

"You may not recall, but I do, that not so long ago the graf offered you a prize with a high price."

"A prize with—?"

Then he remembered.

These are troubled times, sir. That means there is an opportunity for a man of vision to rise—if he has the means, the men and the determination. As I see it, at the least the Lordship of Howe could be raised to an Earldom or more and, at best, the Lord of Howe could become one of the most powerful men in the country.

He had been tempted, of course, but had not believed Mags could deliver what he offered, but now it seemed even the men of the Covenant seemed to think that he could. And Mags had offered it all to Nick, for himself, with no need for the Covenant and their insane notions of a new religion and a new empire.

Then he recalled that Mags had said all he wished was to be acknowledged as a legitimate scion of the Couplands and Tempests. As if such was even in Nicks' power.

But it was in the power of the Covenant men.

Nick shook his head. He felt as if he must be missing something crucial.

"I remember," he said, settling his horse as it danced away from a leaf that the wind had caught and skirled around in its face. "But how does that fit?"

Bristow didn't reply for a while as they went on. Then gave a shrug of his shoulders as if disowning responsibility for the consequences of what might flow from whatever he said.

"It seems to me that if we allow these men to make a connection with the graf and he puts to them what he put to you, they may think that a fine prospect for saving themselves an excessive fee on his services."

"The thought had crossed my mind," Nick agreed.

"Well, correct me if I am mistaken Sir Nicholas, but were it to be decided that he was legitimate, then he would be in a place to claim that he should have inherited Howe Hall and all that estate instead of Sir Bartholomew Coupland, that he should be the rightful baronet and Lord of Howe. In other times it would be no more than a legal headache for you, I am sure. But in these times, as you favour the king, and he is aligning with those of Parliament..."

Nick reined his horse so hard it reared in protest. He turned his mount across the road as he did so and was now both facing Bristow and barring his way. The icy rain that was being driven at them with ever greater persistence was warm compared to the frost that gripped Nick's heart and filled his lungs making it hard to breathe. What Bristow didn't know was that even though Nick had been granted a patent to allow him to inherit, he had yet to be confirmed in his title.

"Before God, there must be a way to stop that," he said.

To lose Howe after all he had done... To even think the thought was to twist his stomach into nausea.

Then like a man throwing a rope to one being sucked down and drowning in a whirlpool, Bristow said, "There is indeed a way, but it would put us both in an unconscionable amount of danger and you might prefer to keep on safer ground."

Nick shook his head and with some effort, pulled his horse around and persuaded it to go on.

"We are going to stop at the first inn or alehouse we come to and get out of this appalling weather, then you can tell me. Unless you are unwilling to face whatever of peril it might bring?"

Daniel Bristow, his face wet from the rain, grinned then.

"Oh no, sir. Not at all. I told you before, I never wanted the life of a mercer."

II

Of course, the tempting bait with which Essex thought he might set a trap for Sir Philip Lord was Sir Philip Lord's wife.

"Will you be missed?" Essex asked and Gideon's exhausted brain, reeling from that blow, struggled to make sense of the question. Essex frowned at his obvious confusion. "Prince Rupert, will he notice you are missing tonight?"

"No," Gideon said, then wondered if it was the right answer. Committed, he stumbled on. "The prince will be with his men all night."

Essex looked thoughtful.

"No doubt to harry our withdrawal with his cursed cavalry." He turned to the two men in the room an lifted his voice. "Robert, can you get a message sent right away to Kineton that they are to begin before first light?"

The long-haired man left the room with Gideon wondering if he had done some harm to the prince's plans, about which he knew nothing at all. He cudgelled his thoughts to focus on what mattered most. Kate.

"Would it be possible to speak with Lady Catherine? I am well known to her. It might be that I could convince her I am a friend."

Essex made a snorting noise, sounding rather like a distressed horse and his broad moustache fluttered. "Do you think she would trust a man whose coat she would see as being turned both ways?"

"But she will not know that my lord," Gideon pointed out. "I can tell her I have been misleading you in my reports and am loyal to the king as she is."

Essex strode over to pick up a familiar-looking folded document from a side table and then turned to hold it out. "Take this and use it as you need to. Haws told me you are a man of great invention. I will trust you to come up with a scheme to entrap this man, Lord, then we can send the two of them to London." Gideon crossed the room to take the pass with a polite bow, but Essex held it a moment longer. "You will need to be quick about it, I have to leave here within a few days. Be sure to tell me of the details of your design before you attempt its execution. I have no wish to be left in the dark about such manoeuvrings."

"Of course, my lord," Gideon agreed, with no idea of where that left his hopes of arranging a rescue. "Might I have my sword back?"

"Of course, I will see to it and as you have no requirement to leave tonight, I will see you are accommodated here."

Gideon was powerless to protest that. Hoist by his own petard and too tired to think of any argument that

THE DEVIL'S COMMAND

would not arouse suspicion, he gave in.

He was given quarters of some luxury and provided with food. As he ate, a soldier appeared to return his sword. Then, lying in bed, thoughts of Zahara troubled him enough that for a time he feared sleep might elude him. But being exhausted and having a warm bed and a full stomach, ensured he fell quickly asleep.

He woke to the sound of military orders being bellowed and hooves and boots on the stones of the bailey. Looking from the window he could see little more than mist and shapes moving in it, but the sounds were enough to tell him that Essex's army had begun withdrawing from Kineton and its vanguard at least had reached Warwick.

Having washed and dressed he emerged to find the house full of soldiers. On the way out he had cause to be grateful for his pass as he was challenged twice and taken for a clerk on a third occasion. Outside, the mist was the wispy, clinging kind that swirled thicker and then parted for a sudden moment to give the view ahead before closing in again.

Gideon's first instinct was to return to Lord to see what kind of plan he might suggest that could be presented to Essex. He had a painful and guilty awareness that whilst he had been sleeping under warm blankets and on a feather bed, Zahara, Lord and Shiraz had faced a cold night in the hovel with no more their clothing for warmth and comfort and Kate, wherever she might be held in the castle, would have suffered an even colder and more bleak night still. He debated whether he should try to see her first but decided he would rather take her hope of redemption at the least.

It was difficult to find direction to his mare in the tumult of soldiery and in the end, he resorted to using Essex's authority to command she be brought to him. Even so, it was nearly an hour after he had left the house that he was riding back out through the narrow throat of the gatehouse.

Once over the bridge, he found the mist had begun to lift but it did so to reveal that the fields behind the inn were being turned into mustering grounds for the army that was pulling back from Kineton. By the time he reached the hovel, he knew he was too late. The building was empty and silent.

It was as if he had imagined ever being there the night before and a search of the trees nearby showed all traces of the horses having been picketed there were gone. But that was unsurprising, there would have been patrols through in advance of the retreating troops. Lord would have needed to move them all well before dawn.

Going back to the hovel he opened the door and crossing the small room in three swift strides, dropped on one knee beside the hearth, fingers probing around one of the flagstones.

He lifted it and peered beneath, half-expecting a small fold of paper to be secreted there. But there was nothing. Just the hard-packed dry earth. There was no message and nothing he could see where the flagstone had sat which might offer any indication of one ever having been there.

Heart sinking and wondering if after all they had been captured, he was about to put the stone back

THE DEVIL'S COMMAND

when he saw a small design on the underside of the stone itself. It was a bit blurred from where the flagstone had been set on the ground, being drawn in charcoal. He moved the stone a little to get more light on it. They looked like a sort of extended letter M written twice over. Gideon stared at the symbols for a few moments in confusion.

Then suddenly he knew.

It was an astrological symbol. Virgo. Drawn twice.

The Two Virgins. The name of the inn where Lord had sent the stableboy.

But Kenilworth was five miles away.

With one hand he wiped over the charcoal marks until they were no more than a smudge on the flagstone. Then, putting the stone back he decided he would have to return to the castle first. He would see Kate and then take word to Lord.

Chapter Ten

I

It was not hard, armed with the warrant from Essex, to discover the whereabouts of Kate and gain access to her. She had been placed in a room in one of the towers, secure but no dungeon, as befitted her status.

The gaoler who took Gideon up spoke of being Lord Brooke's man and had much to say about the flooding of the tower basements with prisoners of war from the Kineton fight.

"Making more work than I have the time for and still expecting me to climb these stairs when someone wants to talk to one of the better sort."

Gideon made a sympathetic response, but his mind was elsewhere as the door was unlocked.

There was a single slender window, shuttered and barred but not so much as to exclude the cold grey light or the sounds of the troops withdrawing into the castle having marched through the mist from Kineton. It was cold and the room had no hearth. Kate had a truckle with a flock mattress and Gideon counted three blankets as well as the warm lined cloak she wore. Her dress was of a faded rose which sucked the fire from her hair and the colour from her face, from the way it fitted he guessed it was not her own.

Of course there had been no chance to warn her.

She had expected something unpleasant because when the door was opened by the gaoler, she wore a wary, weary expression. But perhaps that was a mistaken assumption. Even when Gideon walked in, and she must have recognised him, the look remained. He had feared the gaoler would insist on staying in the room and he would need to make some awkward comment to alert her to his supposed identity, but he turned to ask the man to go, to find he had already stepped back outside.

"Bang on the door when you're ready to leave, sir," he said.

"I will be at least half an hour," Gideon told him. "If the door is locked, I see no reason you need to remain outside."

He added a coin to the incentive which the gaoler took, then looked from Kate to Gideon, his speculative thoughts plain on his face.

"Right you are, sir," he said and left, locking the door.

Once the key had been turned and there were the sounds of footsteps descending the spiral stairs, Kate crossed to Gideon holding out both her hands to take his.

"What are you doing here?" she asked, real concern in her voice.

"I'm here as Ned Blake," he said. "He has been serving Essex these many months. Essex, however, had not met him until I arrived last night. I took his safe conduct and used it to access the castle."

Her face shifted at the news as she absorbed it and the implications.

"Blake has been serving Essex? That means the earl will know all I—" She stepped back, released his hands and managed a thin smile. "Forgive my dress, I was in my male attire when I was taken and they would have left me in nothing but a shift, however Lady Brooke stepped in and insisted in the name of decency that I had this of hers. She was also kind enough to let me have a cloak and extra blankets. I am sure I have suffered much less than the men they have brought here from the battle." She gave a small sigh. "I have had no news of how that went. Here there is talk of victory, but I am wondering why Lord Essex has come north to this place if that is so." The one question she must have most wanted to ask stood silent in her eyes. For all her courage, Gideon could see she was afraid to hear the answer.

"He is safe," Gideon confirmed, and she closed her eyes, shoulders slumped, as if relief itself was too hard to bear. "He came after you and it was all Shiraz, Zahara and I could do to follow him."

That made her eyes open and a smile tugged her lips.

"He is nearby?"

Gideon nodded.

"He left a message for me that he would be at the Two Virgins in Kenilworth... or perhaps he has left word there, since the whole area is thick with Essex's men so he may well need to keep on the move."

"And the battle?"

"I am not sure myself who won the battle, though I believe it was the king."

"Thank God," Kate said, and Gideon had to wonder whether it was for his news of Lord or of the king's victory. "You are here in the castle as Blake, that I accept, but why are you here in this room? Did you ask to see me? Have you some scheme to see me set at liberty?" She drew a breath then as if realising how she must sound. "I ask because, if so, it needs to be soon. I have been told they plan to send me to London for questioning, trial and execution as soon as they can arrange to do so."

"The Earl of Essex himself has given me permission to be here," Gideon told her. "I think for now you are safe enough, as the Earl has charged me with a task that requires you to be here."

"What task?" Kate demanded, stooping on the word like a falcon to her prey.

"The earl wishes me to use you to lure your husband into a trap. He has an order from Parliament to secure Sir Philip and send him to London."

"*Sir* Philip?" Kate's eyes went wide.

Gideon cursed himself for his slip of the tongue.

"Yes. I should have left it to him to tell you though. Your husband distinguished himself with bravery in rescuing the Banner Royal from enemy hands and the king rewarded him with a battlefield knighthood."

He had thought she would be proud and delighted, but the last of the colour washed from her face.

"After he swore to me he would keep himself safe and take no foolish risks. I cannot believe he would have…" She trailed off, then collected herself and shook her head. "I am sure he thought much the same about me taking the risk with the amnesty letters and there he is with a knighthood and here I am a prisoner. Such are the fortunes of war."

"We will remedy that," Gideon promised.

She went over to the window, her fingers on the

shutters. From outside came the sound of the troops arriving from Kineton, so many men and horses that seemed as if they might fill the massive bailey before they were done.

"That vile man who showed you up here would not even open these to let me see out." Then she turned back to Gideon and gave him a brave smile, but the lines engraved at the edges of her eyes spoke to the worry and fatigue she must be feeling. "Why does Parliament want Philip?"

"I have no idea," Gideon admitted. But even as he spoke the words, he realised there was one possibility. Lord himself believed he came from a lineage which would make his mere existence sensitive in the extreme and if someone in the Parliamentary party was aware of that…

Kate cut across his thoughts, her words sharp.

"You know I will have nothing to do with any plan that will place Philip in hazard."

"And neither would I," Gideon assured her. "But in the last he wrote to Essex, Blake spoke of being able to have some influence with Sir Philip."

"Essex thinks you, as Blake, can somehow persuade Philip to walk into an ambush?" She shook her head. "I will admit I think even were there no doubt as to his loyalty Blake is not the kind of man Philip has ever been inclined to give much heed to."

"Essex doesn't know that," Gideon pointed out. "He seems to have a high opinion of Blake and his ability."

"And to think I believed the man to be harmless." Kate spread her hands over the skirt of the dress as if wiping something from them. "Is there any reason your grand design to capture Philip could not be couched in terms that mean we ride out of the castle together this morning?"

"I wish it could be that simple."

"But it is not?"

"I have a free hand to plan," Gideon explained, "but Essex expects me to bring the plan to him when it is conceived for his approval."

Kate studied his face.

"And you have no plan," she surmised.

"I had hoped to get something convincing from Sir Philip," Gideon admitted. "But I came to see you first so I could let you know how things stand and take word of you to him."

Kate smiled. "Oh, I don't think you need to trouble Philip for a stratagem."

For the first time since he had come into the tower room, he noticed a spark in Kate's eyes.

"You have a plan?" he asked.

Kate laughed and there was real delight and humour in it. Gideon was grateful for that. If nothing else, he had brought her hope. But for all her restored confidence, he was not sure that he could offer her anything else.

"I may have. You have the pass from Essex?"

Gideon reached into his doublet and pulled it out. Kate's eyes glittered.

"Then yes, I do have a plan," she said, "but it is better you have no knowledge of it."

Gideon opened his mouth to protest that he was the one who would have to take any plan to Essex for scrutiny, when Kate's expression changed. Staring over his shoulder at the door behind him, her eyes grew round with horror, and she opened her mouth as if to scream.

With no conscious thought, Gideon spun round to follow her gaze, his hand reaching for his sword. The door was still closed, but in that moment of confusion, something hit him, and he was on the ground, his head spinning. Groaning and dazed, thoughts scattered to the winds and his body refusing to obey him, he tried to get up. But the point of his own sword was in front of him with Kate's smiling face behind it.

"I apologise for this necessity, but this must be done so no suspicion will rest on you. When you are set at liberty you can simply leave the castle."

A couple of minutes later he had been stripped to his shirt, gagged with a ball of fabric cut from blanket cloth and with his hands and feet bound with his own stockings. Left face to the wall and covered with a blanket, he could see nothing of what Kate was doing.

"You have legs that are much too long," she complained, sounding unperturbed as if this was something she had done before on more than one occasion. "I will have to hope our gaoler has shorter."

The wait was not long. Over the sounds of troops still milling and being mustered in the courtyard outside, footsteps could be heard coming up the stairs and Gideon found himself wishing Kate had been a bit less quick to render him helpless. The guard had looked to him like a man who could handle himself and he did not think, even armed with his sword, that Kate would be able to overcome him alone.

She shouted through the door even before the man had reached it, sounding plaintive and terrified.

THE DEVIL'S COMMAND

"Please. Help. Please. I think he has fallen sick."

Then the door was unlocked and opened.

"What's happened?" The gaoler sounded harsh and wary.

"I don't know," Kate whimpered, the terror in her voice convincing, "he was asking me questions then he collapsed. I put a blanket over him to keep him warm, but—"

The blanket she spoke of was lifted and then there came a choking gasp and a moment later a heavy weight dropped on Gideon, driving the air from his lungs. At first, he didn't realise what had happened. Then he saw the blood. It had been the gaoler landing on top of him, and the gaoler was now dead.

"One day," Kate said as Gideon felt the body lying on top of him moving a little as she worked the breeches from it, "men will learn that women can be as dangerous as themselves. But until then, I am happy to exploit their ignorance." Her tone chilled Gideon. It had a cut of triumph but an undercurrent of pure glee.

Kate was enjoying this.

A short time later she moved into his view, clad in his doublet and coat and the gaoler's breeches, stockings and shoes, her face darkened with dirt to give a fleeting impression of a shaved chin, the scar that ran from eye to ear vivid on her now masculine-looking face.

"I apologise, Gideon, but this way you are much safer. Essex can in no way hold you accountable for my escape." Then she smiled at him. "Thank you, and I am sure I will see you again soon."

Then she was gone, and the key turned in the lock.

Gideon wondered if she would indeed be able to slip from the castle and the city with Essex's safe conduct. In the current chaos, he thought she had a good chance.

Meanwhile Gideon was left to bear the consequences, but beneath that anxiety and the horror of being trapped under a dead body, was a chilling admiration.

If ever two people had been made for each other in this life it was Lady Catherine and Sir Philip Lord.

II

Having made the decision to seek shelter, Nick pushed the pace northwards as much as he dared. In normal weather, they might have expected to make it back to Newcastle by dinnertime, but by the time they reached the next wayside inn, a place called The Dun Cow, it was late in the morning and the icy rain had turned to a persistent sleet and hail. Getting out of the weather and into the dry warmth of the inn had become the highest priority.

While Bristow saw to the men, Nick demanded a private room to dine.

"I would be happy to oblige you, sir," the innkeeper told him. "But both the rooms are taken even though it is so early, the weather being what it is and the roads right clarty."

Nick reached into his purse and found a crown.

"Would this be enough to recompense the travellers?"

The innkeeper shook his head.

THE DEVIL'S COMMAND

"It is a party of Hostmen back from arguing with the mine owners of Durham and it'll take more than a crown to persuade them out."

Which was when Daniel Bristow reappeared.

"There is a problem, Sir Nicholas?"

"It seems both the private dining rooms here are taken. Our host here thinks his guests won't move."

"They are Hostmen," the innkeeper repeated as if that placed them beyond any ordinary mortal, which, Nick reflected, to such a man as this it did. Their wealth was legendary as was their brutal grip on the coal trade from Newcastle to London.

"Then I'm sure they must be reasonable men," Daniel said, putting a hand on the innkeeper's shoulder whose expression contradicted that sentiment. "If you will excuse me, sir?" He gave a smart bow to Nick and vanished in the direction the innkeeper indicated.

Whether they dined in private or in common, they would still need to eat and drink. Nick arranged for that and as he finished Daniel Bristow returned to say that the smaller of the two rooms was now available.

"I persuaded the merchants out of the kindness of their hearts to let us have the room," he told the worried looking innkeeper with a smile.

"What did you really do?" Nick asked as they placed their coats to dry and took seats at the table beside a warming coal fire.

Daniel gave a small shrug as if disowning his own actions.

"Coal is more boring even than cloth," he said, reaching for the jug of ale left on the table by the previous occupants. "So those men have no imagination. Everything to them is shaped in black slippery stone. I told them that the men in the room next door seemed to be celebrating and then led them to believe it was something to do with them making some deal with the coal men of Durham." He finished pouring himself an ale and set the pewter down again with care. "Well, they were not so keen on that so felt obliged to insert themselves in their colleagues' pockets to find out the truth." He finished the account with a grin which was so infectious Nick found himself returning it and then laughing at the thought of the merchants scurrying out for fear of missing out on a beneficial trade.

"I will admit," Nick said, "from the speed of things I assumed you might have used your sword."

"My sword is always a last resort, not a first, sir. That is perhaps the hardest lesson to learn for most. If I draw my sword, unless I am standing on a battlefield, it means I have failed."

Nick frowned.

"That is an odd notion from a man deemed a master with a blade. How could you teach such a philosophy? It is like telling a man that to be capable with a sword is to admit the need to embrace failure."

Daniel inclined his head, drank down the ale, wiped his mouth and burped loudly.

"I think you put it well, sir. We all need to learn to embrace our own failure and learning to use a sword is one way to do so."

It was difficult to tell if he was jesting or serious and Nick was still wondering when the door burst open. The room would have been filled with half a dozen

THE DEVIL'S COMMAND

angry Hostmen, but before more than one had stepped through the doorway, Daniel was on his feet facing them, standing with his sword in one hand. It was impossible not to admire the lethal speed and grace with which he did so. Nick stood and had his sword out moments later.

"Can I help you, good gentlemen?" Daniel asked and offered them a pleasant smile.

It seemed clear he could not because to Nick's relief they made no further progress into the room and withdrew with murmurs of outrage.

Daniel closed the door behind them, slid his sword home and resumed his seat.

"And that proves my point. If I had succeeded in persuading those gentlemen, they would not have come back. I was forced to draw my sword because I had failed."

"That seems a strange way to view things," Nick said, sitting down again. "Whether it means embracing my failures or not, would you teach me?" He paused and made a decision. "Would you teach me, Daniel?"

The other man took off his hat and got up to set it with his coat to dry by the fire. He moved to sit down then changed his mind and added his doublet to the drying clothes before sitting again now in his shirtsleeves. Nick got the impression he was trying to avoid giving an answer.

"I would pay for the lessons," Nick added.

Daniel picked up the jug and refilled his cup.

"I don't teach," he said.

"Why not?"

Daniel kept pouring until the cup was full. "I don't teach, Sir Nicholas."

"But you are both trained to do so and qualified as a—"

Daniel put the jug down with a crash loud enough that Nick jumped.

"I don't teach," he said a third time. Then as if a dark cloud was lifted, he smiled. "Unless you would learn the mathematics of Pythagoras or Euclid? That I would teach and make no extra charge for doing so. Besides this is the future," he pulled a short-barrelled pistol from where it was thrust into its baldric and set it on the table. "A man with less than an hour of training to use one of these can defeat the best swordsman in the world."

It was perhaps as well that their meal arrived then. There was a decent lamb hotchpot with bread and some fresh apples. The tension that had been between them seemed to ease as they ate, the conversation light and humorous and by the time the remains were being cleared away, Daniel seemed restored to his usual self. Nick accepted the offer of some mulled wine and bought a pipe and a twist of tobacco. It was almost like sitting with a friend.

Except of course he wasn't.

"What is this idea you have to work around what we have been instructed to do?" Nick asked as the pipe smoke began to fill the room like a heavy incense.

"Oh that," Daniel sounded as if he had forgotten about the matter. He leaned forward, dropping his voice conspiratorially. "I say we kill Mags and take control of his company. Then we will hold something of real value for you to use to bargain with those men."

THE DEVIL'S COMMAND

Chapter Eleven

I

Gideon lay in ever increasing discomfort and wondered if he should try to summon assistance. Not that he was even sure he could do so. Bound and gagged with the dead weight of a heavy man across him, it would not be easy. Besides he had no wish to raise the hue and cry after Kate any sooner than necessary. Resigning himself, he decided to wait it out and give Kate the best chance to make her escape.

It seemed a cramped eternity, though it was probably less than an hour before he heard footsteps on the stairs and a key in the lock. He lay still then, giving a muffled groan from behind the gag when the body of the gaoler was lifted off him and blinked up at the faces looking down at him.

Freed, he gave his account to the men who rescued him, was leant a shirt and coat, and had his head tended by the Earl's personal physician. By then it was mid-afternoon, and he was sure that Kate must have made it to safety. All that remained was to leave Warwick himself at the earliest opportunity.

He contemplated trying to do so without a pass but realised from watching those who were going in and out of the gatehouse that there was no prospect he would be permitted to do so. Chafing at the delay, he was informed that the earl wished to speak with him.

The earl was in the same room as he had been

THE DEVIL'S COMMAND

before. Gideon removed his hat, his head beneath covered by a cloth coif, tied in place by the physician to keep a compress over the wound. There were two men writing at a table in the corner of the room who didn't even look up as Gideon was shown in. Essex himself was standing by the window. Before, Gideon had seen it by night, as a dark mirror reflecting the room. Now, in daylight, it gave a view of the river and the countryside beyond. The earl turned his back on it and acknowledged Gideon's polite bow.

"I am glad to see you are on your feet. My physician tells me you should be resting, but then he tells me that too." He shook his head as if that was clearly ridiculous. "What happened?"

There was something in his expression that warned Gideon he was not the first to render an account of the events.

"I went to speak with Lady Catherine and attempted to convince her that I was on her side so that she might trust me enough to join my plan to ensnare her husband. However, I made the mistake of showing her the pass you had given me. I was distracted and she hit me from behind. The next clear memory I have is of when I was rescued."

"You were fortunate," Essex said, his tone grim, "Garvey was murdered, but she took the time to subdue and secure you. There are those who have suggested that you were spared for being her partisan. I think it more likely from what you say that it was because you left her in some doubt as to your true allegiance." He paused and fixed Gideon with a hard look. "I hear you went out this morning."

Gideon nodded. That was something he had expected at least and had an answer prepared.

"Yes, I did. I went out first thing, with some thought to send a messenger from the inn to Prince Rupert to explain my absence. Then I realised with the amount of cavalry on the road it would be unlikely anyone could get through. But I should return as soon as I may, sir, or I will be missed and find it difficult to explain my absence."

"No," Essex said, a weight of finality in the word that made Gideon's heart stand still in his chest. Then the earl sighed and shook his head. "You can never go back now. It shames me to admit it but, I have learned that some of my documents were amongst things that were left behind in Kineton. There will be evidence in them of your true loyalty. If you return to the prince now it will be to face a traitor's death. You have served me too well for me ever to countenance such a fate. When Haws returns he will have an idea of what you might next do best. Until then you—"

He broke off as the door was flung open and the long-haired man Gideon had seen with the earl at their first encounter strode in.

"Thanks be to God, we have the bitch!"

II

Kill Mags.

The audacity and simplicity of Daniel's idea left Nick without words for the rest of the meal. It stayed rooted in his thoughts when they were back on the road, braving the persistent sleet that blew in the face like snow but drenched through clothing like a

THE DEVIL'S COMMAND

downpour.

It was, he assumed, the way of such men as Bristow to see a problem in bald, existential terms. A man stands in the way of what you wish to achieve? Then kill him. It was a compelling, attractive philosophy and one which Nick much preferred to the view that drawing one's sword was tantamount to an admission of failure. Indeed it seemed to contradict it.

Once back in Newcastle, he ignored the attempts by Cummings to get his attention and told the man to talk to Bristow about any problems that needed sorting. Instead, he went to his room and after changing out of the wet travel-stained clothes, took out the document he had been given by Gold and Portly—or Gabriel and Michael, or whatever their true names might be. It was addressed to *Francis Child, Graf von Elsterkralle*n and sealed with the odd symbol which he knew was somehow significant to the Covenant. A circle with a dot at the centre above which a crescent intersected the circle, like horns and below, touching the rim of the circle, an equal armed cross which sat on what looked like a flattened letter M.

He turned the sealed document over in his hands and held it up to a candle, but there was no way to read the contents without breaking the seal. Nick had heard there were ways to open a seal without leaving a trace of having done so. Indeed, he was sure his uncle Sir Bartholomew had been a master of the art because he recalled seeing documents, seals intact, but open on his writing table. A thought occurred as he was about to put it in his locked chest and he slipped it into his doublet instead, then sent his servant to find Daniel Bristow.

The lad returned to tell him that Lieutenant Bristow had gone out and not said where to or when he would be back. Nick resisted the impulse to snap, instead saying he should make sure Bristow reported to him as soon as he returned.

That request came back to haunt him when an hour before midnight, he was brought from sleep by an abrupt double-rap on the door. Tempted as he was to call out that it could wait for the morning, Nick pulled himself up and threw on a night mantle to open the door, his mood sour.

Bristow stood there holding a jug in one hand and two cups in the other.

"I know it is late, but I have some good news, sir," he said, before Nick could begin his snarl. "I brought some fine and expensive peter-see-me to celebrate." He held up the jug of Malaga wine, with the freckle faced smile of a schoolboy caught stealing apples.

Nick stepped back and let him in.

Daniel set the jug and cups on a table then crouched by the hearth and built it up into a blaze, taking off his gloves and rubbing his hands to warm them when he was done. Then poured the wine and served Nick with a cup. It was, as promised, an excellent wine and Nick let himself be mollified by it.

"You said you had good news?"

Daniel nodded as he drank his wine.

"Yes. Yes indeed. A couple of days ago I was asked by the commissar-general if there was any way to apply wine gauging techniques on barrels of powder to assist with an effective inventory. It was interesting, because liquids and powder have a lot in common in the way they lie in a barrel, but I was not sure it would work. It was at best an estimate, and I did warn him I might be as much as one tenth from true. However, he was pleased enough with what I did and wished me to try and teach some of his men. I tried that today, but they seemed to struggle to grasp the idea that 'pi' could be anything other than a coffin of pastry with pigeon inside."

"Where is the good news in that?" Nick demanded.

"The good news is that the commissar-general is looking for a reliable man to command the company guarding his warehouses."

Nick felt his heart sink. "Command? A captaincy?"

"Indeed so, sir."

This might be good news for Daniel, but the last thing Nick wanted was to lose his services and if the commissar-general requested him…

"He wants you," Nick tried to sound as if it was a matter of little importance. "That is understandable. You would be an excellent choice for such a position."

"He does indeed want me," Bristow agreed. "He is thinking to gain from my mathematical skills more than my command ability." Then he put down his cup and reached into his coat to pull out the pouch that held his deck of cards. "The thing is, I am no merchant and he would make me one." He put the cards on the table. "Could I persuade you to a hand or two of piquet, Sir Nicholas?"

Under any other circumstances Nick would have refused. But somehow, he knew this time he had to walk on the ground Daniel Bristow had chosen if he was to have any chance of keeping the man with him.

He lifted his hands in defeat.

"Why not?"

The question was answered a dozen times in the next hour as he lost more than he won. He was tired and on more than one occasion Daniel tapped a card and pointed out where he had been remiss in a declaration or in playing out the hand.

"You need the mind of a mathematician to play this game," Nick protested.

Daniel swept the pile of coins that had accrued during the game towards himself.

"It helps," he agreed and then picked up the jug and looked into it. "So little left." Then he poured the last of it into Nick's cup. "For you, since I appear to have taken the game."

"You always do," Nick observed. "I can't think you find it any challenge or much entertainment."

"It keeps my mind occupied," Daniel said.

"So does reading."

"Reading makes you think. Cards…" He picked up the deck and shuffled back in the ones he had removed which were not required for piquet. "Cards I can play without much thought at all."

Which made little sense to Nick, although he had no care or inclination to unravel it. More pressing was the issue that had occupied him all through the game.

"I am sure if the commissar-general asks, you will be given the promotion. When do you expect it to happen?"

"I don't," Daniel said, his tone blithe as he put the cards back in their pouch.

Nick stared at him in confusion. "I thought you said

THE DEVIL'S COMMAND

it was all arranged?"

"I value my life a little more highly. Your two friends at Newhall—"

"They are not my friends."

"Your two *masters* at Newhall," Daniel corrected. "Indeed, they are *our* two masters and would take it ill if I left you to pursue another career. They were most insistent that I should understand their displeasure came with consequences." He slipped the card pouch back into his doublet. "I persuaded the commissar-general that Cummings would be much the better choice. I said that Cummings is a solid man who will keep his precious provisions safe and one with the accounting skill he needs to balance the books." Daniel smiled then as if he had achieved a great deed and expected praise for it. "As I said, good news. You get to keep me as your lieutenant and Cummings need not feel his over-large nose is being pushed out of joint by my presence. And," he got to his feet as he was still speaking, "that means he will not be there to question your orders when we are required to do anything strange to satisfy those men."

"You are not going to accept the promotion?" Nick's mind was sleep fuddled and his thoughts curdled by the wine. It seemed enough to hold on to that one significant fact at this point.

"No, sir," Daniel assured him. "I told you that I am your man. Thank you for the card games. If you wish, one day I will teach you how to play."

"I know how to play Piquet," Nick protested.

"You know the rules," Daniel agreed. "You don't know how to play the game." Turning, he picked up the empty jug, gathering the cups in his other hand, then made a smart bow. He had one hand on the door to leave when Nick remembered something important.

"A moment, lieutenant, there was something I would ask you."

Daniel turned back, arms burdened, expression quizzical.

Reaching into his doublet, Nick pulled out the letter. "Can you unfasten seals without it being visible that you have done so?

For a moment Daniel stared at the letter as if it were a live snake in Nick's hands, then he walked back to the table and deposited the jug and cups again.

"If you wish me to," he said.

That was when Nick realised that what he was doing was flouting the orders he had been given by Michael and Gabriel. That not only was he flouting them, but he was also asking Daniel to do so as well. And that Bristow had accepted it whilst knowing he was putting his head into a noose at Nick's behest. That last hit home like a hammer blow. For the first time he began to understand and believe what Daniel meant when he said he was Nick's man.

He looked at the letter in his hand. Its seal seemed to mock him.

"It is asking a lot," he said, knowing that sounded weak, "but if we were to know what they wish to say to Mags…"

Daniel stepped forward and lifted the letter from his grip, studying the seal under the candlelight. "I think from the look of this," he said after a few moments, "they expected you to do so. It is set almost with an

THE DEVIL'S COMMAND

invitation stamped in it. That being so, I have to wonder why bother to seal it at all."

He placed the letter on the table, drew the flat bladed eating knife from his belt and held the tip of it in the candle flame, wiping it on his sleeve to remove the soot. Then he slid the blade over the paper and the seal was released from its lower seating so the letter could open. Smiling his satisfaction, Daniel stepped back to allow Nick to be able to get to the table.

"As I said, I think they expected you to open it. If they had wished to make the letter secure, they could have used a simple folding technique to make my job a little bit more difficult than that."

Nick knew that notion had significance, but he had no real idea what it might be. If the Covenant men intended that he would open the letter, then they must have put something in it they wished him to know. So it was with trepidation he unfolded the sheet.

He was met by an unfathomable jumble of letters.

"If they expected me to open it, they did not expect me to read it," he said, turning the page so the other man could see. "It is either meaningless or in some cipher."

Daniel's eyes glittered in the candlelight.

"May I?"

Nick nodded and stepped back, aware now of a shift in the other man from a vague curiosity to sudden, intense excitement. Daniel studied the rows of seemingly random letters for a few moments then smiled.

"If the seal was a test for you, this is a test for me," he said softly, and from his tone it was clear he had been given a challenge he relished. For the first time since Nick had met him, he saw Daniel shed completely the pose of being an amiable man of no more than average wit and become something altogether different. It was as if he had unsheathed the sword of his intellect and, like sunlight on a blade, the sharpness of his intelligence was visible on his face.

"You know the cipher?" Nick asked.

"Not yet. It is, I think more than a simple Caesar shift, maybe a Trithemius…" he trailed off. "Look." He stabbed a finger towards but not touching the page. Nick looked and saw the lines of letters. "See? It has countersigns, that slight drop of the letters here and there?" Nick could see nothing but the expected unevenness of handwriting but held his peace. "It could be some Vigenère variation, I think, but how would they expect me to…" He stepped back and made a brief bow to Nick. "If it pleases you to have this unencrypted, Sir Nicholas, I will need ink, pen, and a quantity of paper." Daniel's eyes were drawn back to the sheet as a most men's might be to the face of a woman who had captured their attention and with close to the same degree of passion. "This will not be quick, I am thinking." Then he grinned. "I like your demanding masters more by the moment."

Feeling as if he had stepped into a puddle and the waters were now closing above his head, Nick opened the door and shouted until his servant, bleary from sleep, appeared. He commanded the writing materials Daniel had wanted and told the lad to find more wine, even if that meant waking the innkeeper.

A short time later he sat watching Daniel creating a complex table of letters.

"What is that for?"

"This is a *tabula recta*," Daniel informed him without explaining, "I am hoping we have a simple letter shift, in which case this will work. If not, we could be here sometime. But I can't help but think they would not have made it too hard for me."

"For you?" Nick was confused.

Daniel looked across the table at him. Hat discarded and tawny hair half covering his face.

"Of course. For me. You think Mags could deal with something like this? If you hadn't asked me to open it, then when he did, he would have needed to give it to me to decipher for him."

"But how would they know you could do such a thing?" Then Nick remembered that Daniel had spoken to the two men alone.

"They took some interest in my mathematical skills," Daniel said, his attention back on the sheet, pen working fast filling in the square of letters. "I had not expected this though. It has a certain style. I like it." he glanced back up at Nick, quill hovering over the page. "This will take me some time. You might wish to get some sleep. I will wake you as soon as I have managed to wrest the meaning from it."

"Very well." Nick gave in to the inevitable. "Be sure that you wake me."

Like himself, Daniel had been up since dawn and endured a hard ride. According to his own account whilst Nick had been sleeping in the evening and the start of the night, Daniel had been working out complex mathematical formulae and trying to teach algebra and geometry. But where Nick's brain was unable to string one thought behind another for want of sleep, Daniel seemed as fresh as if he had just woken.

Before he had even pushed himself to his feet by the table, he knew he had been dismissed from Daniel's thoughts. As he got into bed, he wondered if he had made a wise choice in opening the message or a fatal mistake. But even that worry was not enough to keep him awake. He was asleep as soon as he had settled himself under the covers and woken it seemed scant moments later, with Daniel shaking his shoulder, holding a candle and looking grim.

"I would have let you sleep, Sir Nicholas, but you asked me to be sure to wake you as soon as I had it deciphered. It was indeed a Vigenère cipher, and it took me longer than it should have to work out what they had used as a keyword." He gave a thin smile as Nick pulled himself out of bed again. "I told you it was meant for me. The keyword was 'Bristow'."

That did nothing to make Nick feel any less uneasy. It was as if the Covenant men were playing a game with him. He crossed to the table and grabbed at the cup of wine set there for Daniel.

"What did the message say?"

Daniel pushed a sheet of paper towards him with a scrawled handwriting over it that seemed to have been written in a hurry. Whatever else his ability, Daniel Bristow was no master of the art of writing well. It took Nick a short time to unscramble the hand and insert his own punctuation, so it made sense.

Francis,

THE DEVIL'S COMMAND

I am sure you will recall we met many years ago. I made you a promise that if ever there was any way I could further your suit, I would do so.

That time is now.

The man you will use to transcribe this will be able to tell you how you may contact us. I promise you will not be the poorer for it. We can offer you more than any regular paymaster.

Michael.

If when you receive this, it has not already been opened and read, then you will be performing a great service to us by dealing with the man who brings this to you. He will be no use to us if he lacks even that level of basic initiative.

Nick felt the hairs on the back of his neck prickle as he read, and the last paragraph brought a taste of cold bile into his mouth. He grasped the wine cup and swallowed a gulp to cover the moment, then realised his hand was shaking.

"They are mocking us, playing games with us. They are—"

"Testing us," Daniel said, silencing him. "This is a test. A test of skill and loyalty. We are being pitched against Mags." Then he drew a breath. "It is not what it seems."

"Then what is it?" Nick struggled to see what else it could be. He was being asked to deliver his own death sentence to Mags.

"You were told to hand this over in person?"

Nick nodded. Gabriel had been very insistent on that point. He could use Bristow as a messenger to establish a place to meet, but he was to keep the letter until he could give it to Mags himself.

"The thing is that the postscript was in a completely different cipher. Even if I had shown you my work on the first part in detail you would not have been able to read it."

Nick felt sick as the implications of that sank in.

"That means—"

"That means," Daniel said, "that this man, Michael, is playing a very deep game with us."

Chapter Twelve

I

"Thanks be to God, we have the bitch!"

Gideon felt as if he had been punched in the stomach. He was grateful that the attention of everyone in the room had moved to the new arrival or he would have betrayed himself. He could feel the blood drain away from his face and lowered his head to hide that.

He needn't have worried; his presence was forgotten.

"Lord Brooke, what news?" Essex demanded. "And no matter her crimes, Lady Catherine is still of gentle birth and not to be dishonoured by such words."

Lord Brooke? Robert Greville? That was the man who owned Warwick Castle, Baron Brooke.

"Indeed so, I am at fault. My apologies, my lord," Brooke made a small bow to the earl. "In my defence, she murdered a good man and a loyal servant of myself and Sir Fulke before me."

Essex gave a brief nod acknowledging his apology. "Lady Catherine is taken?"

"Indeed, yes." Lord Brooke pumped one leather-clad fist into the palm of his other hand. "It was a stroke of good fortune. When she tried to leave and offered the safe-conduct you had written for Blake, one of the men who had been on duty earlier was, by pure chance and the grace of God, present. He had seen Blake go out and back that morning and was alert enough to realise the same pass was not being carried by the same person. Their appearance was unalike, and they rode different horses."

"She was apprehended immediately? That was well done."

There was a pause that spoke volumes and Gideon, seeing Lord Brooke's face felt his heart miss a beat.

"Unfortunately, no. She had already been allowed through at that point and a pursuit had to be mounted."

"Out with it, sir," Essex sounded impatient. "You are withholding something of more dire consequence."

"We lost two of the men who went after her. Your men, sir," Brooke admitted. "One she shot as he tried to grab her bridle and the other took an arrow in the neck. That was from a man on a black horse who seemed to have been waiting in cover as if he expected her. He came close to rescuing her too, but one of your men managed to shoot her horse from under her."

Shoot her horse from under her.

Gideon had a sudden and urgent need to vomit, he fought it hard.

"She is dead?"

For an insane moment, Gideon thought he had asked the question himself, but then he realised it had been Essex who had spoken.

"No, not dead," Brooke said, sounding as if that fact disappointed him. "Hurt though. Back in her room

THE DEVIL'S COMMAND

and in the care of a physician. I am very aware that there are those in London who will wish her alive to be questioned about her activities."

The relief was almost as intense as the horror had been and Gideon had to draw a breath to steady himself, aware that at any moment Essex might turn back to him and then he would need to look as if he was pleased with this turn of events.

The earl was frowning. "How bad is her injury? Will she be able to travel?"

Lord Brooke shrugged as if he had no real interest, let alone taken the time to enquire. "You would need to ask the physician once he has seen to her."

Gideon was prepared with his face well-schooled when Essex looked over to him.

"This will make your plans more difficult, I think, Mr Blake."

"Not irredeemably so," Gideon said, though the truth was if Kate was injured, he could think of no way now to free her. His ideas had all been based around her being rescued by Lord on the road. "Lady Catherine may still think of me as her friend." He saw the broad moustache flair and quickly went into an addendum. "Of course, your lordship might feel that trying to use such a dangerous and resourceful woman to trap her husband would be unwise now."

It had, after all, been Essex who had suggested he use Kate as bait in a trap for Lord in the first place. Lord Brooke drew in a sharp breath.

"I have to agree with Mr Blake. It would be folly to—"

The effect on Essex was electric.

"Thank you for your thoughts on the matter, but I trust Mr Blake to know his own business better than either of us." He gave Gideon an endorsing nod. "Do what you think fit. We shall have to make sure the lady is kept better guarded."

Gideon gave a swift bow.

"Of course, my lord. I will, however, need another pass if I am not to trouble you at every turn for access or assistance."

Essex nodded again, moustache bristling a little.

"Of course, I will have one drawn up and signed for you right away, but in the meantime, so you may commence your work, perhaps Lord Brooke would be good enough to escort you to see Lady Catherine."

Lord Brooke clearly did not relish such a task. Whether because he thought it beneath his dignity or from the lack of any desire to oblige Essex, Gideon was not sure. But he suspected both might play into the baron's attitude.

To his credit though, Brooke made no attempt to delegate the duty, unpleasant as he might find it. He strode from the house with Gideon in his wake and one of his men behind them both. They went up to the same tower room as before. Lord Brooke spoke to the man now standing outside the door on the narrow stone landing. He wore the muted purple coat that Lord Brooke had purchased for his regiment. Gideon had a moment to be grateful that he wasn't one of Essex's men, who had lost two of their own to Kate and Shiraz and would likely be more inclined to make life even harder for Kate as their prisoner.

"This man is to be allowed in to see Lady Catherine. The earl requires it."

THE DEVIL'S COMMAND

Then, without even a nod to Gideon, Brooke turned and pushed past him, taking the spiral stairs down two at a time.

Gideon had no idea how badly Kate had been injured and part of him dreaded discovering that she might be mortally so. The one thing he wasn't sure he could ever do was take such news to Philip Lord. Then he realised Lord would already know she was hurt since Shiraz had tried to rescue her.

When the door was held open and he could step inside the tower room, he wasn't surprised to be confronted by the earl's physician, the man who had tended Gideon's head earlier. There was a woman there too, her spreading skirts making it hard to catch more than a glimpse of the prone figure beyond.

"Come back in the morning, sir," the physician insisted, taking Gideon by the arm and turning him back to the door. "I have given her a draft to help her sleep."

He got a glimpse of red hair loose upon a pillow.

"How is she?"

"As well as she might be," the physician said. "We will see in the morning. Now you need to rest, sir, that wound on your head…"

"I would know how the lady is," Gideon insisted. "The earl wants a report and I have permission to question—" Then the woman turned, and Gideon saw the bloody cloths she held. Blood? Her horse had been shot, not Kate herself. Why would there be blood? Then a sudden chill ran through his veins as he knew what had happened. He heard Zahara's voice. *...she might be with child.*

"The questions will have to wait," the physician told him and, unresisting, Gideon let himself be steered from the room and the door closed behind him.

The sickness gripped at his guts, but there was nothing he could do. He couldn't even decide which duty held him more. Should he seek Lord or to stay and do whatever he might to shield Kate? In the end the decision was clear. He had no choice but to stay. He wasn't sure what he might be able to do, but she needed him to try.

This time, despite the privilege of a comfortable bed in a comfortable room, sleep eluded him for much of the night. He had not been able to bring himself to eat, his thoughts homing to the woman drugged into sleep, lying in the tower room and his mind churning with ever more desperate plans to secure her release.

He was woken by a request that he attend the earl as soon as he had risen and presuming that meant his pass had been prepared, he dressed and went quickly. He was admitted to see the earl in the room he seemed to have made his own in the castle.

The first thing Gideon noticed after making the requisite bow, was a sword lying on a table beside the earl. His sword. The sword he had taken from a dead man on the battlefield. The sword Kate had taken from him. It was set beside a new leather baldric.

"I am happy to be able to reunite you with such a fine blade," the earl said, picking it up and admiring it before offering it to Gideon. "It would have been a grievous loss, I am sure. A family heirloom?"

His skin prickled as he took the sword from Essex. Something in the earl's tone of voice... It was as if he were stepping into a landscape filled with snares and any misstep could be fatal. The earl had returned his sword before with no such enquiry. Something had changed.

"I am sure it might have been for some family at one time," he said. "I purchased it from a soldier."

Gideon picked up the leather strap and slipped it over one shoulder before sliding the sword home. His answer seemed to satisfy Essex who nodded and brushed at his broad moustache.

"Someone recognised it," the earl said, "or thought they did until I explained they must be mistaken."

Gideon made a quick bow. "Thank you, sir."

Essex lifted a hand. "Oh, no need. It was an error on their part." He turned and picked up a document, holding it out. "This grants you all the authority you might need."

Taking it with another bow, Gideon read the words and felt his heart move from his chest into his throat and back again.

"Scoutmaster? This is—"

"Well deserved. It occurred to me that now you have been discovered, your use to Haws is less than it was. But you did good work for me, and I would see your future secured."

Gideon stuttered his thanks and wondered what duties a scoutmaster might have or where in the ranking of officers such a role might sit. He had no idea if it was something Blake would have known or if his own lack of military knowledge was placing him at risk of exposure.

"It makes things simpler," Essex said. "It also means I will be able to call upon your expertise in

Haws' absence when consulting with my officers." He gave Gideon a bluff smile from behind his moustache. "It is, after all, my folly that has led to you being in such a place. I neglected to secure the documents that would condemn you. This is the least I can do."

Gideon pulled his scattered wits together enough to acknowledge the honour he was being accorded with a formal bow.

He was dismissed then having been reminded that if he needed to take any action, he was to inform Essex in person first. He left the room in company with a lieutenant who was charged with finding him new accommodation as an officer in Essex's army.

As a result, it was midmorning before he was able to head to Guy's Tower where Kate was being held. But when the door was opened, he found himself uneasy. This was not a situation he had ever been in before with any woman and he, a man of words, found he had no idea what words he could offer—should offer. Words of condolence? Words of concern for Kate herself?

She was lying on the truckle, her hair unrestrained in dark red waves around her shoulders, her skin so pale she seemed much the same colour as the bleached linen of her shift. The scar on her cheek looked like a dark line where it puckered the flesh of her face. She saw him and her face was transformed by a brave smile after the door was closed behind him.

"It is good to see a friendly face," she said, her voice stronger than he had expected it would be. "At least I hope you are still friendly after my high-handed actions yesterday."

THE DEVIL'S COMMAND

It was then Gideon realised that he didn't need to find any words. She didn't know that he knew—had ever known. She didn't know that Lord knew. And she wouldn't, now, want them to have ever known. He had to suppress a guilt-ridden feeling of relief that he was spared that ordeal and focus on what he could do instead to bring Kate some hope.

"Of course we're still friends," he said, crouching beside her as she tried to turn towards him. "No. Please. Lie still. The physician will be furious with me if I let you stir. I have no wish to antagonise him as I'm still under his care myself."

He was close enough now that she could drop her voice to a level little more than a whisper.

"I am so sorry, Gideon, what must you think of me?"

"I think you brave and clever," he told her honestly, his own voice pitched to match hers. "I heard how you were recaptured, and it was through an extreme of bad fortune, not any failing of your own."

Kate studied his face as if looking to see any sign that he was not serious.

"I don't know how they realised I was not Blake. I assume I must have done or said something to give myself away—"

Gideon saw her distress and self-blame and spoke quickly across her.

"It was nothing you did. One of the men who had seen me use the pass earlier, by chance saw you do so too."

She closed her eyes with relief as if she was exonerated from some crime. If so, she had only ever been guilty in her own eyes.

"I might still have made it away. Shiraz would have tried to help me, but I couldn't have his life on my conscience as well, and for all his skill there were too many. I told him to go, and to take Philip my love. I hope he was able to."

"He wasn't killed or captured," Gideon reassured her. "They have no idea who tried to help you."

That seemed to hearten her. It was as if each piece of news Gideon gave lifted another heavy stone from her. There was even a trace of colour creeping back into her face.

"You should go to Philip as soon as you can leave. It is more than enough that I am held, I could not bear if any other paid for my folly."

"It was not folly," Gideon told her. "And I'm not going to leave you here." He pulled out the commission Essex had signed and unfolded it so she could read. "As you can see, I'm safe enough for now and I will find a way to help you."

She shook her head and looked at him with eyes that were veiled over by despair.

"You don't understand. There is no way, now. If I hadn't sworn an oath to Philip I would not still be breathing, but I vowed to him I would live."

The misery in her seemed to come from an unbearably dark place and Gideon could only think it was because she had lost the child. He gripped one of her cold hands in his own.

"I was witness to that oath and shall lend you all my strength as your friend, to see you hold to it. And I promise you I will find a way to bring you from here and reunite you with Sir Philip."

THE DEVIL'S COMMAND

Her smile was weak, and her head sank back into the thin pillow she had been provided.

"You are a good friend, Gideon," she told him. "Will you forgive me if I ask you to let me rest now? I seem to be very tired, but you have brought me much comfort. Thank you."

He left her then, wondering how, or even if he would be able to fulfil his promise.

II

The power and reach of the Covenant were brought home to Nick the morning after Bristow managed to unencrypt the message, when he went to ask for leave. But there was no need. He had already been assigned the task of taking some important messages to a handful of key supporters of the king in Yorkshire. His ability to deliver the message to Mags in person had been assured. Perhaps it was a coincidence, but Nick doubted it.

The last time they spoke, Mags had raised the notion that there might be a way to elevate himself, and Mags, to power without needing the Covenant. At the time, Nick had thought the idea of being freed from Covenant clutches tempting enough to risk at least considering it as an idea. But now he had seen the Covenant were already ahead of him. He was convinced that the best way to secure his future was the one Daniel had suggested. Kill Mags, take his men and use that as a bargaining counter to improve Nick's place within the Covenant itself. If the message he was to deliver to Mags from Michael was indeed a test, Nick intended to pass it with a vengeance.

Despite not having slept all night, Daniel himself seemed wide awake and eager to be off. "I have persuaded the commissar-general to await our return before breaking the glad tidings of great joy to Lieutenant Cummings so the good lieutenant can care for your company in our absence," he explained as they rode out on the same road they had taken the previous afternoon.

Nick nodded approval and decided that the nod might also cover the fact he hadn't even considered who should have command if Cummings had been transferred right away. He was lucky to have a man like Daniel to whom such things were second nature. His own concern was more regarding whether they might struggle to find where Mags and his company had been quartered, but Daniel was quick to reassure him on that too.

"You forget I was sent to serve you whilst I am working for him, Sir Nicholas. He left me a way to get in touch and I took the liberty of sending a message in advance."

Nick glanced at the other man, irritated.

"You sent without asking me? Last night?"

"Oh no," Daniel said. "I paid one of the people at Newhall to take a message for me."

"You—?" Nick almost choked.

"I acted just in case, sir. If we'd not been travelling today, I would have sent another message. But I don't think we can expect the graf to set out to meet us until he is sure we're going to be there and if I'd delayed that would have meant we'd be left waiting for him."

THE DEVIL'S COMMAND

Nick bridled at that. There was a fine line between anticipating orders and issuing them.

"I want you to inform me in future if you are acting on my account," he said stiffly.

Bristow rubbed at his beard.

"I can do that, sir, if you insist. But had I asked you at Newhall if I should send the message, would you have agreed?"

Nick said nothing. The mood he had been in that evening he might well have insisted no message was sent.

"That is a risk I will have to take," he snapped.

"As you wish, sir." Bristow sounded both unconcerned and unrepentant.

It struck Nick that, so far, he had only seen one thing ruffle the calm waters of Daniel Bristow and he found himself wondering if that could do so again. As they took the road south towards Durham he prodded at the topic.

"You refuse to teach me how to use a sword. What if I order you to do so?"

He saw the other man's shoulders stiffen and knew he had impacted.

"That is not something you *can* order me to do, sir, and I would suggest you don't try. It would sour our relationship and we are getting on so well." Which to Nick, sounded close to being a threat. He looked over at the man riding beside him and was about to snap back the kind of response that deserved when something about the set of Bristow's jaw in profile gave him pause. He was no longer so sure that he wished to ruffle that calm. But pride would not let him back away.

"I will not ask then," he said. "Though I would know what happened to make you refuse to teach any?"

Daniel didn't reply, nor did his expression change. They rode on in silence and Nick began to feel he wasn't going to get any acknowledgement of his question.

"It is not my story to tell." Daniel said, at last. "It happened some years ago. My part in it was to teach someone who should never have learned. I learned, though. I learned the cost of teaching."

Nick stared at the man riding beside him, unsettled by the bleak bitterness in a voice he had never heard speak in anything less than measured tones. An involuntary shiver passed through his body which he hoped was not visible. He knew then that Daniel had chosen to entrust him with something he held sacred, albeit in a form that was garbled and unclear. He also understood enough about the nature of friendship to realise that were he to seek to trespass further, it would profane that sharing in some way, and drive Bristow from him. He struggled with how to respond. Saying nothing didn't seem a good option.

Daniel turned then and met his gaze. And Nick knew what to say.

"I think you do still teach," he said. "But not the sword."

It might not have been the best answer, but it was good enough to earn a warming of the gaze upon him.

"Perhaps so," Daniel said, the humour filtering back into his face., "If so you should be careful, Sir Nicholas, because my lessons never come cheaply."

THE DEVIL'S COMMAND

"I think if you would teach me to play piquet it would cost me a small fortune before I learned anything like enough skill."

Daniel smiled and tilted his hat so he could look up at the sky.

"I think we could say the same about anything I have to teach that you might learn, but piquet will do to begin. So, tell me, what are the main advantages of being the elder hand?"

The discussion filled the time until they stopped for dinner, and when they did so, Daniel took out his cards and demonstrated a couple of the points he had made as they rode. It was only when they were setting out again and the afternoon was looking inclined to snow, that the topic turned to Mags.

"What will he be expecting from us?" Nick asked.

"I think he'll expect to discuss the offer he made you. You have considered how to answer him?"

Nick shook his head.

"Does it matter? Does he need an answer? I thought you had already said how we will deal with this."

Daniel sucked in a breath and then glanced back at the men behind them, the nearest of which, Nick realised now, might indeed catch something of their conversation."

"You have changed your mind?"

"Not at all, sir, but it's not so simple a matter as you seem to consider it to be. We must choose our moment, and this might not be it. You have to remember there are two parts to our plan. We have to fulfil the first in a way that will ensure the second."

"So we prevaricate until the time is right?"

"We do what we must for as long as we must. Which means," Daniel observed, "you need to decide what you will say to the graf."

Nick thought about that for a time as they rode on in the worsening weather under darkening skies. He was so distracted in his thoughts that the first he knew of any danger was Daniel beside him drawing his pistol and lifting his hand and his voice.

"Have a care, gentlemen, we have company."

Ahead of them, approaching at a brisk pace and perhaps a quarter of a mile away, was a body of horsemen half as many in size as their own.

"Who are they?" Nick asked.

"If I had a decent perspective glass, I could tell you for sure, but friend or foe it won't hurt to give them a warning welcome—with your permission, of course, sir."

Nick nodded assent, his attention on the oncoming horsemen. He didn't understand the order Daniel gave, the words were strange, brief, sharp, and in a language he had never heard before. But the two files of their escort moved to create tight wings, like the flights of an arrow, on either side of himself and Daniel, each a horse width apart and half a length back from the man in front. Each man had a long-barrelled pistol in his hands and one or two were quickly checking their primer.

They had slowed to a walk but at another command picked up speed again to a brisk and confident trot.

The effect of this manoeuvre on the horsemen approaching them was dramatic. They shifted their direction and took off into the open land that ran alongside the road, deciding to give Nick and his escort a wide berth.

Daniel halted the men and turned his head to watch the others go, tilting the brim of his hat up with the muzzle of his pistol. When it was obvious the horsemen had no intention of approaching them and were well on their way, he grinned at Nick.

"Whoever they were, I think they were not keen to meet us." Then he pushed his horse forward. "As you were, gentlemen and well done. You see, Sir Nicholas," he said, dropping his voice again, "good preparation means one can avoid ever drawing a sword."

"We drew pistols," Nick pointed out.

"We did." Daniel frowned at his as if it had appeared in his hand, then slid it away in the holster on his saddle. "But firearms are very different things to swords."

Nick decided not to argue that point, but to his mind the distinction was a very fine one indeed.

"What language did you use to command there?"

"It was not a language. It was a word made from three invented parts, each referring to a specific action."

Frowning, Nick tried to make sense of that.

"It is a command only your own men would know?"

Daniel grinned at him. "That exactly, sir. Concise, precise and fast to say and may even be done with hand gestures. In small groups or where you have no trumpet, such can win you a skirmish. But it is a little beyond what you might read in Markham or even Cruso."

It occurred to Nick that whether he wished to or not,

Daniel was most assuredly still teaching, and he found he was not averse to learning in such a manner.

Chapter Thirteen

Having left Kate, Gideon's feet carried him to the stables. He went in dread, but to his relief found that whatever horse Kate had taken and lost in her attempt to escape, his own chestnut mare was safe. He spent a few minutes enjoying the warm familiarity of her presence, welcoming and undemanding. She was a link with the world outside Warwick castle where he was still Gideon Lennox and not Ned Blake.

He was just ensuring she would be well looked after by slipping some extra coins to the head groom when two soldiers wearing the purple coats of Lord Brooke's men blocked his path from the stables.

"Blake?"

"Scoutmaster Blake, yes," Gideon admitted.

"Lord Brooke wishes to speak with you."

A prickle of apprehension ran over Gideon's skin.

"I have business—"

"I'm sure it can wait, sir," the larger of the two men said. "His lordship did say it was a matter of importance."

Left with scant option, Gideon went with them. On the way to the house he remembered why the name of Lord Brooke was familiar to him. There had been something of a furore in London the previous year when he wrote something condemning bishops wielding political power. There had been another book too. A rather strange one about his personal philosophy to do with the union of truth and the soul. Neither book had been one Gideon felt inclined to read, but it warned him that for all Lord Brooke might seem the man of war, he was also a man of strong religious conviction.

Lord Brooke's own rooms were at the north-eastern end of the house and were grander than the rest, which was already remarkably grand. The room had a view over the river and the land beyond through a large arched and mullioned window, making the space light and airy. The decor and the furniture were modern, even down to the pedestal writing desk in one corner. There were double doors in the far wall that no doubt opened onto the suite of rooms. The baron would keep his family private from the rest of the world, even as the rest of the castle heaved with troops.

Lord Brooke wore a silk shirt, with his purple doublet slashed to reveal it and his long hair brushed to lie on his shoulders. It struck Gideon that for a man of well announced Calvinistic religious tendencies, he seemed remarkably fashion conscious. Brooke had been standing by the window but turned as Gideon entered and made the necessary bow.

"You wished to speak with me, my lord."

For a moment he saw some hesitation in the baron's assessing gaze. As if he was trying to make up his mind if he had been correct in a previous impression or not.

"Yes," he said, but not before the pause had been heavy in the air. Then he lifted and one hand to the men behind Gideon who had escorted him in. "Wait outside, please." The two gave stiff bows of compliance and left, closing the double door behind them.

Then Gideon had to stand there for a while as Lord Brooke moved to the table and opened a book that was on it, a thick book which Gideon was certain had to be a Bible. The baron took some time to find what he was looking for, turning pages and scanning the text, then he nodded and ran a finger along a line, mouthing the words as he did so. He looked up, still facing away from Gideon and stared out of the window for a while. Then he closed the Bible and turned back.

"That sword which you wear, I would like to purchase it."

Gideon's throat felt dry, and he had to wait for a breath to unlock his own voice.

"It is not for sale, my lord, but I thank you for your offer."

Brooke's eyes darkened.

"How did you come by it? And I seek an honest answer not one made to appease me." He rested his fingers on the book on the table beside him. "One you could place your hand upon this and still say is true."

A frisson of panic shivered through Gideon. He decided to skate as near to the truth as he could without confounding anything he had said before to Essex.

"I had it from a soldier who pulled it from the mud after a battle. I know nothing of where it came from before that."

"And if I were to say to you that I know the man who once wielded that blade?"

"I would offer you my condolences on the loss of a

friend," Gideon said, enduring the cold gaze that held his with the same resilience he brought to bear when a legal opponent sought to browbeat him.

Lord Brooke folded his arms and his gaze hardened to a basilisk glare.

"You mistake what I am saying. The sword you wear must have been stolen from the man who owned it. He still lives. He has not fought in any battle for many years."

"Then it is unlikely to be the same blade," Gideon said. There was something about the assumption and insistence which made Gideon resolved to resist the pressure—that and the fact he wanted to keep the sword.

"It is the very same," Lord Brooke said, unfolding his arms to point at the sword. "I have examined it and seen on it the maker's mark and the styling of the pommel."

"I have seen several such myself, worn by various soldiers in recent times. Perhaps your friend's stolen blade is one of those, my lord."

"What if I were to pay you a fair price for it as your finder's fee?"

Gideon resisted the urge to smile. Most men who were not as hardened as he was to endure the intensity of another's hostility in such a way would have crumbled and handed over the sword, accepting whatever compensation they might be offered. But his years of legal practice immured him to such intimidation.

"I thank you for the offer, sir, but I would keep it."

Brook took a step towards him. Surely the baron didn't intend to try and take the sword from him by force? Perhaps something in Gideon's own expression dissuaded him or perhaps he thought better of it, but Brooke seemed to catch himself and stopped after the one step, his hands closing into impotent fists at his sides.

"This matter is not closed, Blake," he said, his tone cold. Gideon realised he had made an enemy. He wondered if the sword was worth that, but before he could reconsider, a tap on the door brought a message from the earl and he was able to make a dignified escape.

Far from bestowing any extra freedom to act, it appeared his new commission gave him responsibilities which left Gideon confined and frustrated. That afternoon Essex set him the task of collating the myriad reports that had come in from the surrounding area with returning troops, supplemented by the occasional foray by a company of horse or intelligence brought by civilians. Essex, it seemed, wished to return to London and wanted to know if the road to Northampton lay open.

He found a room and a table and set to work. Compiling the reports was a straightforward enough exercise, the problem was Essex would know Blake's handwriting. So Gideon commandeered a clerk on the pretext that his hand had been hurt in the tussle with Lady Catherine.

The reports painted a picture of encounters with Royalist cavalry and gave the impression Prince Rupert in person was everywhere at once. It took Gideon a while to cut through the often extravagant tales to the more prosaic truth beneath. What emerged was that far from seeking to re-engage with Essex or force him out of Warwick, the king had moved to invest Banbury. That was about as far south-east of Kineton as Warwick was to the north-west of it. Gideon was confident he could assure the Earl that marching to Northampton would be as safe as a stroll around the castle bailey.

As tapers were brought to light the candles Gideon realised what he was doing was aiding the same army who he had faced over the battlefield at Kineton fight. It was some comfort to know that his conclusions about the location and intentions of the king's army were not going to be news to the earl for long, but he was left with the same uncomfortable feeling he had known before the battle. Lord had noticed it too. Whose side *was* he on?

He was glad to be given no time to dwell on that, because a summons came from Essex. So, dismissing the clerk and taking the report with its ink scarcely dry, he made his way to the room where he knew the earl would be found.

Had it been a couple of months before he would have thought nothing of the touch of shadow that danced for a moment at the edge of his vision, but now it was enough to make him pull up short in the passageway and even step back, to place himself against a wall. It also meant he had time to draw his sword when the two men came out of the shadows to attack.

They had not expected to find a man armed, in a good defensive position and poised to use the blade he held, because they hesitated.

"Hold! I have a very loud voice," he told them. If

they were indeed Brooke's men, as he suspected, they would want their nefarious work done in silence, the sword taken, and Gideon left dazed. He doubted that Lord Brooke would want the inconvenience of a dead body in his own house.

The men hesitated and glanced at each other. Gideon drew a deep breath, the sword blade keeping them at bay. There might be no one in their immediate vicinity, but there were going to be a dozen or more within hailing distance.

Before the breath was complete, the two must have decided the better part of valour was indeed discretion, because Gideon found himself alone again. He noted the direction they took back through the house towards the stairs that went down to the kitchen. Satisfied that he was safe at least for the present, he put his sword away and headed quickly in the opposite direction towards where Essex would be waiting.

Except Essex was not waiting at all, he was already much engaged in a heated conversation with Lord Brooke and another man who had his back to the door when Gideon was shown in. A man dressed in a military style with a sleeved buff coat overlain by an orange sash declaring his Parliamentarian allegiance, and long grizzled black hair, visible from under his hat.

"...heading towards Coventry not Banbury, what do you make of that?" Brooke was saying.

Then the man Gideon didn't know spoke. "I have no notion what to make of it, sir. I wonder, has anyone asked her?"

Gideon felt as if a thousand spiders had erupted from his skin and were crawling over him beneath his clothing. He knew that voice well. The shock of realisation made him draw an involuntary sharp breath before he could regain his self-control and, in that moment, all three men turned to him.

Essex with his usual steady gaze from above the broad moustache, Lord Brooke with widening eyes, surprised to see him there and Sir Philip Lord, skin darkened, face scarred by pox and hair black, flecked with grey. His expression held nothing at all.

Gideon made a prompt bow and stood, heart hammering as Philip Lord turned back to the conversation, his face now in profile to Gideon.

"Well, did anyone ask?"

"The physician is not allowing anyone near enough to do so. It seems that as well as some severe injury from the fall she has miscarried of a child and is much weakened by it."

Ever after, Gideon would keep the image of Philip Lord's profile in his memory. A man told his unborn child was lost and the woman he loved more than life itself had suffered that alone and in the hands of her enemies. But the profile Gideon saw was carved from stone. In another man, Gideon might have seen that as a sign of utter callousness. In this man he knew it to be the mark of inhuman self-control.

"And that is some reason not to question her?" Lord's voice did not even catch.

"Perhaps Blake here thought to ask her," Essex suggested, gesturing to Gideon, who had his mouth open to reply when the face that was, and yet was not, Philip Lord's, creased more deeply and studied him

THE DEVIL'S COMMAND

from narrowed eyes.

"Blake, you say?"

Gideon gave a bow. "Edward Blake, sir, scoutmaster to the earl."

Lord spun on his boot heel, back to Essex.

"I have no idea who this man might be, my lord, but I can promise you he is not Ned Blake. I've met the man on more than one occasion and this," he jerked a thumb towards Gideon, "is not he."

There was a stunned silence in the room. But no one could have been more stunned than Gideon, his mouth opened and closed a few times of its own accord.

"I—I think you are mistaken, sir," he managed at last. "I am indeed Edward Blake."

But Essex was looking at him as he might at something unpleasant he had trodden in.

"Good God, are you telling me we have been deceived? Are you certain? Who is this man and where is Blake?"

Lord Brooke had drawn his blade, but Lord was faster, stepping sideways and back, bringing his sword to Gideon's chest with the same movement.

"Your sword," he demanded. "Whoever you might be."

There was a moment Gideon doubted. A moment when he wondered if this was some kind of betrayal and not a complex plan in which his denouncement was one act of the whole play. Feeling a line of sweat beading on his brow, he was grateful for the coif covering his head which would disguise it.

Brooke had crossed the space between them in swift

strides and reached to grip Gideon's wrist.

"Allow me," he said. "I shall take this sword. I knew it was stolen."

Without seeming to move at all, Philip Lord was occupying the space where Brooke needed to be so he could pull the sword from Gideon.

"You must forgive me Lord Brooke, *it may be that what hath beene disputed, will be granted: but there is yet an objection which requireth solution.*" For some unaccountable reason, Brooke stepped back as if stung, his mouth opening in surprise and anger.

"You throw my own words in my face?" He sounded as if he considered that to be a terrible offence.

"On the contrary, my lord, I am attempting to show that we are of the same nature, bound by the same *covenant* before God." He moved his hand so the pommel of his own sword lay visible to Brooke against the cuff of his heavy leather glove. "This man is *my* prisoner, whoever he might be. I will take him back to London with the woman."

Brooke's face underwent a dramatic series of colour changes, from the heightened redness of ire, it drained to pale marble and then, slowly, restored to a normal hue, before he nodded.

"Is that Geneva talk?" Essex demanded, brows lowered.

"I apologise if it offends, sir," Lord said, his gaze settled on Gideon as if on a dangerous serpent. Lifting the tip of his sword a little, he indicated Gideon should remove the baldric.

"No more than always," Essex said heavily and got a cold look from Lord Brooke who had stepped back and now stood with his arms folded.

Gideon held out the baldric with the sword attached and Lord shrugged it effortlessly across his own body.

"You will forgive me, my lord, my men are waiting. We need to be on the way."

"But how can you get past Rupert's damned cavalry? It is too dangerous. I cannot permit it."

"Then lend me a company of horse, if it makes you feel more secure, but I must leave tonight. I promise you, sir, the longer we wait the more dangerous it will become. At the moment the king is intent on taking Banbury and the worst we can expect to meet are strong patrols. I have subterfuge enough to take us through those, as I did coming here."

"The woman is injured. She cannot ride," Essex said.

That was when Lord could not, for one brief moment, hide his true feelings and Gideon, who noticed where hopefully the others did not, saw the pain stark in his eyes before his expression shifted to a heavy frown, as if the earl's news had put a major obstacle in his path.

"As I already said," the earl went on quickly, "you will stay here. Lord Brooke can accommodate you and your men. Both prisoners will be secure until the road is safer, the lady recovered, and he can provide you with adequate escort. Or you could march with me, I plan to leave for Northampton as soon as the army is regrouped, tomorrow or the day after."

"Either of which would be most agreeable," Lord said, his control restored, his voice back with a hard edge. "Unfortunately, I have urgent duties to undertake of which this is but one. I need to travel tonight and would be grateful if you could find me a carriage of some description, or a covered cart. Failing that, the lady will have to manage on horseback."

"If you wish her to reach London alive, that would be unwise," Essex said. It was clear to Gideon that even though the earl was Lord-General of Parliament's army, whoever he thought the man he was speaking with might be, he didn't feel he had authority to issue him with direct orders.

"I think you can leave it to me to ensure that, sir," Lord said. "I can promise you I will do all in my power to ensure that she arrives safely at her destination. I will take full responsibility on that count and, if you require it, I am happy to sign a receipt to that effect, exonerating you of any culpability."

"*Culpability*? Culpability be damned," Essex snapped. "I am more concerned about the welfare of the woman."

"Which is commendable," Lord agreed. "But perhaps going a little beyond what might be expected when we are talking of a dangerous intelligencer who has killed at least two men."

Gideon had been standing still through all this, aware of the end of Lord's sword still poised close to his chest. He didn't think he was in any grave danger, but the way this was all playing out he was also sure Lord would not hesitate to use the sword to inflict some damage if he decided to move. Lord would have no choice.

As if reading his thoughts, Lord glanced at him and flicked the sword tip towards the wall.

THE DEVIL'S COMMAND

"You. Over there and sit on the floor."

Gideon obeyed and Lord took a step back so he could keep Gideon in view as well as face the two other men in the room.

"Can I send for my men to remove him, my lord? I wish to be sure he is secured."

"But who is he?" Lord Brooke asked, before Essex could respond.

"Does it matter?" Lord was dismissive. "He is not an issue anymore. I assure you we will find out that and all else he might have to tell us of interest when we have him in London."

"I have facilities here," Lord Brooke said thoughtfully.

Gideon felt his blood run cold.

"I am sure you do, sir, but I promise you that you will not have the expertise of the men we have in London."

Brooke looked as if he might appeal to Essex, but the earl lifted a hand.

"The sooner these people are gone from us the better. I find myself disgusted that I was so deceived by this creature calling himself Blake. Do we even know where the man whose name he has taken might be?"

"I regret, sir," Lord said, sounding sincere, "that if it is as you told me before, he will have been arrested and facing trial. I do not think there is any doubt what the outcome of that will be."

At least, Gideon thought, that would mean Zahara need not feel betrayed.

Essex was shaking his head, his moustache

drooping.

"Such a brave man. And in return we have this vile deceiving knave." He strode over to Gideon and glared down at him. "Have you no shame for what you have done?"

Gideon wanted to point out that he had done nothing that Blake himself had not. In fact, he had done less. But he could feel Lord's silent admonishment in the steel gaze bent upon him. Instead, he looked down and was therefore not prepared when the blow came, and it knocked him back against the wall.

Lord grabbed his collar with his free hand.

"Answer the earl, scum."

Gideon gulped air with no idea what he was supposed to say.

"I am sorry for deceiving you, my lord."

Which seemed to be enough because the earl curled a lip and turned away and Lord pushed Gideon back against the wall.

"May I summon my men now, sir? The longer we are here the greater the risk."

Essex nodded a few times, his thoughts elsewhere. Brooke was still staring at Gideon, who hoped that Lord wasn't going to leave him alone with the two of them. Gideon had a strong feeling that Brooke wanted to try and get a rapid answer to his questions.

Lord sheathed his sword and crossed to the door in a few swift strides to speak to one of the men guarding it, before closing the door again and turning back to the others in the room.

"Do you have some form of wheeled transport, Lord Brooke?"

"My own carriage. But that is hardly—"

THE DEVIL'S COMMAND

"Thank you, sir. That will do well. I will leave you a note of sequestration so you can reclaim the vehicle or its value in due course. Will you send to have it prepared or shall I ask for it to be done?"

Brooke's colour heightened and he looked like a man close to rupture.

"You go too far, sir," he snarled. "I'm not going to give you my carriage."

"On the contrary," Lord told him, "It is you who go too far. You are being asked to oblige Parliament and are refusing such a small thing."

Brooke's hand closed over his sword hilt.

"If you were not who you are—"

"If I were not who I am I would not be asking this of you," Lord said.

Essex lifted a hand. "Let the man take it, Robert. I am sure you will get it back in time."

"It was new last year," Brooke protested. "I had it imported, it is steel-sprung and worth—"

"Less than the value of the information it will carry to London," Lord observed. "Which I am sure you will be able to explain to the Committee when you are summoned to account."

The baron released his sword and gave an exasperated sigh.

"Very well. I will arrange it."

The atmosphere seemed a little less fraught once Brooke had gone and Gideon found himself ignored.

"May I speak to the physician who has been attending your prisoner? It may be there is some treatment he would suggest or some medicament he would wish to send with her."

Gideon didn't get to witness that conversation as the men sent as his escort arrived. He knew them both, of course. One was Bjorn Olsen, the brawny Swede who had spent some time teaching Gideon to use a sword and the other a man Gideon knew as Bela Rigó, who as well as a soldier was a skilled farrier with a passion for the horses he cared for so well. But from their faces, Gideon might have been a complete stranger and Olsen's kick to bring him to his feet was not as gentle as it could have been.

"Find his horse and tie him on it," Lord told them.

Knowing what the men he was being approached by were capable of, Gideon decided it was wisest not to resist even for show. He was manhandled expertly from the room and then walked in close escort through the house. There was something of comfort in seeing Jupp's face with the company of cavalry that waited there, even if his expression was as cold and closed as Lord's had been. Gideon realised then that these were men who had worked this kind of subterfuge before and knew the price of dropping their guard even for a moment. Keeping that in mind, he was careful to school his own features into the sort of frightened, petulant look he had seen on the faces of criminals caught red-handed. It was remarkable how easy he found that.

The scene was lit by the lights from the house, the moon a couple of days past full blundering in and out of the clouds and a couple of servants holding lanterns. Even so, most of the men and horses were still but shadows in darker shadow. It was hard to work out how many men Jupp had with him. Someone managed to locate Gideon's chestnut mare and once mounted his hands were lashed to the saddle. That meant he then had a better view of the small but smart carriage, which was brought out, paintwork gleaming with the Brooke escutcheon clear on the side, in gold and black.

Gideon could see why the baron had been upset to part with it. The body of the carriage was slung on strong leather and that was secured to arches of sprung metal. Akin to some of the best vehicles he had seen in London, it would be worth a small fortune. It was also distinctive. He had to wonder how Lord expected Essex to believe any subterfuge could explain its presence.

Then all speculation ceased as he saw four men carrying a straw pallet across from Guy's Tower. On it, swathed in a blanket, lay Kate, who must have had a painful journey down from her tower room and now lay unmoving. One of her hands fell limp from the blanket and it was Jupp who crossed to her and lifted it back to her side.

Gideon couldn't see Kate being placed in the carriage because the door was on the far side to where he sat his horse, but he did see Jupp's taut and troubled expression as he rejoined the men, which was not at all reassuring.

It seemed an age later, though was less than half-an-hour, when Lord came down the steps from the main house at a run, Essex following more sedately. Brooke remained at the top of the steps by his own front door, arms crossed and looking disgruntled. Lord made a gracious bow to Essex and brief one in the direction of Brooke before mounting a horse

Gideon was sure had to be the black one Shiraz always rode. Issuing a series of curt orders, Lord marshalled his company, with Gideon and the carriage in their midst. Then, with a clatter of hooves on cobbles, they set out at a brisk pace through the gatehouse and the outer precincts of the castle, on through Warwick itself, to take the Stratford Road.

Chapter Fourteen

I

They had passed the last of the houses that crouched about the edges of Warwick when they made a brief pause. Jupp, having cut Gideon's bonds, hustled him into the carriage saying it was on Lord's orders. There was little space inside as the entire pallet had been put in and was wedged in place so Kate would not fall off it.

"Here," someone, in the dark he had no idea who, thrust a bundle of leather straps at him through the open door, which he realised was his baldric and sword. Gideon assumed Lord wanted someone with Kate both to care for her needs and to defend her if it came to that.

"Thank you." The politeness was automatic, but the man had already gone. As Gideon shrugged the leather over his body, the door closed and then they were on the move again.

He had feared Kate would be jarred and thrown about, like the Hackney carriages in London, but this coach swung on its sprung straps in a way that mitigated the worst of the bone-shaking.

"Gideon?"

Kate's voice sounded stronger than he had expected, and he wondered if she had perhaps been feigning unconsciousness before.

"Yes, it is. Although I'm not sure I can be of much help, if there is anything you need, let me know."

It was cold in the carriage, even with the windows shut, and for a time Gideon shivered in silence and braced himself as they hurtled along. Then there were sudden shouts outside and the speed they were travelling at decreased to little more than a trot. Gideon resisted the urge to look out, knowing he would see little and knowing that if there was danger, Lord and the company would be dealing with it in the best way possible.

"There is one thing you could do," Kate said, "Roger Jupp pushed a pistol under the pallet when he secured me in here. I can't reach it. Do you think you can free it for me? I think from the sound of things it might be needed."

She sounded calm and her voice, if not ringing with its usual energy, was firm and confident. Gideon reached around under the pallet with care and pulled free the pistol he found there. Jupp had provided a pouch which his fingers told him contained more cartouches and a small powder horn too. He placed the pistol in Kate's hands and felt, rather than saw them close about it.

"If we stop, you should leave the carriage right away. I can defend myself with this pistol at need. You will be of more help outside."

As if she had anticipated the future, there was a sudden lurch and then the shouting got louder as the carriage came to a halt. Shots were going off and then there was a hard banging on the carriage door a moment before it opened. Gideon had a brief impression of fighting in the dark, plunging horses

THE DEVIL'S COMMAND

and running men. It took him some scrabbling to get past the pallet and through the door, feeling exposed as he did so. Once outside, there was utter chaos in the dark. The moon was hidden behind thin cloud, so shadows rose and plunged.

"Give fire!"

The shout came from behind and was all the warning Gideon had to flatten himself on the ground. Someone less lucky rolled beside him and lay still. Then there came a yell from further along the road, and a tight mass of cavalry was bearing down so fast that Gideon had to roll under the coach to get out of their way.

The whimsical, betraying moon chose that moment to slip silent from the shroud of concealing cloud and illuminate the scene as the compact cavalry punched through the musketeers, perhaps twenty of them who were set in a line reloading as fast as they could.

Gideon pulled himself out from under the carriage and found himself confronted by two men wielding their muskets like clubs. One went down faster than he could even think, the sword in his hand moving as if of its own accord. The second forced him to dodge back and the heavy wooden musket butt, edged with iron, smashed into the side of the carriage. But then the man staggered and fell, attacked from behind and Gideon found himself face to face with Bela Rigó, who had been driving the coach. Rigó saluted him with his sword then stepped back speaking soothingly to the horses.

Feeling his back secured by the farrier mercenary, Gideon looked around but those who had tried to outflank the carriage were now being hacked down by the tight knot of cavalry and their comrades, who had been reloading when the moon revealed their vulnerability, had broken and fled rather than face the same.

The moon caught Philip Lord's face in profile. The gleam of his blade looked dark from the blood upon it as he cut into the man before him. Gideon saw the figure beyond him lift a pistol. With Lord, haloed so by the moon and close enough that the man could have touched his horse, there was no way he could miss.

Gideon started forward, shouting a useless warning and then, above the chaos of swords and blood, hooves and shouting, there came two sharp shots, a yell of outrage and a brief volley from the road.

This time Gideon began to run after the horses as they chased down the men with muskets, scrabbling to get back to their own mounts, for these, he realised had not been infantry, but dragoons, set in ambush. He couldn't tell if Lord was hurt but could see with relief he was still on his horse, still cutting with his lethal blade, until the moon once again took sight away.

By that time, Gideon realised he should not try and join the fight, as to them, a man on foot was an enemy and that his place was to protect the carriage and Kate within. And that was when he realised he had made a mistake to move so far from it. Something white fluttered through the open window of the carriage like a wounded dove striving for flight. He ran back and found Kate, clad in a white shift, half hanging through the window. She had somehow heaved herself up to it but lacked the physical strength to recover her place. The pistol he had found for her lay on the ground as if it had been too heavy for her to keep hold of.

The sounds of fighting seemed removed to another world. Kate's hair, dark as old blood, lay over her arms, the breeze plucking at her shift creating the fluttering illusion of movement.

His heart in his mouth, Gideon ran the last few paces and called her name. When she lifted her head, relief weakened every muscle in his body.

"Is he alright?" Kate's voice had lost the strength he had noted before, the fear and concern naked in it.

"He's still fighting," Gideon told her. It was all the comfort he could offer.

"Then God is kind," Kate said. "Would you be kind, too, and help me back onto the pallet? I need to speak to Philip when he is able. Please tell him so as soon as you may."

Gideon had no doubt at all that would be Lord's first intention once this attack was seen off. He did what was needed to help Kate lie down again, which was hard as it was dark inside the carriage. At one point she drew a sharp breath and at another made a small sound that seemed to try and disguise a moan.

"Thank you," Kate said and her grip on his hand was suddenly urgent. "The fighting is done now. Find Philip for me. Please."

True enough a near silence had replaced the shouts and cries and the soft sound of hooves walking back and then low voices and a brief laugh.

Philip Lord's voice lifted.

"Gentlemen, find our dead and we must move out. We did not kill them all and word will reach Essex faster than wildfire. We all know his horse is appalling, but in sufficient quantity, they could still trample us."

Jupp then took over, issuing swift and specific orders and, before Gideon could cross to him, Lord had left his mount and was striding to the carriage. He placed a hand on Gideon's shoulder in passing, but whether to condone or condemn it was hard to say, because his focus was within, and Gideon might as well have not been there.

"Philip!" The whole weight of love and relief was swept up in the name. "I thought I was too late, too slow, I thought—"

"You saved me," Lord said. "I saw your smile."

"That was what I wanted you to see," she sounded proud, as if in the smile she had achieved a greater feat than shooting the man who had been aiming for him. "Who was it?"

"I am not sure yet, we will find out. But you—"

She lifted a hand and put her fingers on Lord's lips.

"You must remember what you promised me, the oath you made."

He nodded and spoke through her fingers.

"The same you made to me. But—"

"I am not going to be able to keep my oath," Kate said, her hand moving to take his and her voice full of calm and certainty. "You will have to keep it for both of us."

There was a silence then, too terrible to be borne. When Lord spoke, it was as if his voice came from a chasm. Pain filled every syllable.

THE DEVIL'S COMMAND

"You are the guiding beacon by which my heart is steered… *Without that light, what light remains in me? Thou art my life, my way, my light; in thee I live, I move, and by thy beams I see…*"

"Others need you," Kate said, her tone gentle as if speaking to a frightened child. "Danny is all alone doing your work. You cannot abandon him. Zahara relies on you. Shiraz and Gideon both need your protection. You have many others who depend on you and your company has to be led by a man who will not abuse their power. Above all, you have your name to clear and claim. And the prince has need—"

"But I need *you* and the prince can manage his own damn war. It is that which has brought you to this." Lord stood up suddenly, the steel in his voice restored and inflexible against the implacable destructive force of fate. "I am going to get you to safety, and Zahara will restore you to health. Men have died tonight to bring you away alive; they are not going to have done so in vain."

"Philip," Kate sounded between desperation and anger, and Gideon was close to grabbing Lord and making him listen to her., "It is in God's hands, beloved, not yours."

Lord took one of her hands in both his and lifted it to his lips.

"I have played that part before, if I have to again, so be it. I am not going to let you die."

"It's not like you have the choice." Gideon realised he had spoken too late to stop the words. He felt Lord freeze beside him and for a moment feared he would lash out. But instead, Lord reached over and grasped his wrist, putting Kate's cold hand in his.

"Stay with her. Look to her. We are going to ride through hell if that is what it takes." Then, to Kate, "I have not forgotten my oath to you, and I never will. This is me fulfilling it."

He strode off shouting new orders and Gideon picked up the pistol and climbed back into the carriage, a sick feeling in his heart. They were still miles behind enemy lines and those they had beaten off had been sitting in ambush. What if there were more such? What if those they had chased off returned in force? No matter how fast they might wish to go, the carriage would slow them and mark them out.

But his thoughts moved to the woman on the pallet he was squashed in beside and wondering how Lord could be so unfeeling at such a time. Kate must have guessed his thoughts because as they took off again at a pace that was neither comfortable nor safe, she found his hand again briefly.

"That is Philip through and through. He would not be the man I have loved if he sat here awaiting the end with me. I am glad of it. I think it means he will manage without me when the time comes." Her voice lifted its tone and she laughed, the sound finishing in a sharp breath. Gideon had to wonder at her strength of will. "But I am blessed, how many are granted a lawyer to hear their final bequests? I have messages for you to carry for me, if you will."

"Of course, but I am sure you will—"

"God has been known to work miracles, but I have learned never to count on them, so I will tell you and you will listen and remember and if they are never

THE DEVIL'S COMMAND

needed, I am sure I can trust you to forget."

"I will," he promised. "My oath on it." Though in his heart he was sure remembering was what would matter.

"You are a good man, Gideon Lennox, and Zahara is a lucky woman to hold your heart. You must tell her I said so, even if you blush to speak the words. There is no more I would say to her anyway, she knows she has had my true affection and highest regard since the day we met, words now could add nothing to that. Tell Shiraz he must write a book, his wisdom is too fine to be squandered in silence. And tell Danny to forgive himself. Tell him I said he is missing out on too much and life is too short, he has worn a hair shirt too long." Then she gave a low chuckle. "But you might wish to be more than a sword's length from him when you say that. And tell him I trust him above all others to look after Philip. Now Matt is gone there is no one else who can."

She fell silent for a time and the only sounds were the pounding hooves and rattling whistle of the wheels over the uneven ground marking the endless jarring motion as the carriage body swayed and leapt on its sling and springs. Gideon hoped they didn't lose a wheel, the speed was so great.

When Kate spoke again her voice was weaker, wearier, and Gideon had to try harder to catch the words over the noise of travel.

"Life is sometimes so strange in how it treats us. I am sure I should be afraid, but I am not at all. I am merely frustrated to be unable to complete so much of what I started, and to be leaving those who love me."

She drew a ragged breath and went on. "Please present my humblest apologies to the prince that I need to leave his service. Inform him I tried my best at all times. My papers should go to him, apart from the personal letters which are held separately." Then there were other messages to people Gideon did not know, but he filed them all away in different bags and boxes in his mind so none would be forgotten.

"I think I'll need to sleep soon," Kate said at last, sounding very tired. "But there is a message for Philip—in case. Please tell him he has held my heart from the moment we met, and I do not regret one moment of my life with him. Not one. And if he would honour my love, he will keep his oath and he will find happiness. For the rest, he knows me better than I do myself and no words can be needed." She paused then spoke in a different tone. "Now, you have those all in your mind?"

"I do, but only so they may be forgotten when you are well again."

"You can't see," Kate told him, "but that makes me smile. Thank you. It is good to have a friend one can count on at such a time. I have been so very, very blessed in this life." She sighed and after a minute or two Gideon was sure she had indeed fallen asleep, but then her voice came from the dark again, weaker but determined. "And what can I say to you, my new old friend? I am sorry we have not had more time to get to know each other, because you mean more to Philip than perhaps you or he realise. He sees himself in you in many ways, I think, and I do too, though you may find it strange to hear. My words to you would be to be careful. If you choose to stay with Philip, you will need to be his truest friend and that is a burden few have the strength to carry, but you, I think, might do so." Her last words came as a whisper. "His friendship is worth paying that or any other price."

The carriage thundered on through the night, its outriders stopping for no man. Gideon sat in its rough cradle, bracing himself in the dark. Unshed tears making his eyes as heavy as his heart, unsure if the woman on the pallet was sleeping or had already slipped the coils of mortality and taken herself to a greater rest.

II

"You took your damned time." Mags got to his feet as Nick followed Daniel through the door and into the large private room at the back of the inn. He had two men sitting with him, both of whom rose when he did. "You're late Danny, I've been here since this morning." Then he caught sight of Nick, and his smile became wolfish. He shaped a brief bow. "Sir Nicholas, you do us an honour coming in person, I was only expecting this miscreant who has no doubt been giving you a lot of trouble. Say the word and I will have him flogged for it."

Nick recalled the last thing Daniel had said before they dismounted. He had seemed hesitant, his expression troubled. Nick had needed to prompt him to speak.

"You have second thoughts?"

"Have a care, sir. This is Mags, he will play a game of divide and rule. You will need to decide if you want to play or not."

At the time Nick had not caught the meaning and there had been no opportunity to ask for an explanation, but now he understood all too well.

"Lieutenant Bristow has rendered me good service on your behalf, I am sure you will be pleased to know."

Mags' eyebrows rose and he looked between them.

"So that is how the land lies." He sounded sour. "You will render me your account later Danny, don't think I'll forget."

Daniel made a precise bow.

"I have carried out the orders you gave me to the letter, sir. I am sure neither Sir Nicholas nor yourself would have any cause to find fault in me or my actions."

The inn was on the edge of the Yorkshire Dales. When they had arrived there had been snow falling and Nick had no intention of returning to the saddle that night.

"If we are late," he said, "that is because it is not so easy to arrange matters when I am at another's command."

"Something any military man can understand," Mags said and gestured to the two men with him as he resumed his seat. They remained standing, flanking him like a variety of honour guard. "Danny will know Tremullion and Turk, they were friends of Aleksandrov."

Beside him, Nick felt Daniel stiffen.

"We've met," he said. Then, his tone shifting to one of mild enquiry. "Were we going to start carving each other up before or after supper, sir?"

THE DEVIL'S COMMAND

Mags gave a guffaw of laughter and thumped on the table in apparent delight.

"That is what makes you the canny lad you are Danny. And no one is about to get hasty, they weren't that good friends, were you now lads?"

The two men shook their heads.

"Owed me. Never paid me," one said. Tremullion, Nick assumed, as there was a marked West Country drawl. "Bit like the Schiavono."

"That is something we can all agree on, and I will drink to," Daniel said, his hand moving from his sword hilt where, Nick realised, it had rested since they entered the room.

"Sit. Sit." Mags gestured, encompassing them all. Turk and Tremullion resumed their seats on either side of where Mags held his place at the head of the table and Danny sat beside Tremullion leaving Nick the choice of sitting facing him or Mags. He decided his authority was greater if he took the foot of the table. After all, it was as possible for it to be the head.

Food was served, though Nick was so much on edge he neither noted what it was or how it tasted, but Mags seemed to approve for he demanded more and then when a serving girl came with it, caught her onto his lap and refused to let her go until she had let him plant a kiss on each of her breasts. To Nick's discernment, she looked far from happy and gave in because it meant she would get away the faster.

"Tell your master I want you in my bed tonight," Mags called after her as she scuttled out of the room, face red with shame. Then, when she was gone, "You should have seen those boobies. Like peaches. And the girls here, they don't get ridden to death like those in town. Clean and fresh. If you see any you like, Sir Nicholas, say the word, I'll speak to the innkeeper. He's a very obliging man."

"With a dozen of the company under his roof, that would make him a man of good sense," Danny observed. "Are you sure they are whores and not the serving maids they seem to be?"

Mags laughed.

"I'm not surprised you ask. You'd get your cock stuck in your breeches if a proper whore tried to touch you. And what does it matter if they are or not? They're the same when you get them in bed."

"I'd rather get it stuck than poxed," Danny said, his tone free from rancour. "And I seldom need to pay for what is given freely. I'll play you piquet for her."

Mags shook his head.

"I've a fancy for that one. Pick one of the others. There are three or four of them about."

Danny shrugged.

"Perhaps." Then his attention went back to his plate.

Under the table, Nick felt a kick to his ankle.

"I have a message I was asked to bring you," he said.

"A message?" Mags' eyes narrowed in suspicion. "Now who would that be from?"

"Mutual friends, I believe."

Mags studied him over the length of the table.

"I'm sure we have some, being kin and all." He stabbed his knife into something on his plate. "Let's eat first. Messages can ruin the digestion. Danny here, can tell us some of his war stories. How about the one where you wound up lieutenant-general in a siege,

THE DEVIL'S COMMAND

where was that again?"

Another time Nick might have listened and laughed along with the rest. Danny was a good raconteur and had the table reduced to near helpless mirth at points. Nick managed to laugh in the right places, but he had no real idea what he was laughing at. His mind had been thrown into a new turmoil.

He had seen Mags had more men with him, sitting in the common room with his own soldiers. But they were not his own. The men who had accompanied them were Bristow's men. The same he had brought with him when he joined Nick. And that could well mean they were men of Mags' company, their prime loyalty to him and not to Daniel or to Nick. That made a prickle of sweat spring on Nick's brow. He took another gulp of the cheap wine they had been served.

The meal was cleared away by the innkeeper assisted by two of his lads, his expression taut as Mags flipped an angel towards him with casual largesse.

"More wine and have someone build up the fire. A man could freeze in here."

A few minutes later they were closeted in the room with jugs of wine and ale, a warm fire in the grate and pipes of tobacco. Nick decided not to wait to be asked and once the door had closed behind the innkeeper, he reached into his doublet and took out the letter, seal intact, dropping it on the table.

"Oh yes," Mags said, eyeing it with seeming disinterest. "The message. Give it here, then." He held out a hand, Daniel picked it up before Nick could move and leaned around the back of the man beside him to hold it out to Mags. Nick saw there were now two folded sheets in Mags' hands.

Mags frowned at Daniel, then peered at the seal and his face seemed to lose some of its colour.

"Do I want to open this?" he asked, but as his gaze was still on the seal it was uncertain who, if anyone he might be asking.

"Do you have any choice?" Nick asked, glad to be able to seize some small moment of initiative.

Mags glanced up at him, then gave a feral grin. "When you put it like that..." He picked up his eating knife, inverted it and drove the pommel hard into the seal, shattering it into pieces. Then he shook the page to remove the last traces and unfolded it. His eyes scanned the sheet for no more than a moment then he put it down and picked up the other folded sheet Daniel had handed to him. "You've been a busy lad, haven't you Danny?"

Mags unfolded the second sheet and read through it, then he put it down on the table in front of him and whistled a breath out between his teeth.

"Well now, that does make for some interesting reading. Hiding your light under a bushel, Danny? Looks like you have been making friends in high places."

Daniel said nothing, meeting Mags' gaze.

Mags lifted a hand dismissively. "No matter. These things happen. The question is, what's to be done about it?"

Now Mags looked down the table at Nick, making it clear that it was not meant to be a rhetorical question. It was close enough to what Daniel had drilled him in for his response to be immediate and confident.

"That depends on you. There are choices we both have to make here, and we can make them to mutual advantage and pool our resources in support of a common aim, or we can allow this to become something which sets us against each other."

Mags nodded.

"A fair assessment." Then, "I heard you married."

Now what had that to do with anything? When he realised a moment later Nick felt the colour in his face rising.

"I have," he said. "Though that is no concern for you."

"But it is, very much so. It is something that my decision could even hinge upon."

This was a wide step outside what Nick had expected and he tried to think what to say to counter it.

"Why would it matter?" he asked at last.

Mags laughed.

"Danny, take this fool outside and slit his throat."

Nick's heart thumped once then seemed to pause with his held breath. If he had made a mistake, then he was dead whatever he might do. For pride he would not run or beg. He forced himself to sit back and let his hands rest on the table, feigning a nonchalance he did not feel.

Daniel sighed and reached into his coat.

"If you wanted high stakes for us to gamble you only had to ask." He pulled his card pouch out and tipped the cards onto the table. You choose what we play. If I win, I get your whore and you have to talk business with Sir Nicholas. If you win, you get a dead Tempest and I'll talk your business with the men who sent you that letter."

Mags' eyes glittered and his lips twisted in scorn.

"You'll talk to who I tell you to talk to, Danny, and spike them if I ask it."

"You have my word on it," Daniel promised. "I will. Whoever, whatever and whenever. *If* you win."

Mags lifted his chin in the slightest upward movement, Turk and Tremullion were on their feet, but Danny's pistol was already in his hand. He had it aimed at Mags unerringly, turned so the frizzen and mechanism were uppermost. There was a click as he pulled the hammer to full cock. The two men froze.

"Well, then," Mags said, a grin spreading over his face. "I find I like you more and more, Danny. So maybe we could play piquet. But not with your cards. I'm not the trusting kind. But I'm sure the innkeeper will have some."

Chapter Fifteen

I

At first, when the carriage slowed to a halt, Gideon assumed there had to be another problem and had the window open and the reloaded pistol in his hand. Once on the hellish journey, there had been a sudden scattered volley and more shouts, but they seemed to have passed the problem before Gideon could look out. So this time even though there were voices and no shots he was wary.

"Be careful where you point that, Mr Fox," Bela Rigó's familiar tones chided, as he opened the door of the carriage, "I'm not sure if anyone showed you how to use it properly yet."

The humour told Gideon that they were in no immediate danger and had reached their destination. He wished he could share the Hungarian's evident relief. There had been no sound or movement from the shadowed pallet since Kate last spoke.

Gideon had managed to ease his way out from the carriage before Zahara was there, giving him a brief troubled smile, with Lord a pace behind, black wig discarded and face wiped clean of the pockmarks. That was when Gideon recognised they were back in Wormleighton. He stepped quickly aside as Lord pushed past him, focused on the pallet in the carriage.

Gideon wanted to warn him, wanted to say that it

was too late, that Kate had given him the final burdens of her heart to pass on and that she had then let go. But somehow the words wouldn't come. No warning could soften this blow. It was not Gideon's place to come between Sir Philip Lord and his grief.

There was anxious and rapid talk from the carriage. Zahara slipping into a language she knew better than English and Lord responding. The last time Gideon had heard him use it had been to hurl callous malice at her and Shiraz, but now his tone was different— patient, attentive, precise.

When Lord stepped back and looked at him, Gideon began to suspect he might have made an assumption too far himself.

"I need your help," Lord said. Then, lifting his voice, "Jupp, Olsen…" The two men appeared from the mild chaos of men and horses. "We must take the pallet into the house. Keep it as level as possible."

Gideon was grateful that it was Jupp who asked, "Lady Catherine, is she alright?"

"No," Lord replied, voice toneless. "But the prince has promised his own physician will come, if—" He caught on the word and drew a brief breath, "*when* he is needed."

Between the four of them, they lifted the pallet and carried it towards the house. As they had to negotiate the stairs a quiet voice spoke from it with evident effort.

"*Write on my brow my fortune… I forget…*"

Lord's head bowed as he completed the words for her.

"*Write on my brow my fortune, let my bier be borne by virgins that shall sing by course the truth of maids*

THE DEVIL'S COMMAND

and perjuries of men. But you, my lady love, will have no need for a bier and we are most certainly not virgins."

There was a small sound of laughter from the diminished figure on the pallet, but then nothing more until they had set her down on a large, canopied bed in a ground floor chamber and that was when Gideon saw the blood soaked through the blanket and how much there was of it.

Zahara was there, and with her Brighid and Gretchen, three of the few women who remained with the company now.

"Leave us," Zahara said with a fierce look for Lord who opened his mouth to protest. Then, to Gideon, "Keep him away. He has done his part. You both have."

Dismissed, the men left the room. Jupp and Olsen, with a nod to their commander, headed back to join the rest of the men. Lord remained outside the door, facing it. Then he placed both palms upon it and leaned his forehead on the wood, closing his eyes. It was the nearest Gideon had ever seen him to prayer.

After a few moments he stepped back, as if recalling Gideon's presence. "I think I need to get very drunk," he said. "Unfortunately, I cannot. However, if you come with me, we will share some wine and perhaps things that seem unendurable right now will become less so."

Gideon was glad that he could carry out Zahara's will. He knew that she was right, Lord needed to not be there. If there was any chance of Kate finding a pathway back from death to life, he was sure Zahara would know it. His task was to keep Lord from the dark grasping fingers of despair which could turn so fast into anger and destruction.

Lord's room was small but well-appointed. Gideon guessed that in happier times it might be the room made available for less important house guests. The hearth was adequate to warm the room and there was a feather bed with a canopy to keep out the chill and woven hangings over the shuttered windows.

Poking the embers back into life, Lord lit the lights and then sighed.

"One of us needs to send for someone to bring the wine," he said.

Something of his concern must have shown in Gideon's expression as he turned for the door because Lord's hand detained him.

"I'll go. My voice carries more authority." Then his tone changed. "And don't worry, I'm not about to start assaulting the servants—yet." The words landed like a blow and Gideon drew a sharp breath then bit back his response. He had perhaps deserved them.

Lord crossed to where his portable desk had been set up in one corner and unlocked it, retrieved a couple of documents and held them out to Gideon. "You can read these whilst I'm gone. I won't be long. I have only to find someone and ask them to fetch that jug. You will not be facing the wrath of Zahara." The slight smile he offered after that reassured Gideon more than all his words.

Taking the folded sheets, he walked over to the light, aware of the door closing as Lord left the room. One was a letter to Essex from an indecipherable name but given under the name of the Committee of

THE DEVIL'S COMMAND

Safety, commending one Captain Jethro Armitage to the Earl asking that he be given every facility he might ask for or require. A scrawled note beneath said 'He is a good man.' and had the initials A.P. The other stated that Armitage would be delayed and might not now arrive until early November and should be given the enclosed document when he did. There was no enclosure.

The door opened and Lord returned, bearing the promised wine and cups himself. These he set down on a small pillar-legged table, applying the one to the other before holding a full cup out to Gideon.

"See, I am back and not a single corpse in my wake and that," he gestured to the letters with his full cup, "was how I came to be able to ride into Warwick and remove you and Kate. The prince found the first in a cache of Essex's documents in the baggage the Parliamentarians abandoned at Kineton. The second was also in the box, but in a packet of sealed correspondence which must have just arrived as it had not been opened and read. The signature is John Pym, 'King' Pym as they call him, a man Essex would not want to cross as he holds the most influence of any in the Parliamentary faction."

"And the initials?"

"That would be the Earl of Northumberland, Algernon Percy, Essex's cousin." Lord took a single swallow of wine.

"What was the enclosure?" Gideon asked though he had a suspicion already.

Lord took another drink from his cup and drained over half of it in one go. Then put it down beside the jug and stepped away from it, as if trying to distance himself from his desire to empty it completely.

"That was a warrant from the Committee of Safety, signed by Pym. As long as Essex was convinced that I was Armitage, we had no problem. I apologise for betraying your assumption of Blake's identity, but it was necessary as Greville had said a few things before you arrived that made me think he was starting to guess something was amiss, that and I badly needed some sand to throw in their eyes."

"Then who attacked us? If Essex and Brooke were convinced by your act…"

"The answer to that is rather ironic," Lord said. "It was a Royalist scouting mission led by a local man who recognised the coach and decided he had sufficient strength to try and capture a prize." He gave a brief rictus grin. "Unfortunately for him, he picked the wrong men to try it on."

"But they were our own side," Gideon protested, horrified.

Lord seemed unconcerned. "Indeed. That was unfortunate. But these things happen."

Gideon let it go. There was another question to ask, hard as it was.

"You said we had casualties." Only they were not just 'casualties' to Gideon now, they were all men he knew, men he had fought alongside.

Lord picked up his cup, refilled it to the brim and drank before he replied.

"We lost Thompson and Garland," he said.

Thompson, the big man with a face like a gargoyle who Gideon had first encountered in a smoky alehouse when he met Lord. Garland was one of the

THE DEVIL'S COMMAND

mercenaries Gideon recalled who had a good sense of humour. Neither were men Gideon had been close to, but both now left a mark on him with their passing. That was three men lost in as many days.

He swallowed some wine himself and wondered how any man could command a force of soldiers as Lord did, laugh and drink with them, then send them to die. But he knew it wasn't that simple. Lord always fought with them. He didn't send them to death, he led the way to it himself, taunting it, daring it and perhaps with some dark corner of his soul, seeking it for himself.

"I think perhaps we should drink to happier times," Lord said and lifted his cup. "Times to come when *I would my sword had a close basket hilt to hold Wine, and the blade would make knives, for we shall have nothing but eating and drinking.*"

"Is that what you would want, though?" Gideon asked, unable to hide his bitterness and sorrow.

"Is that not what any man would want?" Lord got up and refilled Gideon's cup to the brim. "I have changed my mind. I intend to get drunk after all. You may stay and join me. We can talk about politics, religion, literature and music, and call each other brother as we vomit into our boots. Or you may go and sleep, chaste and sober, and dream of a world where law has overcome war and universal bonhomie abounds."

If nothing else in his weeks with Sir Philip Lord, Gideon had learned that facing reality was never a matter of choice, but a matter of necessity.

So, of course, he stayed.

II

If someone had tried to persuade Nick a month before that he would be sitting into the early hours in the backroom of a wayside inn, watching two men play cards for his life, he would have declared that person fit only for Bedlam. But now he sat at the table, with Turk and Tremullion standing behind him to ensure he wouldn't leave before his fate had been decided. Now and then one of them threw another log on the fire at need or arranged for more wine to be brought.

It was agreed to place all on whoever won a *partie* of piquet. Nick's life rested on six hands of cards. It was a complicated game and one more found in places favoured by the better educated and wealthier in society, not a game often played in the backroom of a country inn. But it had the advantage that only two could play.

The innkeeper had provided them with a reasonably fresh deck of cards, though to Nick's thinking there were one or two that were more visibly marked than any Danny had in his pouch. Mags had taken off his hat and the rucked ridge of scar tissue that parted his long greying hair on one side shone in the lamplight. He sorted out the cards they wouldn't need in the deck then cut for the deal and licked his lips as he cut a queen. It was not a game that favoured the dealer and whoever cut lowest had to deal the first hand.

"I think you'll be starting us off then, Danny lad," Mags said.

Shrugging, Daniel flipped the deck open as if it

THE DEVIL'S COMMAND

were a book.

"King," he said. "You deal first."

Mags scowled and gathered the cards, shuffled them and then dealt them in twos and threes until they each had twelve cards. The remaining eight that formed the *talon* pile he dropped on the table face down between them.

Whilst Mags spent a moment moving the cards about in his hand, no doubt to group them by suit and power, Danny left his as they were and chose four cards from across the spread to discard and exchange for four from the *talon*.

"That is generous of you," Mags said, scooping up the remaining four to replace his discards. "I've not often seen a man take less than the full five."

Danny shrugged and scratched at his beard.

"No point spoiling a hand for no reason," he said. "Five for *point*."

"Not good," Mags said, then grinned. "I've six."

The rest of the declaring went on. If the other player agreed the claim they would say 'good' if they could do better, they would say 'not good' and make their own claim. Mags having declared he had the longest suit, Danny declared for and won the longest sequence with four. Then Mags capped his *trio* call for three of a kind by calling it 'no good' and claiming his own *quatorze*, four of a kind, and a bonus *trio*.

The declarations and scoring for them complete, Mags led a card and the playing out of the hand began. The focus of both men was absolute. It was as if the consequences of victory or defeat had left their minds as soon as they started playing. All either of them now cared about was beating the other man. It was more of a duel than a game of chance.

The first three hands of the *partie* had been inconclusive, both had scored points and neither had taken any substantial lead. But the fourth hand changed things. Mags had gained thirty points in his declarations with a steady reply of: 'Good...good...good' from Danny as he conceded the superior hand and was only spared from Mags claiming the humiliating *repique* of a further sixty points, by being able to show his hand was blank, with no card over ten. That he had somehow still managed to take the one trick needed to avoid granting Mags a *pique* bonus in the play, Nick put down to pure luck. But Danny seemed unperturbed throughout as they went into the fifth deal of the six they would play.

"You're not having much luck with the cards today," Mags said as for the third hand running, he called the better declarations. At least this time Danny had taken one of the three and as it was for sets, he had then called three lesser sets, lifting his points and closing the gap to some degree. But with one hand left after this, the score seemed to have slipped beyond all hope of recovery should Daniel not achieve some miracle in the playing element.

"You may have the longest and strongest single suit," Danny said, with a smile, but as I have the lead, and not any one of your spades, you won't get to play it."

He proved his point by taking every trick, the last with the humble seven of diamonds. "*Pique*, I think," he said with a smile and that put the two scores within touching and everything depending on how the cards fell for the final hand.

If his fate had not been tied to the game, Nick might even have enjoyed watching it. He could see now how, despite the fall of the cards, Danny was making better ground with what he was given, but the best player in all creation had no chance of winning with an impossibly poor hand.

Danny got to deal the final hand in the *partie*, which meant the advantage was with Mags. He did so swiftly, two then three, then three then two and then a final two. His favourite way to deal, Nick had noticed. As usual, Danny barely glanced at his cards before putting them down.

At the far end of the table, Mags sat, sweat beading on his brow in the warmth of the room, glaring at the cards in his hand as if they were his enemies. Beside Nick, Danny was now in his shirt sleeves, coat and doublet slung on the back of his chair, his hand of cards flat on the table in front of him, their plain backs revealing nothing of what they might each be, an expectant expression on his face.

"You are taking your five cards?" he asked.

Mags grunted, pulled his chosen discards from the fan of cards he held and grouped them in one palm, tapping them on the table before putting them in a neat pile face down and counting the top five cards off the *talon*.

Danny shook his head. "I'll keep what I have, I think."

Mags eyed him with suspicion. "You going to show us what's left in the *talon* then?"

Which was when Nick recalled the rule that said if the second player, the 'younger' did not take all the remaining cards after the 'elder' had taken theirs, then he could choose to reveal them to both players.

"I'm sure I'll work out what they are if I need to know," Danny said. "Let's get on with the declarations. What do you have?"

"Five," Mags said, then hawked and spat on the floor.

"Equal," Danny said, quietly.

"I have forty-one in it," Mags offered.

"Not good." Danny looked thoughtful. "That is five points to me, and to save you time I'm taking fifteen points for sequence too."

Mags did not look too disheartened. Which was not so surprising. Those scores suggested all Danny's strength was in the one suit. In the card play, whilst a single strong suit was nice, as Danny had demonstrated before it was no use if it could not get played and for this final hand, Mags would have the lead and it also meant that Danny was less likely to have cards in other suits that might spoil Mags' play.

"Tell us your sets then," Danny prompted.

The declarations went on and at the end of them Nick did a rapid calculation and realised that against the odds, they were level on the same score as they began to play. But Mags took a step ahead right away as he received a point for leading. He won the first five tricks with his long suit and Nick was disturbed to see Danny with nothing in the suit, flinging away royalty cards as discards. His heart felt as if a giant fist was set about it and squeezing in. The air with its weight of tobacco, coal and wood smoke seemed

THE DEVIL'S COMMAND

almost unbreathable.

With Mags scoring for each trick, it was hard to see how Danny could win. The next trick would give Mags the magic seven which would score him a bonus of ten points and then there would be no way Danny could recover, even if he won all the rest after that.

Mags looked at his hand with a scowl. Then his expression lightened.

"Looks like I can't stop you getting the lead off me, but I think you will have to play back to me before we are done." He threw a card on the table with a smirk.

The ten of hearts. Nick recalled seeing Danny discard the queen and felt sick.

Danny said nothing, his expression as it had been throughout. He rubbed at his beard for a moment then dropped the knave of hearts on the ten and picked up both cards to put the trick aside.

Mags' face turned puce, then the colour drained from it

Danny smiled at him. "Oh, you thought to force me to play the ace to make your king a winner? I'm sorry to disappoint you."

Nick felt a rush of relief which was headier than a goblet of brandy. Danny had won. He had his strong suit to play through and then the ace of hearts. Nick knew he was safe. Through a haze of emotion, he saw Mags push himself to his feet.

"You wish to withdraw?" Danny asked.

Mags' hand was resting on his sword, his face ugly.

"What is the point of playing it out now? Lay out your hand and claim it."

"We both agreed to play a full *partie*," Danny said, "If we don't play it out, we haven't done that. I am a man of my word, and you are too. We have no choice but to play it out."

There were rumbles of agreement from Turk and Tremullion who Nick was sure had their own reasons for wanting to see Mags pushed further into the corner.

For a moment Mags glared at Danny, then he sat down again.

"Play it," he snarled.

The next five tricks were, as expected, all Danny's winning clubs, Mags throwing away his useless hearts and dropping the king on the final one in disgust.

The last card remained. Danny's fingers moved and the eight of hearts flipped face up.

Mags could not have looked more shocked if a sheep had turned and savaged him.

"I don't think you have any hearts left now, do you? You kept your ace of diamonds instead." Danny said. "And what a shame you discarded the king because the ace," he reached over to turn the cards in the pile he had chosen not to exchange with at the start of the game, "is right there in the *talon*."

For a moment Nick stared at it in disbelief. Then there were chuckles of laughter from Turk and Tremullion which became full bloodied guffaws. The look of fury on Mags' face, twisted into something more feral that Nick recognised with a chill—hatred. But Danny seemed not to notice. He swept the cards up and restored the deck with an easy grin.

"I take the *partie* and I win our wager."

THE DEVIL'S COMMAND

THE DEVIL'S COMMAND

Chapter Sixteen

I

The game was won, but from the way his hand twitched, Nick was not at all sure Mags would accept the defeat. He looked close to drawing his sword. Perhaps something in the way Danny held his gaze, almost as if willing him to do so, made him think the better of it because he got to his feet and spat into the hearth.

"You win," he said and the smile he mustered looked ugly. "We'll play again and next time the game won't be *piquet* and the stakes will be of my choosing. Look to yourself, Danny, I'll not be sending you a letter when the time comes for that."

He screwed up the two documents that had been sitting beside him on the table and threw them into the fire. Then he stalked from the room without looking back, followed by Turk who was still wearing a smirk, but Tremullion paused on the way out and slapped Bristow on the back.

"Well played," he said. "You really made him sweat. I've not seen another man do that to the graf before." He laughed and then left the room, following in Mags' wake.

Nick sat unable to move for a moment, weakened by relief. But as that washed away it was replaced by fury and once the immediate threat was gone as the

THE DEVIL'S COMMAND

door closed behind Tremullion, he exploded.

"How could you have done that?" he snarled. "You stupid half-wit, you gambled everything, on a bluff. My life. On a bluff. And you didn't even need it to be a bluff. You could have taken the cards from the *talon* and won." He still couldn't believe that Daniel had done that. "What would you have done if he'd led with a higher heart?"

Daniel shrugged and filled his cup.

"Firstly, your life was never at risk and secondly, if I had taken the *talon* I'd not have won, it was only the ace that was worth having." He took a swallow from the cup and put it down. "Besides, Mags wasn't going to lead high. He always led low from the first hand, and I'd been feeding him my high cards to those low leads when I could to encourage him."

"But why take such a needless and foolish risk?" Nick wanted to shake the man. "I can see no point to it. No reason. No sense."

"No, I don't suppose you do," Daniel said and picked up the cup again, this time to drain it, wiping his mouth on his sleeve as he put it down and refilled it. Nick realised it was the first time he had seen Daniel drink that evening. "The point was, I didn't want to just defeat Mags, that would have been easy. I wanted to humiliate him too. Make him look a fool to his own." He gestured to the closed door with his refilled cup. "You can be sure Turk and Tremullion will be telling the tale of it to all their company, even if Mags threatens them not to do so. They won't be able to stop themselves. He was taken. Like a little boy still in skirts, and that will be something he can't live down."

Nick shook his head. He still couldn't see the point.

"And what if he'd decided to attack you? We could have both been killed. Three on two."

"I wish he had," Daniel said, staring at the cup he held. "Then I could have killed him, and this would all be over. It wouldn't have been three on two, just him and me." He drew a slow breath. "It was only ever my own life I was playing with."

"Then why not go and find him now? You still could. He will be in his room."

Daniel shifted his gaze then to stare at Nick.

"You have no idea how these things work, do you? If I were to go after him now, I'd have Turk, Tremullion and half our own men ready to cut me down."

"But you said—"

Sighing, Daniel put the cup down. "It is a matter of honour. Mags is their commander. If anyone attacks him, they will defend him. But if he chose to attack me, then it is on him. They wouldn't interfere unless he asked, and he'd never ask as it would diminish him in their eyes. He'd be as good as dead then anyway."

It sounded a very odd version of honour where a man would laugh at his commander one moment and be happy to see him cut down, then the next be defending him to the death. Honour was consistent, a true and binding commitment, not something that could be shaken off in a moment and reforged.

Nick thought of the twisted look on Mags' face.

"You do know he hates you now?"

"Of course he hates me. He knows what I'm doing. He should. He's done it himself enough to others in

THE DEVIL'S COMMAND

the past. He hates me because he's just realised that I might be the man to do it back to him." Daniel got up and stretched, finishing with a yawn. "I should go to my room, there'll be a girl waiting for me. You should sleep too."

The thought of sleep was alien to Nick after the events of the past hour.

"You think we are safe here?"

"I'm not worried. If you are, I can arrange for your room to be guarded. But Mags won't do anything yet. He can't. It would be making too much of what happened. It'd be admitting I'd bested him utterly and he can't afford to do that."

After which Nick hadn't expected to get any sleep at all, so he was surprised when he woke to find he must have fallen asleep almost at once and that it was past dawn.

An even bigger surprise was that as he went to break his fast in the common room, there was no sign of Mags or any of his men.

His own men were there, Danny's men, but not Danny himself. Nick had finished eating before his lieutenant appeared looking as dishevelled as if he had slept the night in his clothes.

"Was she any good?" Nick asked as Danny sat down at the table with him.

"Was who any good?" There was a genuine frown of confusion on the other man's face.

"The wench you won from Mags. And talking of Mags, it looks like he left in the night."

"The wench I won from Mags? I didn't ask her to share my bed," Danny said picking at the food he was brought, "I included her in the stake to keep her from being forced into sharing anyone's bed against her will. And Mags left before dawn. I suspect he didn't want the rot to spread any further than it already has."

"So where does that leave us?" Nick asked, thinking aloud as much as anything. "What are we supposed to do now?"

Danny stopped eating for a moment and looked across the table. "That's your decision, Sir Nicholas. Our masters from Newhall will still expect something for their pains."

Nick thought how Mags had balled their message to him and flung it in the fire. "I don't think their offer was accepted."

"I hope not, but I wouldn't be so sure. Either way, I don't think they will be happy with this turn of events."

"They would be happy to see me dead," Nick said.

Danny shook his head. "If they'd wanted you dead you would be so. This is just their way of testing you and so far, you have shown them your mettle."

"Testing me? I don't see—"

Danny cut in over him.

"They wanted to see if you could secure my allegiance, which you did and then if you could stand up to Mags. Which you also did. Your life was never in any real danger. I think they will be pleased with you. It is me they will have an issue with if anyone."

He went back to eating and Nick wondered if that was indeed true. But whether it was or not, far from becoming the bridge between Mags and the Covenant men he had wanted to be, Nick had become aligned with one Mags now knew as an enemy. Which meant either he would not consider any approach from the Covenant or, worse, he might seek to make contact with them on his own.

It seemed whichever way he looked at it they came back to the same simple solution.

"We need to kill Mags."

Still eating, his mouth full, Danny nodded. Then he swallowed the mouthful down with some small ale.

"We do, sir," he agreed. "Last night we began to work on that."

Which made little sense to Nick.

"*Began* to work on it? How hard can it be when you are talking of sliding a sword through his brisket? I thought that was what you are good at."

There was a brief shimmer of something dark in Danny's eyes and he looked down at his food before he spoke.

"The thing is sir, to the men he leads he is a living legend. They don't follow him because he's good with a sword—though he is, very. They follow him because he has a name for making good money and finding good paymasters. Because he's worked for men like Wallenstein and got made a graf. Because he has a reputation and a name they know. Because he's survived again and again against the odds, and that is a kind of magic they hope will rub off on them too." He looked up again then and pushed the food away. "But to them, I'm just good old Danny Bristow. Great for a laugh and a game of cards and the man you ask for advice when you have big guns to play with. If I'd killed Mags last night, they would have carried on with their new paymaster. We need those men and that means we need them to see someone who can best Mags. Then they will come to us. Or many will."

Nick shook his head.

"I don't see how—"

The four men who pushed into the room, passed the protesting innkeeper, wore cuirasses over their leather coats and were well-armed, although their swords remained at their thighs and pistols holstered on hips. Their leader wore a hat with a cluster of pheasant feathers pinned to its band. With some surprise, Nick recognised the man as Tremullion.

Danny glanced at the men and if their presence impacted him at all it was that he started to eat a bit faster. Tremullion approached them and took his hat off, making a sharp bow to Nick, whose hand had somehow found his sword hilt and rested there.

"Sir Nicholas, I was hoping to have a word with Lieutenant Bristow. If that was acceptable."

Danny looked up then, the slightest trace of a frown creasing his brow. Whatever this meant it was not something he had expected to happen. He glanced at Tremullion then looked at Nick, awaiting his word.

"Whatever needs to be said can be said here." Nick was far from certain the aim of these men was not to get Danny on his own and either murder or abduct him, although Danny himself seemed not to show any such concern.

Tremullion looked between them then glanced at the men behind him. One shrugged and the other two gave small nods.

"We heard you might be recruiting," he said, eyes sliding from Danny to Nick as if uncertain. "I mean,

THE DEVIL'S COMMAND

last night the word was about that you'd—"

"Yes," Danny said, sounding untroubled. "I am. Sir Nicholas has employed me to find more experienced men to fill our ranks. If Sir Nicholas has no objection, consider yourselves hired."

Sir Nicholas sat in astonished silence. He had no idea how Danny imagined he had the right to employ men on Nick's behalf. If it was on Nick's behalf and not his own. But he nodded anyway. At that moment he would rather have these four men with him than against him.

"Does Mags know you are leaving his employ?" Danny asked.

The four shifted a little uncomfortably at that.

"More I was turned off," Tremullion said.

Danny's eyes widened.

"He let you go?"

"He were nae gonna," one of the men behind rumbled.

Danny pushed himself to his feet and made a neat bow to Nick.

"If you will allow me, Sir Nicholas, I will go and make the necessary arrangements. You will want to be on the road as soon as we may, I am sure."

Nick bit hard on his irritation. It was dawning on him that Danny was very good at seeming to offer him obedience whilst at the same time setting the agenda and giving the orders himself.

"See to it, lieutenant," Nick said sharply, hoping he managed to retrieve some measure of his authority by saying that, but suspecting that it was clear to these men who was the one leading them.

As they left, it dawned on him that he was still being tested by the Covenant men. He had shown he could win Danny Bristow to his side, but could he command the man, or would he be the one commanded? That was perhaps the greater test and one he had no intention of failing.

Danny was back a short time later and walked in whistling a marching tune.

"We've done better than I hoped, sir," he said when he reached the place where Nick still sat. "Mags is unsettled. Tremullion is lucky he has good friends, the men with him, or he'd have been spiked for sure. But I believe we should leave soon. I don't think Mags is going to take this well and he knows where we are. The men are ready to leave as soon as you are."

Nick was already on his feet.

"Then we shall leave right away," he decreed.

Danny gave a brief bow. "Yes, sir."

After all the uncertainty, it felt good to Nick to have simple agreement and compliance with his command, and he was determined to ensure things remained that way into the future.

They left the inn with the morning still young and the new men riding in with the rest, marked only by their lack of uniform appearance. Nick made a note to send Bristow to get a further requisition of those green coats. He liked that they were distinctive and was contemplating having his entire company clad in them. Intent on asserting his authority, he placed himself alone in front of the twelve and Bristow.

Then horsemen appeared a field away, hidden by a rise of high ground. They were well equipped, in grey

THE DEVIL'S COMMAND

coats with blue sashes, and they outnumbered the twelve men Nick had with him at least three times over.

Sir Ferdinando Fairfax's men.

Parliamentarians.

Mags' new paymasters.

Every instinct told him to turn and flee whilst there was still time, to order his men around and head away. He heard a flurry of sound behind him, wood and metal scraping free of leather and knew his men were better prepared for this than he was. Then, from behind him, someone cleared their throat.

"If you will allow me, Sir Nicholas…"

All his determination to keep command whatever the cost, ran flapping back along the road.

"Do it, lieutenant." At least that made his delegation sound more like an order, even if all knew it was not.

A moment later, Danny was beside and then ahead of him, calling the odd words Nick had heard before, which the men behind moved to as a flight of sparrows, or a shoal of fish might move as one. Nick found himself the centre of an arrowhead of men who, far from fleeing, were picking up speed as they approached the advancing group which was trotting towards them. It was the same manoeuvre he had seen them do the previous day and then it had scared the men ahead of them enough that they left the road to avoid any contact.

Whatever response the commander of the approaching cavalry might have expected it was not that and there was a belated shouting of orders and a trumpet. But the effect was to disorder the troop even more than it had been. Then Danny gave the most bloodcurdling scream Nick had heard issue from a human throat, and before it was halfway done many of the men behind him added their roars and the faces of those that they bore down on were shocked and pale.

A moment before impact the pistols fired in rapid succession, close enough together to be a resounding volley and saddles emptied, whilst the odd shot from the grey-coated men seemed to do little. Then they were in amongst them. Nick had his sword out and swung it at a man with a blue sash who was trying to cut at his arm. His blade took the hand at the wrist, nearly severing it and a back thrust went through the man's throat. About him, close-packed, Danny's men—his men—were scything through flesh and bone like a harvester through wheat, and the sky seemed to rain blood.

Then they were through and at another command, Danny brought the men wheeling round to face the enemy. The carnage they had carved was plain on the road, Nick counted over a dozen fallen, dead or injured and the men they had carved through were not waiting for a second attack. The moment Danny wheeled the troop, despite the desperate shouts of whoever was their commander, they broke and ran, leaving their wounded and dead, fearful for their own lives.

Nick marvelled then at the power of the weapon he now commanded. He shivered with exultation, thrilled at how easy it had been. The slaying, the mayhem, the fear in the enemy, the blood, red and wet on his sword. He knew then it was worth whatever the

THE DEVIL'S COMMAND

price he was having to pay.

II

Gideon woke to someone shaking his shoulder. His head felt hollow and his mouth dry, tasting as if he had been swilling it out with vinegar.

"Time to wake up, I regret it was indeed the lark and not the nightingale that pierced the rather grubby hollow of thine ear."

It was no surprise to see Philip Lord immaculately clad, hair neatly combed, white against the dark mulberry of his silk doublet, cat's head sword at his thigh.

Gideon had to suppress a groan as he swung his legs over the side of the bed. He recalled, vaguely, Lord helping him escape from his doublet and putting him on the bed. Where, or if, Lord himself had slept Gideon had no idea. He also had a vague memory of singing some disreputable songs from his student days, being surprised that Lord had known more verses than he had ever heard and throwing up in a chamber pot.

As he was getting dressed, he remembered why they had been getting drunk. He doused his hair in cold water set in a bowl on the corner table and then, running his fingers through his hair to order it a little, wondered how he could ask.

"I am waiting with some impatience," Lord said, standing by the door. "Zahara has told me if I try to demand entrance to see Kate without you there, she will have Shiraz remove me."

Gideon paused mid-rake.

"Me? Why?"

"That is what we will find out as soon as you are ready to face the world. Or at least that small feminine corner of it." Then, "I did," Lord said, "assume from Zahara's response that Kate is considered well enough to receive us uncouth male visitors, which at least suggests she is still alive." He closed his mouth hard like a man who had said too much and realised the fact.

Gideon finished his ablutions and pulled on his boots. He had his sword scabbard in hand before it struck him how much a part of his life it had become to wear one. In London, it was not something one would think of wearing in the house, but now it seemed strange whenever he was not wearing it and instinctive to reach for it as much as for his hat when he got dressed.

Lord's impatience showed more in his stillness than his activity. He leaned on the wall and watched Gideon, straightening when he was ready and opening the door without a word, striding to the stairs. Gideon caught up with him by the time he had reached the bottom.

The door to the room where they had left Kate was guarded by men Gideon did not recognise wearing red coats.

"Prince Maurice's men," Lord explained as they approached, "Injured in the battle and pleased to be able to serve here." He nodded at the two, who straightened and stepped aside so Lord could open the door. But for Gideon, it was another reminder that the company was stuck in ever-diminishing numbers. He wondered if Lord would be looking to recruit at some point, but then how he could begin to replace men like Garland and Thompson?

He followed Lord into the room, thoughts pushed into terrible speculation about what he would find there. He had been less sure than Lord that Zahara's words meant Kate was still alive. So it was with extreme trepidation that he looked over to the canopied bed. Zahara was sitting beside it on a stool pulled close in. She rose as Lord strode over and gave Gideon a weary smile, which he was uncertain how to interpret.

Kate lay with her eyes closed, her hair vivid and dark red against the linen sheets and her skin the colour of porcelain. For a terrible moment, Gideon thought she was indeed dead, but then Lord moved and took her hand in his.

"*Wake now my love, awake; for it is time,*
The Rosy Morne long since left Tithones bed,
All ready to her silver coche to clyme,
And Phœbus gins to shew his glorious hed."

Kate opened her eyes and smiled up at him.

"I am sorry I can't answer you in kind," she said, her voice not strong, and Lord dipped to place a gentle kiss on her lips.

"I have poetry enough for us both," he told her.

"You always have," she agreed. Then her gaze found Gideon. "I need to thank you for being so kind last night."

"It is already forgotten," he said, knowing she would take what she needed from his meaning, but she closed her eyes for a moment. When they opened again she managed a sad smile.

"No," she said firmly. "It should not be forgotten."

Gideon's chest tightened.

"Then it will be remembered," he said and that seemed to satisfy her. Zahara touched his arm and drew him away from the bed to give Kate and her husband the privacy of each other's company.

It was the first time Gideon had been able to talk with Zahara since he had returned from Warwick and somehow, he managed to resist the urge to take her in his arms.

"I was afraid for you," Zahara said. "When you did not come back—when Lady Catherine came out alone and…" She reached out and gripped his hands in her own, her coifed head lowered so he could not see her face. When she looked up her face was tranquil again and she studied him with care as if committing him to memory in a new way. "Lady Catherine said she hurt your head. May I see?"

For the next few minutes, Gideon sat on the stool Zahara had been occupying, which she took over to the window where the light was good and submitted to having the wound on his head examined.

"It is healed mostly now," she assured him, "though I am sure it will be sore to touch for a time but better to leave it uncovered as much as you can. The air here is clean enough."

"But what of Ka—Lady Catherine?" He had to know.

Zahara looked away.

Gideon shook his head. "I know she… she miscarried, but surely—?"

"It is not only that." Zahara lifted her gaze to meet

his, a depth of sadness marring their usual green serenity.

"Then what...?" Gideon was at a loss.

"She fell when her horse was shot, and she broke her pelvis when she fell. The physician in Warwick must have been capable as he bound her well, so the bones do not move. But it is not certain that she will heal from that. There can be damage inside her from the break, damage we cannot see, nor see how bad it is. It means although she is comfortable, she is weak from blood loss and could still die."

Gideon felt the constriction in his guts tighten.

"She is not afraid for herself," Zahara went on. "She is afraid for the Schiavono. She is afraid of what he will become without her. That is why she wants you with him."

Gideon felt the weight of that burden settle on his shoulders. He wondered if he could do what was needed. Could he keep Sir Philip Lord from the darkness that stood ready to devour him whole if his foot slipped from the narrow way, if Kate faltered? It took little imagination to see the kind of monster that would be unbound in Lord if he lost Kate. Gideon was not at all sure he had the degree of strength needed, but he also knew that were it to happen, he had no choice but to try. The alternative would be unconscionable.

"Danny would be a better choice," he said, knowing that was true.

"But he is away in the north. There is no one else at this time and in this place apart from you who could even attempt the task."

Gideon knew what Zahara was asking of him, what Kate had made clear she expected of him. But the brutal fact remained that if Kate died and Lord fell, the creature that would rise in his place would be an angel of vengeance, nothing human remaining. He would become in reality all Gideon had first believed him to be—a dark legend made flesh.

"I am not sure I can," Gideon said, hating himself for having to face that truth. "I can try, of course, but what if I fail?"

"Then," Zahara said, "at least you will have tried."

There was no chance to say more because Prince Rupert's physician arrived and with him was a messenger commanding that Lord and his men rejoin the army. A royal summons which could not be refused, but Lord, from his expression, seemed half inclined to do so.

"You must go," Kate insisted. "I have the best care and it will do you good to have something else to think about for a time."

So, reluctantly, Lord left her.

"You can stay here if you wish," he told Gideon after he had arranged for the messenger to receive refreshments and issued the necessary orders to prepare his men. "You are not enrolled on my fighting strength."

But Gideon remembered what Zahara had said and shook his head.

"I will come. You are down two men as it is, and Shiraz will be here."

Lord accepted his decision with a nod. "Ride the bay, we will be working."

Then, farewells made, they left the house with the

remaining men of the company and took the road to Banbury.

THE DEVIL'S COMMAND

Chapter Seventeen

I

"I've never been to Banbury," Roger Jupp confided, "and the only thing I ever heard about the place was that they're shysters. That a Banbury tinker, when he mends a pot of one hole will make the means for three more."

Even though Jupp was not by nature a garrulous man, Gideon realised that he was making an extra effort to be so for Lord's benefit. He must know as they all did the cloud that hung silent and pall-like over their commander, and although they made a good pace Jupp had still managed some good-humoured banter riding alongside Lord and Gideon.

"That is what they say about Banbury tinkers," Lord agreed. "I've heard a better tale of Banbury folk though.

In progressu boreali,
Ut processi ab australi,
Veni Banbury, O profanum!
Ubi vidi Puritanum,
Felem farientem furem,
Quod Sabbatho stravit murem."

Jupp looked askance at his commander then sent a despairing glance to Gideon.

"You have Latin, Mr Fox, what's the Schiavono on about there?"

THE DEVIL'S COMMAND

Gideon sighed. "I've read Braithwaite too," he said to Lord.

"I am not surprised. He was another lawyer who made a journey to the north from London. I would have thought he might have been your role model." Lord, riding his blue roan reins in one hand, put out his left arm, elbow bent and palm open, grasping at the sky, like an actor declaiming on the stage.

"In my progress, travelling northward,
Taking my farewell of the southward,
To Banbury came I, O profane one,
Where I saw a puritane one
Hanging of his cat on Monday,
For killing of a mouse on Sunday."

Jupp gave a snort of laughter so sudden it made his horse dance.

"So I am guessing they won't be holding a big welcome party for us when we get there then?"

The people of Banbury I am sure will be pragmatic enough to recognise superior force when it turns up on their doorstep," Lord opined. "The bigger question is what will the castle do? It has a good-sized garrison and if it is well supplied it could hold us up for a while."

"That shouldn't be too terrible," Jupp said. "We can find quarters in the town perhaps. But then if they are that puritan, they might not run to a decent alehouse in the place."

"No town in England is *that* puritanical," Lord assured him.

Banbury lay less than ten miles riding from Wormleighton, but the road took them around the high ridge of Edgehill, the shadow of which brought memories back to Gideon of the battle he wished he had never seen.

His fear, as they rode to another town of innocent civilians that had been besieged, was that he would be forced to witness more of the same. Then he realised that was not his biggest fear. His biggest fear was that he might discover that these men he rode with and thought of as friends, were in truth men of the same cast as Digby's.

Not much more than an hour after they set out, they had been challenged at and allowed through the outer pickets of the king's army. Soon after that they clattered through the town where soldiers were clearing away makeshift barricades some of the townsfolk had put up in a vain attempt to offer some resistance. Mercifully there were no signs of looting or ill-treatment of the people. No obvious signs at least.

"I have to find the prince, but I think you had better see if you can make yourself useful, Jupp," Lord said. "And I don't mean in emptying the local meagre alehouse." He nodded at a smart-looking inn they rode past with what looked to Gideon like a stylised deer hanging above its door.

"Place like that they will have a sign saying, 'No soldiers served here' anyway," Jupp said, adding a grin. Then he lifted a hand as he gave a terse command to the rest of the company. Gideon was about to obey and go with them when Lord's voice stopped him.

"With me, Gideon."

So instead, he turned to follow Lord towards where

THE DEVIL'S COMMAND

the castle sat on the edge of Banbury by the river. A square keep on a square island in square curtain walls, brooding over the town as a mother hen might over her clutch. Except this time the castle had failed in its task of protection. The town had been taken and now artillery was being placed to bring down the walls. Beyond the guns were regiments of foot, ready to move should a breach be prepared for them.

The prince, they had been told, was with those guns, which were being lined up on the open ground beside the river. Gideon could see it was a water meadow that had been churned to a muddy morass by the hooves and shoes of the king's army. Beside the guns, was a knot of well-dressed and well-attended men, amongst whom the figures of the two princes stood out,

There were occasional musket shots from the castle walls, which served to encourage them to give the fortress a wide berth as they rode beside it. Lord picked up the pace and then cursed as the wind stole his hat, leaving his head exposed and his hair trailing like a white banner. A loud whistle came from the walls of the castle, dipping in tone, then lifting and breaking, carried by the wind.

Lord's mount seemed to take a marked exception as it curvetted before he checked it, and they went on. Except Gideon was left wondering. He had seen what no other observer could have seen, that Lord had used reins and legs to make the horse perform. He wondered, but was unable to ask, as Lord then pushed the roan to speed and Gideon's bay was left to catch up.

They reached the knot of men and Lord dismounted, throwing his reins to one of the attendants and strode off before Gideon could do the same. The group around the princes parted like the red sea at Lord's approach, closing fast enough behind him that Gideon was hard-pressed to keep up.

"Sir Philip, I am glad you have come so quickly," Prince Maurice greeted them. His brother was talking in a language Gideon did not understand, to a young man who was pointing out details and making calculations on a sheet of paper spread on a tree stump. "The report you provided on Essex, his troops and intentions could have been written by the earl himself."

Which, Gideon realised, it probably had been. Essex must have entrusted Lord with a report to take to London along with his supposed prisoners.

"I am glad it has been of value," Lord said, offering a bow.

The large white dog which had been lying beside Prince Rupert stood up and trotted over to Gideon demanding attention. Embarrassed, Gideon petted it.

"You brought us that report?" one of the other men asked, sounding impressed. Gideon recognised the speaker as the king's Lord-General, Patrick Ruthven, Earl of Forth. This was the man to whom Lord had deferred the offer of command in the council of war before the battle.

"I had the privilege to be able to serve the prince in such a way," Lord said.

"But how the devil did you get such information?" Now there was a touch of suspicion.

"I went in disguise, sir," Lord told him, "I bought a

THE DEVIL'S COMMAND

load of cabbages from a man who was going to sell them in Warwick. In such a way I managed to enter the city, even into the castle, and note what was there, ask questions, discover what was needed and come away again."

"Cabbages?" Forth echoed, as if less certain that his leg wasn't being pulled.

"Nets of cabbages," Lord agreed, face straight, but a slight glint of humour in his eyes that Forth must have missed. "And I borrowed the fellow's hat, coat and sunk-backed horse so I could enter undistinguished. Then when I was finished, I returned them to the man who had lent them to me and said that Prince Rupert thanked him for the loan."

At which those around them started laughing. Whether that was from thinking the whole story a huge joke or from the notion that Lord might be taken for the prince, Gideon was not sure. But it kept anyone from questioning how, in truth, the report had been come by.

The laughter had caught Prince Rupert's attention, or perhaps it was mention of his name, because he stopped what he had been doing, clapped the young man with him on the shoulder and turned to Lord.

Gideon, his hand still occupied petting the dog, found himself the object of Prince Rupert's attention. He was not sure if the look was curious or hostile, but the prince clicked his fingers, and the dog went back to its master.

"I think Boye likes your Mr Fox, Sir Philip," Prince Maurice observed.

"Boye likes anyone he can fool into giving him a

fuss for five minutes." Prince Rupert sounded exasperated. "Never offer him anything to eat or he will follow you to Hades."

There was more laughter and Gideon managed to smile but was sure his face must be scarlet. The last thing he wanted was for the prince to feel he might be trying to win his dog's affection.

"This could be a little time consuming, gentlemen," the prince went on once the laughter had died down. "De Gomme assures me that we can punch through the outer walls this afternoon but then we would need to work on the inner and the keep which, if well defended could hold a while."

"I assume we have offered terms?" Lord said.

The prince nodded.

"Generous enough too, but the commander is the youngest son of Lord Seye, Richard Fiennes. Not yet twenty and determined to prove he can hold the castle against all comers. He has the support of some good troops. Two hundred or so of his father's men and twice as many again of others. The town tells us some of them are foreign."

Lord looked thoughtful.

"Would you be willing to consider allowing me to try to parley, sir?"

The prince frowned at him.

"What do you have to offer that I did not?"

"Nothing, sir. But I can be persuasive. If I succeed it would save us much time and manpower."

The prince pulled a pocket watch from his fob pocket and consulted it.

"You think you can do this?" he asked, looking at Lord who was far enough away from Prince Rupert and tall enough himself, that the prince did not seem to look down on him.

Lord nodded. "I believe so, sir, or I would not suggest it."

There was a short silence with all eyes on the prince, whose own gaze remained on Lord. Then he nodded.

"Very well, Sir Philip, we'll send a flag and see if Fiennes is willing to talk. Though I think after he threatened to beat senseless the next man who came to ask him to surrender, it might be unlikely."

There was more laughter at that as the orders were given and someone took a horse at the prince's instructions and rode off to make the necessary arrangements.

Gideon found himself ignored as Lord was drawn away by Prince Rupert to talk with the military engineer, de Gomme and the great men about him moved to join them or fell to talking amongst themselves.

"You have served Sir Philip for a long time?"

Gideon turned and looked up to meet the brown eyes of the prince's younger brother.

"Not long, highness," he admitted, flustered by the attention. "Since September."

"He seems to think highly of you, though." This prince had more of a French accent to his speech as if less practised in his English than his brother. "You are much in his company nowadays."

Put like that, it did seem strange. After all, why would a man like Sir Philip Lord favour him with friendship over other men who were more of his kind? Even men like Roger Jupp, who was well regarded by

Lord, but never taken into his close circle in the way Gideon had been.

"I believe he finds me useful," Gideon said, wondering why the prince would take such interest in him. Something of his uncertainty must have transmitted itself to Prince Maurice who gave him a smile that held a shyness to it Gideon wouldn't have expected.

"I do not wish to make you uncomfortable," the prince said. "That is more my brother's way. But I find myself curious as to why Sir Philip needs the company of a *lawyer* over that of others at such a time. You are doing some specific work for him?"

Somewhere deep in Gideon's mind, an alarm bell started to clang. It was easy to forget sometimes that Lord was more than a much-admired mercenary commander, he was also a man with a hidden heritage that could prove fatal.

"I work more as a copyist than a legal advisor," Gideon said. "Much of what I need to handle is sensitive intelligence which requires more understanding and discretion than the average clerk might bring to the task."

Prince Maurice tilted his head forward in a slight nod.

"That was what we thought, Robert and I." He gave 'Robert' its French pronunciation. "And my brother asked me to see if you would be interested in working for him in a like capacity."

For a moment Gideon was speechless.

He was being offered Ned Blake's post. The kind of promotion which could be the making of any man. With such a position he could offer Zahara the home and the security she needed. He would be close about the princes and even the king himself. He would become an intimate of the court, trusted with the secrets of those in power, talking daily with princes, dukes, and earls. Such royal patronage could even lead to a knighthood, lands... It was a dizzying prospect. True, he had promised Zahara he would stay with Lord, but then whatever happened Lord would remain with the prince as it was what Kate would wish, so he would be there too.

A saying his physician friend Anders Jensen had told him once came unbidden to his mind. *The requests of great men are commands.* And they were. It was his duty to acquiesce and obey. Lord would see that and understand. A heady vision of his future danced dazzling bright before Gideon's eyes and acceptance hovered on his tongue.

Then he remembered and felt sick.

To Prince Maurice and his brother, he was not Gideon Lennox, he was Mr Fox. How could he begin to explain that, or excuse it, without sounding as if he was engaged in some nefarious deception?

The prince's pleasant gaze was still on him, expectant but patient.

"I understand you might hesitate," he said. "Sir Philip is a man who demands great loyalty from those who serve him, but I would assure you neither my brother nor I would ask you to betray anything of Sir Philip's that you might have been entrusted with to date."

Gideon knew then that the only way forward was through honesty. If he explained and the offer remained, then perhaps all would be well. If it was deemed unacceptable for him to have kept his true name hidden, at least he would have tried. He drew breath to explain that Fox was a nom-de-guerre, but a hand rested suddenly upon his shoulder.

"Please excuse me, highness, I need Fox with me."
Lord's voice.

Prince Maurice stepped away as if he had been caught out in some social *faux pas*. He gave his shy smile to Lord then a glance back to Gideon which told him the matter was deferred not set aside for good.

"Of course. I must not detain you, Sir Philip. Mr Fox and I were having a pleasant *private* conversation that we can continue in due course."

Which, to Gideon's relief, placed a royal seal of silence on any enquiry Lord might make regarding the topic of their conversation.

Having made the appropriate bows and his arm gripped in a vice-like hand, Gideon was pulled through the men about the princes, from the inner circle of nobility and senior command, through a middle layer of officers and out through those charged with guarding their betters, and then the servants and junior officers waiting to be summoned, dismissed or commanded.

Mounted again, they headed back to the town where a rutted, house-lined road led to the drawbridge-protected castle entrance.

"What did you say to the prince's offer?" Lord asked as they reached the edge of the town. His curiosity sounded mild.

"You know?" Gideon was reluctant to break that royal seal of privacy.

THE DEVIL'S COMMAND

"Of course. They came to you because I had told them no."

The strength and suddenness of his own anger took Gideon by surprise.

"You turned it down without even asking me?"

"Yes," Lord sounded unrepentant. "There was no opportunity to mention it to you. At the time you were in Warwick, and I assumed that once I made it clear I had no wish to lose your services, that would be the end of the matter. I saw no reason to trouble you with the issue as I believed it to be closed. My mistake. Had I known the prince would get his brother to ask you whilst keeping me occupied, I would have given you due warning."

"But this is my life you were disposing," Gideon protested. "Without even telling me."

They were close to the Bargate now and Lord shook his head. He sounded sharper than usual. "The prince asked me as I am your present employer. I made a decision about your career that I deem to be in your best interest. There is nothing unusual about that, it is the way of the world."

"And what if I wish to work for the prince?"

Lord looked at him with a frown that contained something of concern and something of surprise.

"Why would you wish it? You are not the kind of man Blake was. You would not survive as long as he did. You are too honest."

Gideon wanted to say he wouldn't be disloyal as Blake had been, but then he realised that was not the point Lord was trying to make. Before he could think how to answer, they had stopped, and Lord was talking to a well-dressed man mounted on a tall and noble-looking grey.

It took a short time to organise the parley group. The man on the grey was one Sir William Howard, a man in his forties, who Gideon gathered had volunteered for the duty. Bearing in mind the threat that Richard Fiennes had made, Gideon decided Sir William was a brave man.

Gideon was handed a plain coat to wear in place of his own and Lord disappeared to return a couple of minutes later, mounted on an ordinary-looking horse and also wearing the coat of a common trooper with his hair hidden beneath his hat.

"When we get inside," Lord explained, "Sir William will be allowed to go alone to present the latest offer to Richard Fiennes and we will be detained as he does so. The first bit, us on horseback, is for show. We will have to dismount to be allowed in. Can you carry a flag? Never mind, I will. Oh, and give me your sword, I promise it will be quite safe. See? It has mine for company. And remember to do what I do, or what I say, and keep your mouth shut."

As Lord had said they needed to dismount by the drawbridge and under the white flag he held, Sir William walked forward towards the closed castle gate. Behind him, Gideon felt his skin prickle as the silent muzzles of a dozen muskets could be seen tracking their progress from the walls. That was when Gideon realised he had been deceived about the castle. This was a significant fortress and if its commander decided to hold out, the king would be forced to delay or leave an enemy strong point in his rear as he advanced towards London.

THE DEVIL'S COMMAND

There were two moats. One around the curtain wall, separating the castle from the town and a second, deeper, from which the castle proper rose and within the walls of which the keep sat high on a raised knoll. The town had managed to spread its way in part behind the curtain wall and the moat there was little more than a ditch, but extra earthworks had been added to the corner of the castle walls.

Walking across the wood of the drawbridge, approaching the high walls, Gideon felt small and impermanent. This castle had stood for many hundreds of years before he was born, its stone facing the world and keeping those within secure, generation after generation. No matter what happened to him inside it today, the castle would still stand and be here for many hundreds of years to come. A solid stone bulwark.

Cold. Impersonal. Daunting.

They had to stop when they reached the gate and wait whilst the wicket was opened. The thundering trundle of chains echoed as the portcullis was lifted. Under the cover of all the sound and perhaps guessing his fear, Lord spoke.

"It might look like a stronghold, but these walls would come down like paper if we brought big guns to bear on them." He nodded to the new earthworks protecting the castle. "Those are all that would make a difference."

Then there was no more chance to talk as the gate was open and they stepped through into the inner bailey. Close to, Gideon could see the fortifications here had not been maintained at their best. Someone had made a recent attempt to repair the places where the weakness would show, but this was a stronghold that was past its prime.

The men who approached them were wearing blue coats. One held a polearm and the other two carried muskets, ported across their bodies so they could be swung down at a moment's notice, and each had a curl of lighted match between their fingers.

"We are here to parley," Sir William protested, "there is no need for such a show of force. I am Sir William Howard, and I am unarmed except with the goodwill of the king who would seek a way for us to resolve this matter peacefully."

The three men were very clearly common soldiers of no standing, but they made no show of deference to Sir William. Instead, the one with the polearm gestured to the stairs into the keep.

"You're to come with us, Howard."

Gideon was shocked. He had heard the 'prentice boys in London and some extreme puritans talk in such a way as if social rank meant nothing, but he had never expected to hear it in the provinces.

Sir William was an able diplomat because he didn't allow their rudeness to ruffle him in the slightest. He turned to Lord and Gideon as if they were in truth the humble soldiers they appeared to be and instructed them to await his return. "You need have no fear, we are here under a flag and that means these people will not abuse you."

Gideon made a brief bow, following Lord's example and stood unmoving as Sir William was escorted up the steps to the keep.

"You two." Another group of four blue-clad

THE DEVIL'S COMMAND

soldiers approached, their faces grim. "Get in the gatehouse, not having you gawking at our defences."

"Bit late for that," Lord murmured.

"You what?" The musket butt came up with the words and would have pounded through Lord's teeth had he not stepped back and used the pole which carried the flag he held to block the blow.

"Leave them be, Bezaleel." The voice came from behind them, and the blue-coated man stepped back.

"Course, sir. I wasn't meaning anything by it. But we had orders—"

"I'll see to it. You four can take yourselves back to the keep."

Gideon risked a glance around as the soldiers walked off, looking unhappy. A man stood there with hair, so short it was barely visible beneath the helmet he wore. He was dressed in a drab grey and the old leather buff coat he wore was stained like a butcher's apron. He had the weathered, wary look that Gideon had become used to seeing in those who lived by the sword. A look that aged any who possessed it. His gaze was dark and compelling, but more compelling was the short-barrelled pistol he held in one hand and the two men behind him who wore similar expressions and cradled muskets.

The man who had spoken before gestured to the door behind him.

"Inside," he snapped. "I don't want to do this with anyone watching."

Furling the flag he carried, Lord obliged and Gideon, sweat breaking out on his shoulders and heart hammering in apprehension, followed him through the door.

THE DEVIL'S COMMAND

Chapter Eighteen

The room in the gatehouse held tables, chairs, a few personal items that had been discarded or forgotten, and five men playing dice in the corner. They glanced up as Gideon and Lord were ushered in the door, then went back to their game.

Gideon was expecting violence and he had little doubt how that would go. Three armed men and the five playing dice, against himself and Lord, who were unarmed, apart from the pole Lord held with a white flag attached to it.

But the first thing Lord did when they got inside was set the flag down beside the door. Only one of the other men who had been outside, came in behind them, and he propped his musket beside the flag then closed the door.

"It's a good thing you can still whistle," Lord said, looking at the brown-haired man who was sliding his pistol back into its baldric.

"Been a few years since I needed to, Schiavono, sir. And maybe is more a good thing you lost your hat."

Lord clapped the man on his shoulder and smiled, shaking his head. Gideon felt a familiar sense of reality spinning itself in a new direction, then he let out a slow breath of relief.

"I thought you were set on going home," Lord said.

"Well, I did, for a time. But things didn't work out, so I came back. I was over in France then I heard things were happening here so me and some boys decided to come along and see if we might help out."

Lord nodded, then he glanced at Gideon beside him and put a hand on his arm, still facing the other man.

"Mr Fox, this," Lord gestured, "is Argall Greene. Mr Fox is my man of law." Greene gave Gideon a brief bow of the head and shoulders as Lord kept talking. "Greene must be one of the very few that can claim the distinction of having been born and raised in our American colonies. He is from Jamestown, Virginia."

"I've not met many men grown can say as much, and none this side of the Atlantic, for sure," Greene agreed.

"And that is how it should be. We have colonies in the new world," Lord explained, "so we can send people over there to get rid of them—dissenters, criminals, undesirables, the masterless, the younger sons of younger sons, heedless adventurers and insane idealists. It is intended as one-way traffic. We don't expect them to start breeding and sending people back."

Greene gave a shout of laughter and the men with him grinned in appreciation.

"Then 'tis my good fortune, that as such a colonist, I don't have to keep to those rules of your old world."

"That is true and is why many men of all sorts and stations have gone, so those rules need not be kept." Lord's expression grew more serious. "But there are rules we must all yet obey. Are you contracted to this man Fiennes?"

"Man?" Greene gave another shout of laughter then his lips curled in contempt. "He's a *boy*. Worst kind. A boy who knows he's not a man but wants the world

THE DEVIL'S COMMAND

to think him one and will do anything to prove himself so, even if it is something no sensible man would countenance."

"You think he won't surrender?"

Greene shook his head.

"Not unless pushed. And no, he's not bought us. We were passing through and the town were so impressed they asked us to stay as they'd heard some German princeling was out raiding and feared for their gold and their women. They gave us some of that gold and then when we showed too much of an interest in the women, decided they liked us less than they thought, so we came here to the castle. That was just in time for word of a fight we missed and then your whole army turns up."

"Not mine," Lord said, "but I'm with it for now." Then he paused and something in the atmosphere changed. "Would you want to work for me again?"

Greene didn't answer at once, then lifted his shoulders.

"You see, we were heading north," Greene said. "I had the word Mags is somewhere in Yorkshire or those parts and has an eye for more good men and the money to pay for them."

Mags recruiting? Gideon felt sick.

"Unless you are set on that course, I could save you the walk and your men would thank you for it. After all, *generally, all warlike people are a little idle, and love danger better than travail.*"

"That is truth told," Greene agreed., "Besides, why should we walk further to serve a lesser man?" He thrust out his right hand and Lord gripped it with his own. "I was going to ask why you had your lawyer with you, sir, but now I see it." Greene nodded at Gideon. "You can contract us on the spot."

"It can be useful to have a man of law to hand," Lord agreed, "but they are *in their nature, a contrariety to a military disposition*."

That earned another shout of laughter which all joined in. Gideon managed to smile but could not help reflecting on the truth of Bacon's words.

"What would you have us do, sir?" Greene asked, and Gideon found himself once again forgotten.

"You can pressure the youngster to surrender?"

Greene looked thoughtful. "We have provisions enough to hold out a month or more and weapons for a thousand men, good stores of powder. But most of Fiennes' men are unseasoned as fresh withies—farm lads or apprentices not soldiers. We've been having to teach them one end of a musket from the other. A handful are fortified by their faith in God, but the rest are scared shitless of what they see going on outside. So, I'm going to say yes. Though it might take a bit of a show of force from your side, sir. Maybe fire some of those guns? But the boy will have to fold if he faces a rebellion from his men and I can arrange that."

The door opened and the man who had remained outside put his head in and said something in German. Greene nodded then looked at Lord expectantly as the man closed the door again.

Lord moved to pick up the flag.

"It seems the talking is over. You had better show us from the premises."

A short time later they were walking back across the

THE DEVIL'S COMMAND

wood of the drawbridge, with an unhappy-looking Sir William Howard.

"I hope, Sir Philip, your ends were achieved," he said. "I have never had to endure such a lecturing from a beardless child in all my life before."

Lord didn't answer him until they were once again in the relative safety of the Bargate where they had left their horses, clothes and weapons.

"Thank you for your assistance, Sir William, the king will soon thank you himself, I am sure when he is resupplied with much-needed munitions and is one fortress and perhaps five hundred men better off."

The older man looked at Lord then, as if seeing him for the first time.

"If you have worked that miracle, then it would have been worth the same a dozen times over indeed. But Fiennes did not seem to me to be at all inclined to surrender."

"He will, and that will be to your greater credit."

Gideon was not permitted to see how it played out from the view he might have had by the guns. Instead of heading straight back to the prince to report their success, Lord detoured to find Jupp, who was with the better part of the cavalry at the edge of the town, waiting to see if they would be needed for any work that day.

"We have some recruits joining us," Lord told him, "I think we have developed a brigade of foot, but there is no need for you to worry about them too much, they will come with their own commander." Then before Jupp could do more than nod his understanding, Lord gestured to Gideon. "Keep Fox with you and keep him safe." He was already turning the blue roan as he spoke and trotted away.

Gideon knew that kind of phrasing well enough by now to translate its meaning. He would not be permitted by Jupp to go anywhere until Lord returned. If need be, he would be prevented from leaving by force. He also knew why, and his anger blazed at the high-handed way Sir Philip Lord had assumed all rights over him as if he were indentured.

A small rational voice pointed out that Lord was right when it came to working for the princes. It would require him to be as duplicitous as every other courtier, every day of his life until he would no longer know what he valued beyond ambition. He would become the kind of man he had always despised. Lord's action was taken to keep Gideon from being subjected to a royal command he would be powerless to refuse.

But the louder voice bellowed in outrage that even if this offer from the princes was not one he should accept, or even could on account of his misconstrued identity, he should still have been told of it. He should have been allowed to consider it for himself. What if it had been one that would offer him preferment without the hazard? Would Lord have kept that from him too?

"What was the Schiavono on about?"

He was so caught up in his own issues it took Gideon a moment to decipher the question Jupp asked.

"About the recruits?"

"That's the thing. We are parlous low on men right now, so low we can't do anything useful as a unit except scouting, but I can't think the Schiavono would be wanting to take on the kind of recruits I've been seeing here. The ones with horses are either too much the gentleman to take orders, or more used to walking behind the horse with a plough than able to ride one, and the infantry are worse. Half only joined because they were told they'd get a pike if they did and thought it meant they'd have fish dinner."

"These seem a bit more experienced than that," Gideon assured him. "They were with a man called Greene. He was someone known to the Schiavono, from Jamestown in Virginia."

Jupp's expression changed.

"Was it Argall Greene? Then the men with him won't match his surname. He's a bit too much of a bastard to keep anyone on his roll unless they can earn their keep."

"You don't like him?" Gideon hazarded.

"Oh, it isn't a matter of liking. I'd have him beside me on any battlefield rather than against me." He looked thoughtful for a moment then shrugged. "It'll work out. The Schiavono knows his business. We need the men. How many?"

Gideon had little idea and had to admit it, so Jupp lost interest and Gideon was left alone nursing his resentment. But at least it stopped him from having to think about the things that were happening that he could do nothing about. Things like Kate.

There was a brief thunder of cannon, the sound echoing off and between the close pressed walls of the city. Some of the horses about them danced around in terror. Gideon's bay flicked his ears and then kept them attentive for a little on the sound that followed. Silence. As if the whole town had been hushed by the roar.

Noises returned, voices, movement, doors shutting and dogs barking. Gideon's gelding relaxed again and for a while, nothing much seemed to happen at all, and Gideon was restored to his brooding. Then there was a cheer from somewhere towards the castle which was repeated a few times. The castle, Gideon assumed, had surrendered as Greene had promised.

A rider came by and said something to the officers of the red-coated regiment Jupp had been attached to and then Jupp was ordering the men to their horses.

"Looks like we're done here," he said to Gideon. "I'd say you should wait for the Schiavono, but he asked me to look after you, so you'd better keep with us, though I've no notion where we'd be going."

"Oxford," one of the men from the main regiment they were with suggested. "The king, I heard, is halfway there already."

Jupp scratched at his beard.

"How far is that?"

"Oxford?" The other man considered. "Thirty miles maybe."

Gideon realised his expression must have given away how appalled he was feeling at the thought of being that far from Wormleighton and Zahara because the soldier gave him a strange look.

"Thirty miles?" Jupp said, his tone considering. "Then I think we'll be staying here after all. Unless my colonel tells me otherwise. I need to send someone to—"

"I'll go," Gideon said quickly.

THE DEVIL'S COMMAND

"No, you won't." Jupp's tone allowed no argument and Gideon's fists balled with frustration. "Olsen, go find the Schiavono and ask if he wants us to march to Oxford or wait on him here. Better be quick."

"I will not go to Oxford," Gideon said between gritted teeth. Jupp shook his head and turned back to the remainder of the company.

Soon they were alone in the field, the other cavalry that had been waiting there all left to take the road south. But they were not the only troops in the field for long.

Gideon spotted the neat ranks of infantry marching towards them from the Bargate. Behind them, straggling a little were a number of women and even some children. At their head was Argall Greene and he lifted a hand in greeting as he caught sight of Gideon.

"God's wounds, the bastard's bringing us half a bloody regiment."

For some reason, Jupp didn't sound delighted.

He shouted some orders at the company, and Gideon fell in with the rest, his knowledge now of the basic drills enough that he did not disgrace himself or Jupp. The dozen men on horses looked like a small honour guard as Greene brought his men to a halt.

"Sergeant Jupp? Or are you Quartermaster now?" Greene asked, looking up at the row of mounted troops and Gideon felt the man beside him bristle.

"Captain," Jupp said.

The atmosphere between the two men was so tense it spoke of some history both would much rather have not had to encounter again. For a moment Gideon thought there might even be swords drawn. But Jupp sat like granite and Greene drew a breath.

"Congratulations, Roger, you deserve it if any man does. The Schiavono always chooses his officers well."

It was as if a boil had been lanced and a moment later, Jupp had swung himself from his horse and the two men were pounding each other on the back like long-lost brothers.

"As you were, gentlemen," Jupp told his men and most dismounted and there were more shouts of delight as old friends were reunited and introduced to new ones. Gideon, as often at such times when those who were comrades in arms were being exactly that, kept to himself, feeling very much an outsider and in some ways glad that he was.

In the midst of it all, Olsen returned with orders for them to remain until Lord came back. However, far from joining the general milling of men on the field, Olsen rode over to where Gideon stood holding the reins of his horse and dismounted beside him.

"I saw a sight I have no wish to see again," he said gravely, "and I would not have spoken of it to anyone else, but I think you should know, sir."

Gideon stared at the Swede wondering what kind of dire news could be heralded in such a way.

"I should know what?" he asked.

"When I found the Schiavono he was with Prins Ruprecht, and they were arguing. It is never good to argue with a prince on any matter, but the Schiavono was furious. I have never seen him so angry, and the prince was white with wrath." Olsen shook his head looking worried. "It was not good. Not good at all."

THE DEVIL'S COMMAND

"So why tell me?" Gideon asked though a corner of his mind suspected he already knew the answer.

"Because it was *you* they were arguing about, Mr Fox. I don't know why, or for what, but I heard your name spoken several times as I was waiting, and I doubt I was the only one who will have heard and marked their quarrel and understood that you were the cause. This could go ill for you."

"I don't see why. It is not as if I have been—"

Olsen gripped his arm as if to make him listen.

"The Schiavono is too important to the prince for him to allow a breach between them. Word is it was he who led the castle here to surrender. But you are not so important in the scheme of things, and it is times like this we who are of little account can be crushed between those who are of much." Olsen released him and stepped back. "Have a care, Mr Fox."

Then he went off to talk to Jupp who was sharing what seemed to be an uproarious tale with Argall Greene, leaving Gideon feeling like a fish that had been left behind on the beach by a giant wave.

Gideon did know enough of the way things worked in this world to understand that by telling him, Olsen had placed himself in some peril. If Gideon were to let Lord know Olsen had spoken to him, the man would be disciplined and maybe even turned off. It was a mark of trust that he had done so, and Gideon knew he would need to be careful to keep that quiet.

But he had little time to consider what, if anything he could or should do about what he had been told. A shout went up and then there was cheering as Sir

Philip Lord rode from the town and rejoined his men.

Dismounting by the first of them he encountered, Lord threw the reins of his horse to the man and then took the time to talk to all those who seemed to know him. Shouts of laughter and more cheers marked his progress, and he was smiling and clapping men on their shoulders. The women pushed forward too, one Lord even embraced and was scolded by, which led to much good-humoured amusement.

Like a man returning to his own, a family reunion of sorts. Lord, exhausted as he must be, afraid for Kate as he was beyond doubt, and desperate to return to her as soon as he could, moved slowly, giving each man or woman he spoke to his full, undivided and unhurried attention.

When he reached the front of the company and stood by the horse lines, he saw Gideon and acknowledged him too with a smile and a nod before turning to face his men.

"I am not sure," Lord began, lifting his voice, and they all fell silent to listen, "I am not sure why you have all come here. France has better weather, better food and better wine."

"And better women," someone from the ranks called out, which earned jocular shouts of outrage and laughter.

"That, Blaise, is a matter of opinion," Lord said when they had quietened again, earning some more laughter. "But what is not an opinion is that there is no finer fighting infantry force on English soil at the moment than the men I see standing here. You will be given the best because you deserve the best—because you are the best."

THE DEVIL'S COMMAND

The cheers that provoked were the loudest yet and it was a while before Lord could make himself heard again.

"I have made provision for you and though you will march as my regiment, under my colours, with Captain Greene as your commander, the Lord-General of the King's Army, the Earl of Forth, has given me his word that you will be provisioned and quartered with his own." That only earned a few calls and not much enthusiasm. "Gentleman, you will be marching to Oxford where I will join you shortly. Until then, if you have to fight, make sure you win."

There were shouts and cheers then, Lord making a point of standing with Greene and saying some things to him that the noise of the men drowned out. Then Greene nodded, gave a smart bow to Lord and shouted to his men.

As if by magic the random groups that made a crowd formed up into neat ranks and files and a few minutes later, to the tuck of their drummer, they had turned to march back through the town to start on the way to Oxford.

Gideon watched the women with handcarts at the rear and a small child sitting on top of a pile of possessions in one sucking its thumb. What kind of world, he wondered, would this war have wrought into being when that child was grown? For at that moment, it felt to him as if this war would be like the Dutch war, eternal and unending, lifetime after lifetime.

Sir Philip Lord spoke beside him.

"We should get back to Wormleighton," he said. "I

have been given permission by the prince to do so on Kate's account."

Gideon nodded but could not bring himself to meet the other man's gaze. Sometimes it was as if they dwelled on separate continents, and right then he felt the distance acutely.

The ride back was made at speed with little talking. Lord was at the front setting a punishing pace whilst the rest of the company were left doing their best to catch up on the varying qualities of horse flesh each man owned. Gideon's bay fell into an easy ground-eating stride which was enough to keep him with Jupp but not to match the stamina and speed of Lord's roan.

As a result, when they clattered through the gates of Wormleighton and into the stable yard there, Lord was already inside the house, and someone was leading his roan away. As Gideon dismounted, Jupp was beside him.

"I'll make sure your horse is tended. You go after him. I've seen that expression on his face once before and that was when they told him Captain Rider had died."

Fearing the worst, Gideon ran up the steps and looked along the passageway. This time there were no guards. He saw Lord standing by the door to the room where Kate was lying. Lord lifted one hand as if to open the door, then lowered it again and leaned his brow against the wooden panels as he had done the previous night.

"I am not sure," he said, straightening up as Gideon reached him, "whether knowing is worse than not knowing and I wonder if that makes me a coward?"

Which was when Gideon had to remind himself that

THE DEVIL'S COMMAND

Lord had no notion that Gideon knew he had been arguing with the prince about Gideon's fate. His anger evaporated and the tight knot of resentment sank from view.

"Let me," he said and tapped on the door.

Chapter Nineteen

The scene was as it had been before, Zahara sitting on a stool beside Kate. The hangings were down on three sides about the bed and the heat from the fire was stifling as every sick room needed to be.

Zahara stood as they entered. Her eyes were hollow in her skull with exhaustion, but she somehow managed a smile for them.

"Lady Catherine is sleeping," she said. "She wanted to stay awake for your return, but she was in so much pain I insisted she took something for that and then she fell asleep."

Relief was chased by concern across Lord's features, and he strode over to look at the sleeping woman, reaching out one hand to brush a hair from her face.

"There is no fever?" he asked.

Fever, as Gideon knew, could be the harbinger of death even if the blood loss had been staunched.

"No. No fever. But pain." Zahara swallowed as if something had caught in her throat. "She is very brave."

"What did the prince's physician say?"

Zahara shook her head. "He was loath to examine her too closely for fear of causing more harm, as he says she will need to be moved. He says once she is in Oxford more can be done. He sets great store by the king's physician Dr Harvey who he was very keen

THE DEVIL'S COMMAND

should see her as soon as possible. Then he left something for her pain. We are almost the only ones here now. All those who were able to travel have gone to rejoin the army. They say this place is now too close to Warwick and it has no proper defences."

Lord nodded and his lips tightened.

"That is true. This is more house than fortress and little has been done to put it into any state of defence. Tomorrow, we will leave ourselves."

"But—"

"I know." Lord's words cut like a whip across Zahara's, and she took a step away from him. He saw her expression and his own changed. He brought both his hands up to cover his face for a moment then released his breath as a shuddering sigh as he removed them again. "I should not...I..."

Zahara moved to him and took his hands in her own.

"You must sleep, Schiavono. You cannot help Lady Catherine if you are so tired. I will wake you as soon as she wakes again." Only then did Gideon realise that Lord had slept little if at all the previous night. Between the sympathy and understanding, Gideon felt a cold sliver of doubt. How far could Lord go without sleep before it began disrupting his judgement? Was that why he had argued with the prince?

Lord was nodding slowly as if even that was too much effort.

"You need sleep too," he said.

"Brighid and Gretchen are coming to take turns and watch, as soon as they have made sure the men have enough to eat. I will sleep in here on a truckle in case

I am needed."

"I could—"

Zahara stopped him with another shake of her head.

"I will look after Lady Catherine. You need to sleep well. You have the world to face for us all and only you can do that."

Lord nodded again and spent a moment more gazing at the sleeping figure on the bed, then he turned back to the door. He hesitated as he reached it and looked at Gideon.

"You had better come with me."

"I will come soon," Gideon said, aware that his tone was too stiff. Seeing Lord's eyes widen he went on, "I wish to speak with Zahara."

Lord gave a nod that was part way between granting permission and acquiescence, then opened the door and went through, closing it behind him.

"You should go rest," Zahara said, standing with her hands clasped as if she was unwilling to let them free.

Gideon crossed to her in two swift strides. Taking her hands, linked as they were in his own and holding her gaze, he lifted them to his lips to kiss the back of one.

"I will if you are," he said. "You look more tired than I feel."

"As soon as Brighid or Gretchen comes, I will sleep," she promised. "You should go now. The Schiavono needs not to be alone."

"The Schiavono wants to dictate my future," Gideon said, the words out before he could recall them.

Zahara studied him, then freed her hands from his,

crossed to where a jug was placed on a table by the bed and poured some of its contents into a cup and brought it to him.

"Tell me what is between you two and drink this, it will help you sleep." He took the cup and sipped the contents. It tasted as old hay might if mixed with honey, the usual flavour of such remedies.

"Prince Rupert wishes me to serve as his privy clerk and the Schiavono refused on my behalf without even asking me. As if it were none of my concern. He even argued with the prince about it. I am not allowed to decide my own path now, it seems."

Zahara said nothing for a few moments as if giving deep consideration to what he said.

"And do you wish to serve the prince?" she asked.

"It would mean I could offer you a future," he said, then felt the colour rise in his face as he realised the assumption that lay behind that.

Zahara's gaze on him was wide and green.

"If I have a future," she said. "I am hopeful you will be with me in it. But I do not see how that could be if you were to work for the prince. I do not think I would like the kind of man you would have to become to do so." She paused and then shook her head. "I do not think you would like to become that kind of man, either."

Her words flowed over him more healing than the remedy she had given him to drink. But the resentment had spent too long burrowing under his skin to release him.

"It's not even about this post. It's that I'm no more than another playing piece that Sir Philip Lord can dispose of as he chooses on the gameboard of his life. He decided for me."

"Did you tell him you wished to accept the prince's offer?"

Gideon frowned.

"Well, no, I—" He broke off.

"Do you want to take it?"

He shook his head.

"No. Not now."

"Then the Schiavono did the right thing when he argued with the prince on your account. Everyone knows the prince has a temper, but everyone also knows it is wise not to provoke that temper. You are fortunate. There are not many who would do such a thing for a friend."

The enormity of it struck home and Gideon shook his head.

"I didn't think—"

Zahara nodded at the cup he still held.

"You should finish that," she said. Then, as he drank the last of it down, "The Schiavono told me the prince asked him for you when you were in Warwick. He was angry that the prince should think you were like a dog or a horse that could be given or taken whether you wished to be or not, and he said that he would not allow it to happen to you."

Gideon choked on the mixture he was swallowing.

Zahara took the cup from him as he coughed, just as the door opened and Brighid Rider slipped inside to join them, smoothing her hair down when her eyes met Gideon's gaze and making a small curtsy.

Zahara touched the back of his hand.

"You should get some sleep now," she said, her

voice soft.

Gideon nodded and then left.

The servants seemed to be already asleep or gone as there was no one around that Gideon could see. Lit by a candle taken from a sconce, he managed to get lost on the upper floor of the house before he found Lord's room, and he only found it because Shiraz was outside the door. He shook his head as Gideon approached and jerked his chin towards the room next door.

Feeling more than a little awkward about entering a room to which he had not been shown in a stranger's house, Gideon consoled himself with the thought that the owners of the house, although not in residence, had seemed to be happy enough to have the princes and their cavalry staying and Lord's much-diminished horse were not a comparable burden.

The room was cold, and he was pretty sure the bed was well slept in, but he was too tired to care and troubled to remove no more than his sword, pistol, coat and boots before climbing into it and falling asleep.

He seemed to be awoken moments later.

"Gideon. Get up. We have to go. *Now.*" Lord's voice came from close by, urgent and commanding.

Blinking himself awake, Gideon pulled back the hangings and saw Lord had lit the candle he had extinguished before sleep. The first trace of light was framing the window as dawn drew breath to break.

"Good," Lord said, seeing him. "Hurry."

Then he strode back across the room and was gone.

Thankful he had slept in his clothing, Gideon pulled

on his boots and fought back into his coat before slinging his sword to hang on one thigh and his pistol on the other. There were sudden shouts from outside and he rushed to the window in time to hear shots and the cold sound of steel blade on steel blade.

The glance he got was enough to tell him what had happened.

Though the mist and frost still held, a small patrol of Parliamentarian cavalry, perhaps a dozen, had come to investigate the house. Lord's men had waited until they were in the stable yard and then launched an effective and bloody ambush. Men and horses, breaths misting in the cold air, heaved in the confined space. There were two bodies already on the cobbles and as Gideon looked, an arrow sliced through the neck of another man and he was thrown, choking. A horse had been cut open and blood and guts from it were trailed over the ground. Another man who must have been dismounted before the attack began, slid and fell to be trampled beneath the hooves of his comrades as they tried to turn to flee. The horses' dying screams echoed off the walls and drowned the shrieks of the dying men.

"We need one alive," Jupp's voice carried over the chaos.

Gideon had stood by the window for perhaps as long as it might take to count to five, but what he had seen was more than enough. It was burned deep into his memory and would haunt him always. Feeling sick, he grabbed his hat and ran from the room, taking the stairs down in twos. The door to the hall was open and Gideon heard Zahara's voice, so he changed his destination and went that way. The big room was

THE DEVIL'S COMMAND

filled with a huddle of terrified servants, and Zahara was there talking to them, her voice calm, assuring them they were safe. She gave Gideon a brief smile.

"The Schiavono is outside," she told him.

"Keep these people inside if you can," he said. Then lifted his voice so they would all hear. "There is fighting going on outside. We are winning and all will be well, but right now it is dangerous to leave the house."

The chance shot that came through one of the large windows, shattering some panes, but missing anyone inside, added extra credence to his words and most of the women and many of the men crouched or tried to get under the big table.

"Yes, keep low." He had to shout to be heard. "Keep away from the windows and keep low."

"Go," Zahara told him. "We are safe here. Gretchen is with Lady Catherine. I will be with her as soon as the fighting is done."

Gideon had no wish to leave her but knew his duty was to join the defence and that was also the way he could best ensure her safety and that of the others inside the house. He ran through the empty building, only stopping when he reached the door to the stable yard.

There were no sounds of ongoing violence now, only voices. He heard Lord's raised in cold anger.

"You had no right to promise him quarter, what if he finds out we are heading west to Stratford and Worcester? If his friends find him and release him, then they will be after us more quickly and in greater numbers than if they had to split their force not knowing where we were going."

"I'm sorry, sir," Jupp sounded crestfallen. "I thought it seemed the fastest way to get the information out of him at the time."

"You mean you did *not* think," Lord snarled. "By God, I'll have you flogged for that. Now make sure we are ready to leave for Worcester within the half-hour."

Gideon felt a sick kind of sorrow coursing through his veins, which meant he was unprepared, as he stepped outside to see Jupp grinning and Sir Philip Lord, gripping him by the shoulder in a gesture of approval.

"Fox," Lord said, as he turned. Gideon froze, his confusion complete. Lord strode over, his voice lowered. "I need you to get my desk, it will have to go in the carriage. We're not taking any wagons. Everything and everyone are on horseback, except for the carriage. I'll need to use both your horses. You will have to decide which to ride."

"Why are we going to Worcester?"

Lord's mouth opened and then he closed it again and shook his head with an expression of exasperation. He spoke in a low voice.

"*He is deceiv'd, and in his great deceit, he doth deceive the folly-guided hearts.* If we are lucky, that is."

Then Gideon realised and felt his colour heighten. But greater than any embarrassment was a wash of relief that he had been wrong about Lord.

"I see," he said, knowing how weak that must sound.

"We have very little time. The sounds of those shots

will carry and if the man Jupp interrogated is telling the truth, we can soon expect a visit from a regiment or more of cavalry who are sweeping this area to clear it of any lingering Royalist malignants such as ourselves. Get my desk, put it in the carriage." Lord pressed the key into Gideon's hand. "We don't want to make the same mistake as the Earl of Essex and leave incriminating documents behind."

Lord turned and strode off, calling new orders and Gideon went back into the house and ran upstairs.

The portable desk was locked already but there was a packet of documents sitting on top of it, so Gideon opened it and put them inside before locking it again. He had picked up the heavy wooden case by its leather travelling strap when he saw another document that must have slid between the bottom of the box and the table it was set on. Rather than reopen and relock the box, he pushed the document into his doublet for safekeeping. He took a moment more to look around and make sure no more papers had escaped, then heaved the heavy box onto his shoulder and headed back down the stairs.

He had feared he would be required to go into the stable yard with its burden of carnage and gore and had steeled his stomach to manage if he had to do so. But at the bottom of the stairs, he caught sight of the carriage, still with its distinctive black and yellow livery, outside the main door. Bela Rigó stood holding the horses. Grateful that he was spared the stable yard, Gideon loaded the portable desk and secured it as best he could. Then he went back into the house to make sure Zahara was managing the household.

The first thing he heard was Lord's voice, lifted to carry, addressing the household staff.

"You should all leave now. Go to friends, family, anywhere you may. The soldiers who will come will not be kind as we have been kind. They will not protect and respect you as we have protected and respected you. They will treat you as their enemy because you have treated us as your friends—and they may be brutal."

A clamour of voices answered him, and he had to call for silence to be heard.

"Those of you who have nowhere to go, come and speak with Brighid and your Housekeeper Abigail here, they will tell you what you must do. The rest go now and gather what possessions you may carry. You need to be gone from here within the half-hour. Now hurry."

Gideon stepped aside to avoid those of the household staff who came out through the door, though most it seemed had either taken the route that led to the kitchens and thence to various outbuildings or were those with nowhere to go. He assumed Zahara must be with Kate if other women were dealing with the servants and was about to go towards her room when Lord strode from the dining hall and saw him.

"Did you get my desk? Good. Then I need you with me, we have to move Kate to the carriage."

He didn't break his stride and Gideon followed him along the passageway. Shiraz was standing by the bed, his hand falling back from his sword when he saw who entered, Zahara didn't turn, she was tucking the blankets around her patient.

THE DEVIL'S COMMAND

Kate was lying swathed in a cloak and blankets to protect her from the cold, her face as pale as the linen cover on the pillow beneath her. Someone had taken a door from one of the rooms in the house and that had been pushed under the feather bed beneath her. Gideon could see that Zahara had made some effort to put her hair in order as it lay about her face.

Seeing them Kate mustered a brave smile

"Are we off and away again?" Her tone was light as if they planned a pleasing outing for her.

"We seem to have outstayed our welcome," Lord told her, returning her smile and putting his hands around one corner of the door that was her support. He gestured to Gideon who moved to help lift at another corner. With a bit of repositioning, Shiraz and then Zahara each managed to take a corner.

"I thought we had been good company too," Kate said and sang softly as they lifted her.

"Company with honesty
Is virtue vices to flee:
Company is good and ill
But every man hath his free will—."

She broke off on a sharp breath as the board caught on a door jamb jarring her. After that they navigated through the house in silence, taking great care when going down the steps at the front.

At first, Gideon couldn't see how they could get Kate into the carriage, but then he realised there was no intention of leaving her on the door. Somehow, they managed to move the featherbed onto the carriage seats. Zahara slipped into the carriage too. Lord dropped a kiss onto Kate's lips and closed the door.

As they had been struggling with getting Kate stowed, the rest of the company had formed up around them, the women all riding pillion, bags and boxes over horses' backs. The horses they had won from the scouting force that had been ambushed in the stable yard, more than doubled their available mounts.

"Fox!"

Gideon looked around to see his bay furnished, reins held by a mounted Olsen. Beside him, Jupp was holding Lord's roan and was riding his cremello. Mounting, Gideon glanced around at the throng of men, and a few women, on horseback. There were one or two unfamiliar faces, which Gideon could only assume were servants who had nowhere else to flee. He caught sight of his chestnut mare now demoted to being a pack animal.

"Gentlemen," Lord's voice brought virtual silence, except for the scraping of hooves and the snorts of horses. "We do not fight unless we have no choice. Our sole purpose, our duty, is to get ourselves and Lady Catherine to safety." He paused and Gideon was sure he was holding the gaze of one or two of the more hot-headed. "And," he added in a different tone, "if that is not good enough for you, think of the warm bed, the good meal and the fine ale that awaits us, and that will spur you to speed if nothing else does."

There was laughter, breaths misting, and a subdued cheering as Lord led them away from Wormleighton, their home for the past week.

They had not gone more than half a mile before Lord took a path into a coppiced woodland, the naked

THE DEVIL'S COMMAND

trees with their bolls spiked like giant clubs rooted in the soil. For a moment Gideon was confused as this was a difficult route for the carriage, but then he saw there was a wide track, well rutted and used by local people.

Lord called to Shiraz and with a single upward nod of his head in acknowledgement, Shiraz turned his black gelding to follow the track to the west. Gideon was pretty sure he knew why. If any of them could attempt setting a false trail well enough to convince their pursuers they had indeed headed towards Worcester, Shiraz was the one best able to do so.

Then the company headed south and east, rejoining the road below the trees. Helped by ground that was flat and cold enough to be hard, the pace was a steady ground-eating one which Gideon knew from experience they could maintain for several hours. Unencumbered by any lumbering heavy carts, they made good time and they only had to reach the environs of Banbury less than ten miles away to be safe. Even taking a less direct route should not add more than a couple of miles to their journey. By mid-morning all being well, they should be safe in Banbury and able to take the journey on from there to Oxford at a more gentle pace.

The shout from the rearguard after they had put perhaps three miles between themselves and Wormleighton made heads turn. Lord reined, gesturing Jupp to keep going. Looking back, Gideon saw a plume of dark smoke rising to join the grey clouds above. It took him a moment to realise what he was seeing, then he knew and felt sick.

Now he understood why Lord had told all the household servants to leave. Gideon hoped they had gone fast enough and far enough. A keening cry from one of the women he didn't know was hushed by another and burdened now by the knowledge of what their presence had done to Wormleighton, the company ran south. Gideon hoped that their pursuers would either be misdirected by the ruse or not wish to venture this close to a Royalist-held town, but with the main body of the army already well south of that, it was hard to be sure how far or hard they might be pursued.

They had been following the river southwards. Jupp explained they were heading to the bridge at Cropredy so they could cross there to reach the main Banbury road. Indeed, they might well have made it through without incident had not Bela Rigó, who was driving the carriage, called Lord over as they left a village called Claydon. Lord halted the company.

"We have to find someone with the tools to fix a loose wheel," he told Jupp, and Gideon felt his stomach sink. It was not that surprising. After all, they had not granted the carriage much for its needs and the roads which were not so difficult for a horse would be wrecking at speed for a vehicle, and this one had already endured more than its makers ever envisioned for it in the run from Warwick.

"We could go to the priory, sir."

The voice was young and female. It was easy to spot who it belonged to as she had turned bright red as she sat her pillion, as everyone looked at her. She was one of the young maid servants they had brought with them from Wormleighton

THE DEVIL'S COMMAND

"The priory?" Lord asked.

"We're close by Clattercote Priory, sir," she told him, speaking like a river in spate, her words tumbling out in a nervous flood.

She said had been born in Claydon and everyone in Claydon knew that Sir Henry Boothby, who had lived at the priory since the death of his mother Lady Judith two years ago, was a king's man. But that was not so surprising seeing as his half-sister was married to the Earl of Newcastle, and the Priory was a big house, bound to have what would be needed to fix a wheel as it used to be a proper monastery once, with real monks, where they looked after lepers. In fact, there was this big pond where the lepers used to bathe, and her mother said that the local children—

Lord held up a hand as if to shield himself from the flow of words.

"Thank you. Martha, is it?"

The young woman nodded.

"A sixpence for your help," he said and pushing his horse forward, pressed the silver coin into her hand. To Gideon, it seemed very much as if he was buying her silence.

"Where is this house?"

Martha pointed along the road. "You see that bent tree? The road to it is there, you'd see the house from here but for the trees."

Another shout went up from the rearguard. A lone rider coming towards them at speed. Shiraz. He made a wide gesture with one hand as he saw them, and Lord swore loud enough to make Martha and some of the others they had rescued from Wormleighton draw a quick breath.

"We will have to take the carriage to this Clattercote Priory and hope for the best. Jupp, you will take the company and these our guests on to Banbury and bring out support if there is any to be had. If we can get the carriage out of sight, they should chase you and you should have no problem keeping ahead of them. I will keep Shiraz and Rigó, stealth not numbers will be what aids us here."

Gideon's voice clashed with Jupp's.

"I'm coming with you. Zahara is in the carriage."

"Sir, we can't leave you—"

Lord was looking back along the road. He spoke with a terse authority.

"Fox, you can stay with me. Jupp, you have your orders, obey them and get these people and the rest of the company to safety. Now ride on."

He matched deed to word himself and headed to the tree Martha had indicated, waiting there as a tight-lipped Jupp led the main body of the company past it. As Rigó turned the carriage into the side path, Gideon saw Shiraz wheel away through the trees again.

"As fast as you think we can in safety," Lord told the Hungarian as the carriage began along the track.

"That would be a stately walk then, Schiavono, sir," Rigó said, but nonetheless gathered the reins and pushed the horses into a pacing trot, the carriage bumping in an alarming manner, its body swinging on the suspended straps as the impact of the loose wheel made itself more obvious.

Chapter Twenty

Gideon's first impression of Clattercote Manor was that it owed more to its remote monastic past than the last century of secular life. The house itself had been remodelled in a style that spoke to more recent times, but somehow that didn't make it seem any less austere, with its high walled gardens and bleak front under glowering gables.

Gideon heard the sigh of relief from Lord as they passed under the arched gate that must once have been the entrance to the religious foundation buildings and they were finally invisible from the road. A high walled barn was set, doors open, on one side as if eager and ready to embrace the carriage.

But even as Lord gestured Rigó towards it, Gideon could see that the reason the door was open was that two horses had been offered temporary accommodation within and were in the process of being fed. Rigó swung down from the driving seat and led the coach horses into the barn ignoring the protests of the boy feeding the ones already there.

A group of ten men had emerged from behind the house. Most were clad in red coats of varying shades, all wore swords, and carried muskets. Except for their two officers. One was a man in middle age, who Gideon presumed must be Sir Henry Boothby, as he was dressed in a fine black worsted and wreathed in fury with a fowling piece held in his hands. The other was a younger man in the same red as the men but armed with sword and pistol. Behind them were two sturdy-looking servants, clutching long poled agricultural tools.

The younger officer barked an order.

"Make ready. Present." A light clatter of sound as hammers were cocked and frizzen pans uncovered. One or two men were blowing on their match.

Gideon joined Lord, dismounting to face the righteous wrath of Sir Henry.

"What in God's name do you think you are doing, sir?" Boothby demanded and behind him, eight muzzles were lifted matchcords burning. "How dare you ride in here as if you own it all." His outrage made his moustache quiver. "I know you rebels have no respect for rights and property, but you have made a mistake here. Whoever you are, you are now a prisoner and I demand you lay down your weapons or my men will shoot you like the treacherous curs you are."

Lord stood beside Gideon still holding the reins of his horse and made a bow.

"I fear you are mistaken, Sir Henry, we are as loyal as you are. I am Colonel Sir Philip Lord, and I am here to seek your assistance. The rebels you speak of are indeed not far from us and in some strength."

"A likely tale," Sir Henry snarled, "You are Lord Brooke's men. I saw the carriage and I know that poltroon is more than proud of it.

"The proof I can offer is inside that carriage," Lord said, "which I took from Lord Brooke much against his will."

"If there is such proof, we will uncover it presently. But I would suspect whatever it might be. Now your

THE DEVIL'S COMMAND

weapons, man, whoever you are, or I will order my men to fire."

Gideon, seeing no other option, started reaching to remove his baldric, but Lord's free hand gripped his wrist stopping him.

"That might cost you two fine horses as well as two loyal men," Lord said as Gideon released the leather strap again, heart hammering. There were times he wondered if Lord's arrogance was going to be the cause of his death.

He jerked his hand away from Lord's grip and, as he did so, he caught and pulled at his doublet beneath his open coat, ripping a button and some stitches. The paper he had stuck in it in his rush to leave Wormleighton fell out.

He bent with the instinct of years that meant every document was precious and needed to be treated with care and respect. Then he saw the signature and realised this one was indeed precious.

"If you will forgive me, Sir Henry, I have the proof you seek. You will know this signature and it will confirm Sir Philip is indeed who he says he is."

Lord frowned at him.

"Then bring it here man, and let me see it, whatever it is. But if you try to touch your weapons or if this is some tomfool trickery…"

Clutching the document at arm's length and feeling as if it were a periapt that might keep him safe from the hollow-mouthed muskets, Gideon walked over to Sir Henry.

Sir Henry snatched the document from him, opened it, squinted at the page and then blinked.

"This is Prince Rupert's signature," he agreed. Then he handed the document to the younger man beside him who read it, frowning.

"This says it is to Sir Philip Lord asking him to join the prince at Banbury immediately. It is dated yesterday."

Without missing a breath, Sir Henry pivoted his wrath.

"You are late then, sir," he snapped at Lord. "You should have joined the prince yesterday."

"I did, Sir Henry, but that was yesterday," Lord said. "I had to return to Wormleighton to rescue my wife. It is she who is in Lord Brooke's carriage, and she is badly injured."

Sir Henry snatched the note back from the man who had read it and squinted at it again, then thrust it back at Gideon.

"And who are you, sir, to be carrying such notes in your coat?"

"My lawyer and regimental clerk," Lord said, "Gideon Fox. He was named by the king for his courage at Kineton, as you may have heard."

Sir Henry had not, but the officer beside him was nodding.

"I recall hearing that name," he said, "and I recall Sir Philip was one of those knighted on the battlefield for redeeming the royal standard."

"Then why didn't you say so?" Sir Henry roared. He strode over to Lord, and the officer turned to the musketeers.

"As you were. Cover your pan. Uncock your match. Slope your musket."

The change of mood was dizzying. Gideon felt

THE DEVIL'S COMMAND

much safer once the muskets were no longer pointed towards him.

By then Sir Henry had his arm around Lord and was trying to draw him towards the house.

"I was released by the king to be sure my house was safe, but I will be rejoining the army tomorrow. You must stay for dinner at least. Tell me how you managed to steal Robert Greville's damn carriage. Your man Fox is a lawyer you say? Is he a good one? I need a good lawyer. My damned brother thinks he should have this house and has gone crying to the law with it."

Lord tolerated it thus far, then Gideon saw something inside him snap.

"I regret, Sir Henry, there is no time. The force that pursues us set Wormleighton ablaze for harbouring us, your own house is at risk if we are found here and—" he broke off as Shiraz appeared riding hard making a high gesture. "They have sent a scouting force this way, it will be here at any moment. Deny our presence and they may leave."

"You mean I should *lie* to these rebels?" Sir Henry made it sound as if he was being asked to pot-roast his firstborn.

Lord shook his head.

"I mean, Sir Henry, that if you do not convince these men that you have not seen me and the carriage, they will summon their main force and treat this house the same as they treated Wormleighton. Worse perhaps, because we rescued the women and servants from there and you do not have men here in adequate numbers to defend this house."

Sir Henry stood there blinking for a moment then seemed to come to himself.

"Yes. I see that," he said. He drew a shuddering breath and pulled his shoulders back. "It is needful in the king's service, so it is honourable, and I will do it."

Lord clapped a hand on his shoulder. "I will ensure the king hears of your courage."

Sir Henry looked at Lord then as if seeing him for the first time.

"Knight banneret. That is quite remarkable," he said. "Well done, sir. I will do this. Have no fear."

Then he made a stiff bow to Lord who rewarded him with a tight smile.

"Remember you have not seen us, that is all you need to say. Now, you should go back into the house and quickly."

Shiraz had gone into the barn already and Gideon followed Lord into the building and helped pull the doors closed.

"How did you happen to have that message to hand?" Lord asked as the doors shut.

"It was on the table after I picked up your desk. I had no time to unlock it again."

"You damaged your doublet," Lord observed. "Give it away. You have earned a new one. In silk, with slashes. I do not look after you anything like as well as I should."

Gideon might have answered that, but the sound of hooves reached them.

"If Boothby messes this up…" he murmured.

"If he does, we kill these scouts and hope Jupp can bring support before the main force get here," Lord

THE DEVIL'S COMMAND

said, his voice tight.

He didn't need to say what would happen if Jupp failed, Gideon's mind was full of what he had seen Digby's men doing to the Parliamentarian baggage. As those who pursued them had fired Wormleighton, he knew to expect little else at their hands.

Shiraz stood beside Gideon, his bow ready and Bela Rigó, grim-faced, was checking his pistol. Gideon glanced at the carriage and saw Zahara standing by the horses soothing them and the stable boy huddled in a corner looking terrified.

Gideon gripped his sword. If anyone came through the door, he would kill them before he would let them get near the carriage. There was no doubt in his mind that he would, and could, do so. The three men he stood with, he knew, were as committed.

It all depended on a rather unintelligent middle-aged gentleman with a profound sense of honour and social aspirations. Gideon found himself wondering not so much if the man *would* lie as if he *could* lie. Or if he did, could he do so in a convincing enough manner?

The horses stopped outside the barn and Gideon decided from what he heard there must be ten or twelve. Enough that between Boothby's men and themselves they should be able to put them down. But then any gunfire would bring the main force onto them.

"Search the place," an officer snapped and as footsteps came closer Gideon felt Lord tense beside him and nod to Shiraz who moved to the far side of the carriage, nocking an arrow as he did so.

"What the devil do you think you are doing, Thomas?" The outrage in Sir Henry's voice was perfect. "This is my house, if you think you can walk in and take what you want you are much mistaken, sir. Get away from my barn, there is a pregnant mare in there near to her time and needing shelter in this cold. I'll not have your men terrifying her. Whatever it is you want, just tell me and then you can go."

The footsteps had stopped when Boothby shouted, and Gideon could picture the same scene that had greeted them. The row of musket barrels levelled and ready, but he suspected that these men would not have been taken by surprise and would have their weapons to hand.

"I have no wish to quarrel, Henry," the officer, presumably Thomas, said. His tone was more placating than Gideon might have expected and his voice strangely similar to Sir Henry's. "I have come to recover stolen property. Some renegades made off with an expensive coach belonging to Lord Brooke. They are dangerous men, traitors to the king and his parliament. I am sure you would not countenance theft or shelter thieves."

Gideon had a sudden conviction that this must be some relative. One ranged on the opposite side of this war to Sir Henry. Whether that boded well or ill was much harder to judge. Would Boothby be willing to kill a relative to protect strangers? Gideon found he was holding his breath and beside him, Lord and Rigó were like statues, their faces cold and hard.

"Fine words from a man who would be a thief himself if he could," Sir Henry snapped. "You will not turn me out of my house. Mother wanted it for me, she told me as much before she died. Her exact words were 'do not let that false and cruel, unnatural eldest son of mine take the Priory from you'. She rewrote her will nine years before she died and no matter what you might think, a later will takes precedence over an earlier one."

This was the kind of matter which had formed the bread and butter of Gideon's work in London, but here, with the brothers ranged on the opposite sides of this war, there was not going to be any simple legal solution for either of them. More to the point, what if brother Thomas decided that this was a good chance to rid the world of brother Henry? Or vice versa? His hand tightened on his sword hilt, and he managed to find a small corner of his mind where he could offer up a prayer.

"False and cruel?" Thomas made a snorting noise. "Is that how she described me? If anyone was unnatural it was her. A woman running around as if she was the equal of any man, making decisions about this place without even consulting me."

"Our mother rebuilt the house with her own resources," Sir Henry snarled. "She enclosed the land, grew our flocks and cattle. She was better at managing the estate than most who call themselves 'gentlemen' around here. How dare you—?" Then something must have reminded him that there was more at stake than a family quarrel because he broke off and snapped. "It will be settled in court."

"In court. Quite so," Thomas echoed. "But this matter that brings me here cannot wait. Have you seen the desperate men I spoke of? They would be travelling with a carriage painted in Lord Brooke's colours."

"Do you think I would tell you even if I had?" Sir Henry said, his tone scoffing. And Gideon's blood ran cold. "Now take your men and get off my property."

"I can order a search and—"

"Search? Search what? There is nowhere to hide a carriage in the house and if anyone had tried to put one in any of the outbuildings you can be sure I would have been told about it. You wish to sack and burn the Priory? What would be your inheritance then? Now run back to your rebel masters before I start shooting your horses."

There was a silence in which Gideon could almost hear the thoughts that must be running through Thomas Boothby's mind. No doubt he had volunteered to scout Clattercote, and he would have much in mind what had been done to Wormleighton already that morning. If he was indeed seeking to take possession of the house one day, he would not want to risk something like that happening here.

"All you have told me betrays you have no knowledge of those I am seeking," Thomas said at last. Then his tone shifted, and he sounded almost weary. "You never were a clever man, and you have made a mistake in choosing your loyalty. I can be patient and the Priory will be mine. But for all that, we are brothers and I hope not to be forced to fratricide on the battlefield. God keep you."

"I hope God will forgive you, Thomas, because I am not sure I ever can," Sir Henry spat back. "You are a vile, ignominious, arrogant and yes, unnatural, son and brother. Now get off my land."

THE DEVIL'S COMMAND

Gideon was sure that must be more than any man would take, brother or no, but the tense silence stretched on for longer than seemed possible.

Then, "Mount up, we are leaving," Thomas' voice was sharp and hard before the sound of hooves retreating. As they faded into the distance, Gideon lifted his hat to wipe the sweat from his brow and realised he was breathing again.

Bela Rigó moved to open the door, but Lord caught his arm and then shook his head. Some five minutes later they heard Sir Henry's voice, as tired and worn as his brother had sounded.

"They have gone. I think they will not be back." Then the door was heaved open from the outside to reveal Sir Henry, the young officer and the two servants who had been with them before.

Lord made a bow. "You have my thanks and my sympathy. It cannot be easy to have one's family divided by this war."

Sir Henry shook his head.

"We were divided long before that," he said and now there was a touch of sadness in the anger. "But come, it is not safe for you to remain here longer. I will have Joseph show you the back ways to Banbury."

"We cannot depart yet," Lord said. "The carriage has a loose wheel and if that is not corrected…"

"Can you not leave the wretched thing here? It will be safe enough and you can send someone to fetch your ill-gotten gains when the opportunity arises."

"My 'ill-gotten gain', as you call it," Lord said, and Gideon could hear he was restraining his impatience, "is a necessity not a luxury. It contains my wife who has been severely injured and is unable to ride. I need to get her to Oxford and safety as soon as I may. Banbury is a way station, and that carriage is the best means we have for her to travel."

Sir Henry looked at his men.

"I could fetch Bill from Claydon," one suggested. "He's good with wheels."

"Is he someone to trust?" Lord asked.

"He's my brother-in-law," the man said. Which answered the question less well than he thought it did.

Lord nodded. "There is no one here with the skill?"

"Oh, I could put a wheel back on that had come off, well as any man. But if you want one repaired to get you to Oxford, you need Bill."

"Very well. I will send one of my men with you. Promise Bill an extra crown for his trouble and there is a shilling for you if you bring him right away. I'm sure I need not tell you that secrecy is needed."

After the man had set off accompanied by Rigó, Lord turned down the offer of dinner in the house but asked if they might impose on Boothby's goodwill for some food to eat in the barn. "I have not had much time to spend with my wife recently," he explained.

Lord sat in the carriage with Kate and the murmur of their voices reached Gideon where he sat with Zahara. The stable boy had shot from the barn like the bullet from a musket as soon as he saw the way clear to do so and Shiraz had taken some of the food and vanished outside, no doubt to keep watch.

It was the closest to privacy and time together Gideon had been able to enjoy with Zahara for a while. An enforced time of inactivity whilst they

THE DEVIL'S COMMAND

waited for Rigó and Sir Henry's man to return with Bill of Claydon.

They ate, and by unspoken agreement, talked of only inconsequential things, as if they were sat at a table in some inn. Only when Zahara gathered up the remains of the food to keep for later did Gideon broach the topic he wanted to ask about.

"How is Lady Catherine?" he asked.

"She is enduring," Zahara said. "But it is hard for her. She is in a lot of pain and the roughness of the road is far from easy to bear. But she will do whatever is needed. She is brave."

"You are brave too," Gideon said and Zahara smiled.

"I have no need to fear," she said, "not for myself. I only fear for you and for the Schiavono."

Without thinking Gideon reached out to brush away a strand of hair that had escaped from her coif and lay over her cheek.

"Will you always stay with the Schiavono?" he asked. It was a question that had troubled him more and more as time went on and the incident with the princes had highlighted it even more in his mind.

"I do not know," she said. "*Insha'Allah*."

"What does that mean?"

"It means if God wills it."

Gideon felt the distance between them grow.

"But what does Zahara will? What would you like to do?"

For a moment he believed he had said something terrible because her eyes filled with tears and she looked away, blinking them back.

"I'm sorry," he said, "I was not meaning to—"

She looked up and then leaned in towards him, kissed her own fingers and pressed them for a moment to his cheek. Then she sat back and smiled with brimming eyes.

"There is only one man apart from you who ever asked me that question," she said, by way of explanation. "Only one man. Ever."

"And how did you answer him?" Gideon asked, knowing who she must mean and understanding now so much he had not before.

"I told him, 'I do not yet know'."

"And he took you to Kate?"

Zahara nodded.

"And do you know, now?"

She drew a breath as if she was going to answer then released it without speaking and turned her gaze to hold his own. Once he had thought them kitten-green, but now they seemed more like the depths of a mysterious forest.

"I know I would wish you to be with me," she said. "I do not know how that can be in the ways the world would allow to either of us."

"You mean because of your religion?"

That made her smile.

"God would never divide heart from heart," she said. "*Far or near there is no halting-place upon Love's road.*"

Gideon shook his head, the confusion weighing over the hope of a moment before.

"I don't understand," he said.

"And I cannot explain until you do."

He wanted to tell her that was unfair. But her gaze

hadn't faltered, and he could see the sadness and yearning reflected in her eyes that wrapped itself around his own heart.

"But there is hope?"

She reached out and took one of his hands in both her own.

"With the Beloved, there is always hope."

"Zahara." Lord's voice came urgently from within the carriage. She was on her feet in a moment, Gideon close behind.

"I think I might have the start of a fever," Kate's voice said, sounding weaker than before. Lord had to climb from the carriage to allow Zahara to get in and he stood, face pale, staring at the open door, waiting for the words that would bring his world into desolation.

Zahara said something to Kate that was so quiet Gideon did not catch it, and then she came out of the carriage, holding her bag.

"I will mix something," she said. "It will help. You should sit with your wife, Schiavono. Soon we will be travelling again and there will be no opportunity for you to do so." Then Zahara turned to Gideon and before he could speak, she said, "I need you to go to the house and fetch me some clean, hot water, please."

He went.

By the time he returned with the jug of boiled water and a cup, Bela Rigó was back, the carriage was supported in one corner by a barrel and Bill was working to mend the wheel. Lord was standing alone, outside the barn, looking through the open gate to the track beyond and the fields around that.

Zahara took the jug and the cup, thanking Gideon with a smile then nodded towards Lord.

"The Schiavono needs company," she said. "Although he may not know that he does."

If Gideon had been left to make the judgement himself, he would have said the last thing Sir Philip Lord needed was company. His expression was closed. His eyes fixed on the horizon. But Gideon trusted Zahara's wisdom. He walked over and stood beside Lord taking in the leafless trees visible through the gate and the empty earth of the fields. He said nothing because he knew words would never be enough—or would be too much, but he hoped perhaps just his being there might help. So he was a little surprised when Lord himself began to speak.

"*My prime of youth is but a frost of cares,*
My feast of joy is but a dish of pain,
My crop of corn is but a field of tares,
And all my good is but vain hope of gain.
The day is gone and yet I saw no sun,
And now I live, and now my life is done.

And now I live..." He turned to Gideon. "If you wish, I will speak to the prince when we reach Oxford. It is possible that I was wrong, and you would flourish in his service, but either way, *you* should decide."

The words were so far from where Gideon's thoughts had been that he had no reply. Lord misunderstood the silence.

"I know you feel I acted hastily, and perhaps you are right. I still believe it would not suit you, but the truth is..." He hesitated before going on. "The truth is I find I do not wish to lose your service, your company. You once accused me of wanting to keep you so I could have someone to whom I might show off and boast. But there are too many who are happy for me to do so. There are few, precious few, who will gainsay me, not from malice, but for my own benefit. Perhaps I am, as any man, selfish enough to wish to keep about me those I like and trust."

"I don't wish to serve the prince," Gideon said. "I wish you had told me of the offer, but I wouldn't accept it."

Lord looked at him with an odd expression of uncertainty.

"You are sure? It is unlikely that a similar opportunity will come your way again and refusing such service is not without its price."

Gideon wondered how to say what he needed to say, how to encompass in a few words his understanding of what it would mean to accept such a post. In the end, all he could think of was a simple statement of truth. "I am not cut out for the life of a courtier."

Lord laughed. "That is true. But then you are not cut out for the life of a soldier-of-fortune, yet still you ride with me and my company."

"The difference is you don't ask me to stop being myself."

There was silence between them for a short time.

"I think you stopped being the person you were when we met, some time ago," Lord said, his tone reflective. "But I must say I prefer the person you have become, and that person would not be a man who could follow in the footsteps of Ned Blake."

There was a shout from the barn, Rigó calling to say the wheel was set. Lord rested his hand on Gideon's shoulder.

"When we get to Oxford, I will speak again to the prince and make sure he understands it is my will and your contract to me that binds us. He will know not to blame you." Then Lord smiled. "You will need to write yourself a binding contract we can backdate and have witnessed."

Gideon nodded at least then he would be there for Lord when he was most needed.

When—no, *if* Kate...

They walked back to the barn, side by side and the last verse of the poem Lord had spoken before echoed in Gideon's mind.

I sought my death and found it in my womb,
I lookt for life and saw it was a shade,
I trode the earth and knew it was my tomb,
And now I die, and now I am but made.
The glass is full, and now the glass is run,
And now I live, and now my life is done…

Oxford, All Hallows Eve 1642

Oxford was very different to how Gideon remembered it from his year there studying theology before his father's death had freed him to take up law. It had been transformed by the war, with the colleges and students pledging their support for the king, and the town resentful at the army's presence.

Lady Catherine's chamber was hot as all sick rooms must be. In the midst of it, on a bed with red hangings to aid her recovery, Kate lay as if in state, fever abating. The king's physician, Sir William Harvey, who had been tending her for the past day and a half since their arrival, shook his head.

"Unbelievable that the charlatan in Warwick believed she had a fractured pelvis."

"Then what is it?" Sir Philip Lord's gaze seemed unable to remain with Harvey but kept escaping the requirements of politeness to return to the peaceful figure sleeping on the bed, Zahara sitting beside her.

"A bullet wound. Well, a bullet. For now, I have eased the ill humours and removed the putrefaction that was causing. But the bullet remains yet there within her body lodged perilously close to her spine. As long as it remains it is a risk to the lady's health and in time, maybe her life. Should it move, it might leave her crippled but that is in God's hands, not mine. I have done what I can, *medicus curat, natura sanat*."

"Can you not remove the bullet?" Gideon asked, seeing that Lord was finding it hard to maintain his concentration after more days and nights with little sleep, keeping at his wife's side.

"That would require a surgeon," Harvey said, his tone stiff. "A surgeon would be unlikely to have the physician's skill to know how it could be done without causing more harm. Removing this bullet would not be like pulling a tooth." Harvey gathered his things into a capacious leather bag and made a brief bow towards Lord. "Sir Philip, I will visit again in the morning."

There was a heavy silence in the stifling room after he had gone.

"At least," Zahara said, "Lady Catherine is out of danger for now."

"Perhaps there are surgeons in Oxford who come well recommended?" Gideon suggested, but he was sure if a man of the competence needed existed, Harvey would have mentioned his name.

"What we require," Lord said, "is a brilliant surgeon with the knowledge of a physician. Or maybe more an outstanding physician with the skill and training of a surgeon."

Gideon looked at him and nodded, his thoughts already following where Lord's lead.

"That being so," Sir Philip Lord went on, "we need to find Anders Jensen."

THE DEVIL'S COMMAND

Author's Note

This book is dedicated to my children. Both of them have been, in their own unique and wonderful way, amazing sources of support and encouragement in my writing. I hope they know how much that means to me and how incredibly proud I am of the people they have become.

Unlike the previous books in this series, many characters in The Devil's Command have famous historical antecedents.

Amongst others: King Charles himself, his nephews Prince Rupert and Maurice, the Earl of Essex, Lord Brooke, Lord Digby and Boye the dog. I have done my best to place them approximately where and when they were as we encounter them in this story, but not invariably so. Rarely, some of their words are taken in part from the historical record, such as those of King Charles before the battle, but most are purely my invention. Their attitudes and personalities are my interpretation taken from what I have read about them.

Lesser-known historical figures underlie some of the other characters too. Blake was indeed both a private secretary to Prince Rupert and busy betraying all he learned to the Earl of Essex. Papers captured after Edgehill led to that discovery. Blake was tried and hung. And the Boothby brothers of Clattercote

Priory, which still stands not far from the village of Claydon, did indeed have a legal battle for the property (eventually won by Thomas) and their mother, the thrice-married Judith Austen, had developed the house and estate very successfully as a lone widow over forty years until she died in 1640.

My discovery of the Boothby's of Clattercote was one of the wonderful moments that make writing historical fiction such a delightful thing to do. When I was planning the retreat from Wormleighton I needed a house between there and Banbury to set the final scene. I put my finger on the map (on screen - it was Google maps) in the place I needed such to be and found I had pointed to Clattercote. In investigating its history, I met the Boothbys and discovered how perfectly they fitted what I wanted at that point in the story. But I get ahead of myself...

The battle of Edgehill was the first battle of the English civil war. It took place pretty much as I have described, from the initial encounter of some of Prince Rupert's foragers with their Parliamentarian opposite numbers the evening before, through to the capture and rescue of the Banner Royal, the knighting of those who rescued it and the rather uncertain and inconclusive aftermath with both sides claiming victory. Although inevitably, as we ride with Gideon, I only show a narrow slice of what was a highly complex event as all battles are.

I have taken some liberties with the council of war before the battle, conflating events for simplicity, but an argument over tactics such as I describe did indeed lead to Robert Bertie, Earl of Lindsey refusing

THE DEVIL'S COMMAND

command and Patrick Ruthven, Earl of Forth taking over as Lord General of the army.

There were, according to Clarendon (one of the primary sources for the period) amnesty notices printed before the battle but never distributed: *But all men were now so much otherwise busied, that it was not soon enough remembered; and when it was, the proclamations were not at hand.*

Sir Faithful Fortescue did change sides during the battle. Unfortunately, a lot of his men forgot to remove their field sign and so were killed by the Royalists they were trying to fight alongside.

The terrible treatment of the Parliamentarian baggage train by Digby's horse is sadly historical but it was far from the worst atrocity that would be meted out on the non-combatants following each army in a war that became ever more brutal as time went on. That unwelcome accolade must surely go to the massacre and mutilation of Royalist camp followers, mostly women with their children, by the cavalry of the New Model Army after the Battle of Naseby in 1644. A deed that was then celebrated in the London press as being a worthy and righteous act.

The siege of Banbury I have taken a few liberties with, aside from weaving in my non-historical cast. Historically, the garrison surrendered after a couple of shots were fired by the Royalist artillery. The tale of the cabbage seller which Sir Philip Lord usurps was one attributed to Rupert at the time in a contemporary pamphlet.

Wormleighton Manor was owned by the Spencer family (ancestors of Princess Diana). Although it was no longer favoured as their main residence which was even then the much more modern and commodious Althorp Hall. Wormleighton was indeed burned during these wars, but probably not at this point and probably not by Parliamentarians. It was likely burned two or three years later by the highly aggressive Royalist garrison of Banbury Castle, to prevent it from being occupied by Parliamentarian troops.

Another thing that needs mention here is sign language.

There is much evidence to suggest local sign languages of a simple finger spelling variety had been known from mediaeval times at least. But there was a cultural flourishing of one particular sign language at the Ottoman court in the sixteenth and seventeenth centuries with many hearing people learning it including the sultans themselves. In 1605, Henry de Beauveau, the French soldier and diplomat who visited the Sublime Porte escorting the French Ambassador, said this was called *ixarette*, probably a French pronunciation for *işaret* the Turkish word for 'sign'. Later accounts suggested that this language could be used to hold sophisticated exchanges suggesting it was indeed a language in its own right and not just alphabetic finger counting. It is this sign language or something very similar that I envisage the polyglot Shiraz using to communicate.

Finally, a word about marriage in this era.

At this time the strict legal formalities around marriage had yet to be set in stone as they were eventually in the 1753 Clandestine Marriage Act. A wedding licence or banns to be read and a church

THE DEVIL'S COMMAND

service, whilst vital where money and property rights depended on the marriage being legally indisputable, were not technically necessary. Marriage was not a sacrament. In law, to marry all that was required was a spousal. At its most basic this was simply to declare, in the present tense, that you accepted the other as your spouse (the 'I do' of the marriage service). Such informal spousals still occurred into the 17th Century despite the church's best efforts to discourage such. This is demonstrated by the amount of analysis given to the validity of various wordings used in such marriages by Henry Swinburne the ecclesiastical lawyer in his work on the subject written in the 1620s. However, in the Caroline era until their suspension in 1640, the ecclesiastical courts dealt with very few cases, suggesting that they were increasingly rare.

If you have enjoyed The Devil's Command, I would love to hear what you thought about it so please do leave a review. You can also follow me on Twitter @emswifthook or get in touch with me through my website www.eleanorswifthook.com where you can find more about the background to the book including the origins of the various quotations in the text.

Meanwhile, you will be pleased to know The Devil's Command is the third of six books In the Lord's Legacy series, which follow Gideon Lennox through the opening months of the first English Civil War. As he unravels the mystery of Philip Lord's past, he finds himself getting caught up in battles and sieges, murder investigations and moral dilemmas as all the while he is in the grip of his seemingly impossible romance with the beautiful Zahara.

ELEANOR SWIFT-HOOK

Printed in Great Britain
by Amazon